MA...MÍ

©1747

LA
TORTUGA

LABERINTO
DE ÁRBOLES

10

SIGA EL
SERPIENTE

HUBER HILL

HILL

AND THE

DEAD MAN'S

·TREASURE·

B. K. BOSTICK

Sweetwater Books
An imprint of Cedar Fort, Inc.
Springville, Utah

ISBN 13: 978-1-59955-911-7

Published by Sweetwater Books, an imprint of Cedar Fort, Inc.
2373 W. 700 S., Springville, UT 84663
Distributed by Cedar Fort, Inc., www.cedarfort.com

LIBRARY OF CONGRESS CATALOGING-IN-PUBLICATION DATA
Bostick, B. K. (Bryan Keith), 1980- author.
  Huber Hill and the dead man's treasure / B. K. Bostick.
    pages cm
    Summary: When fourteen-year-old Huber Hill inherits a mysterious box from
his grandfather with a gold coin and a treasure map, he decides to finish
the hunt his grandfather started, seeking a treasure guarded for centuries
by Ute Indians and the spirits of long dead Spanish conquistadors.
  ISBN 978-1-59955-911-7
  [1. Buried treasure--Fiction. 2. Adventure and adventurers--Fiction. 3.
Supernatural--Fiction. 4. Ute Indians--Fiction. 5. Indians of North
America--West (U.S.)--Fiction.] I. Title.

  PZ7.B649557Hub 2011
  [Fic]--dc23

  2011023818

Cover design by Brian Halley
Cover design © 2011 by Lyle Mortimer
Edited and typeset by Melissa J. Caldwell

Printed in the United States of America

10 9 8 7 6 5 4 3 2 1

Printed on acid-free paper

Dedicated to my wife
and to the memory of Grandpa Jay—
"Where you are, there's gold they say."

ACKNOWLEDGMENTS

Writing and marketing a book takes a village. Thanks most of all to my wife, JulieAnn, for putting up with me through the whole process. She read draft after draft and helped with so many ideas that found their way into the story. She believed in me even when I didn't. I love you.

Thanks also to the many friends, neighbors, and family members who read initial drafts and gave valuable feedback, especially mom, Jack, and Granny HaHa. Thanks to my wonderful family—Mom, Jack, Kirk, Michiel, Madison, Malorie, Bob, Cindy, Justin, Jeanette, Ray, and my dad, whose presence I miss more than words can say. Many thanks to Angie Workman for picking up and believing in the story. Melissa Caldwell for helping me trim the fat and whip the narrative into shape. Mariah Overlock for helping organize the "Treasure for Alyssa" fund-raiser and blog tour. Thanks to Brian Halley for the map and bookmark designs and the many invaluable creative ideas.

I owe a lot to Obert Skye for taking an interest in my work and giving good advice. A big thanks as well to Frank Cole for his help. I owe a shout-out to Dean Nielsen for his assistance with the cover/map concept designs and creative ideas. Mark McKenna did a beautiful job on the final cover illustration and brought the characters to life. Thanks to Lowell Oswald Jr. for creating the outstanding website/trailer and Tyler Brown, Thomas Naranjo, and Boston Watts for their acting talents.

Most of all, thanks to you, my readers. This is all for you. As long as you keep reading, I'll keep writing. *Dead Man's Treasure* was inspired by my Grandpa Jay who told me countless stories about Spanish treasure hidden high up in the mountains. It's through you, the readers, that his stories and memory live on.

PROLOGUE

"WHERE IS IT? TELL ME NOW!" demanded the man in the black. A tattoo of a black serpent ran the length of his right forearm, appearing as if it had wrapped itself around the flesh. The tattoo ended with the snake's mouth inked seamlessly between his thumb and index finger. The serpent's open mouth clutched the man's throat.

"I . . . already . . . told you! I . . . don't . . . know!" the old man choked.

"Wrong answer," the man in black whispered, and using his other hand, held up his victim's oxygen tube and kinked it sharply. A hissing sound filled the room as the elderly man flailed about wildly.

"*Por favor . . . por favor . . .* ," the old-timer gasped, his face the color of a turnip.

The man in black eased the kink in the tube, allowing oxygen to flow back into his victim's lungs. Heaving in and out, peach-like color returned to his face.

"*Te pregunto otra vez*! Tell me where it is!"

"It does not matter. . . . How . . . many times . . . have I told you? Doesn't . . . exist!"

The man in black gritted his teeth and thrust his face toward the old man.

"You did not look hard enough! You gave up too easily!"

"Maybe . . . but tell me . . . what . . . would you do with it . . . even if you found it?" the white-haired man choked. "Wouldn't matter. Your cup . . . will never . . . be filled. An evil heart . . . is never . . . satisfied."

A wicked grin crept onto the man in black's face. "Perhaps not, but I will fill my cup nonetheless."

The man in black kinked the tube again and watched the old man writhe in agony as the terrors of suffocation gripped him. The old man's sprawling legs and arms sent objects flying off his nightstand, and they shattered onto the floor. A monitor bleeped and rang as bulging eyes pleaded for mercy. The man in black finally released the tube. Gulping for air, it took several moments for the old man to speak.

"*Sobrino mio.* . . . What . . . have . . . you . . . become?"

"A man who will do *whatever* it takes to get what he wants."

"Well . . . you . . . will . . . have . . . to . . . do . . . *worse.*"

The grin returned to the man's face. "I can. I can do so much worse. Yesenia? Your granddaughter. Perhaps you told her where it is?"

Genuine fear now filled the old man's eyes.

"No . . . you wouldn't . . . please . . . ," he said, panicking.

"You know I would. Now I will ask you once more. Where is it?"

The old man hesitated but then uttered between sobs, "Eldredge . . . Nicholas . . . . Carbondale . . . Colorado."

Beyond the beeping of the monitor, a distant siren screamed down the streets of Salamanca, Spain.

"Sounds like *médicos* are on their way . . . I do not think they'll make it on time!" The man in black smiled as he withdrew a long, sharp blade from his side. With one quick slash, the oxygen tube was severed from its tank. The end fell to the hardwood floor and helplessly blew about particles of dust. Once again, the old man's body thrashed about, his muscles constricting. His mouth gaped open and shut like a fish out of water. Stars dotted his vision. Slowly, the old man relaxed as darkness crept in from the corners of his eyes. Hazily, he stared up at the inky figure looming over him. Gently, Juan Hernán Salazar bowed toward his uncle and lightly brushed his forehead with his lips. *"Buenas noches . . . Tío Carlos."*

CHAPTER 1

A SERIES OF VIBRATIONS shook Huber from his stupor. The sound reverberated off his orange plastic chair and echoed throughout the classroom. Heads turned toward the sound, including that of Mrs. Collins.

"Mr. Hill, that better not be a cell phone in my class."

"Sorry, sorry, I'll turn it off."

"I hear it again, and you know what happens."

"Yeah, I know. I'm turning it off."

Huber fumbled through his front pocket, digging out his cell phone. A manila envelope indicated he'd received a text message from 555-3547. He knew that number and also what the message relayed without reading it. Huber flipped the phone open.

"HAPPY H8 PUBER DAY!"

People often wish they could travel back in time to change some word or action. If Huber Hill could travel back in time, he knew exactly where he'd go: the fifth grade maturation assembly. On that fateful day, Huber's life changed in ways he couldn't have fathomed at the time.

"So, at what age do boys usually start puberty?" he'd asked the presenter.

Before the doctor could answer, Scott McCormick had

conjured up Huber's new name—Puber. And it had stuck.

Huber wished he had been named something more normal like John or Mike—anything that didn't rhyme with Puber. His parents hadn't even taken the courtesy to give him a middle name he could go by instead. His great-great-grandpa Huber was a pious Pennsylvanian pioneer who had helped tame the wild Colorado frontier and establish Huber's hometown of Carbondale. Nestled within the Rocky Mountains, Carbondale's current population numbered around five thousand souls. The city boasted two grocery stores, three gas stations, and, to everyone's recent excitement, a McDonald's restaurant.

Huber quickly erased the message and turned off the phone, resolving not to turn it on until he went home.

Fourteen years old and one of the three hundred Wolverines who navigated the hallways of Carbondale Middle School, Huber suffered silently. Each day transpired eerily the same as the last, save the variation in the creatively contrived put-downs by Scott McCormick. Scott, a good foot taller than most kids his age and twenty pounds heavier, intimidated most students and teachers. Buzzed red hair, camouflage pants, and a hateful stare were his trademarks. Today, this tank of an eighth grader wore an insulting T-shirt, displaying the words *I'm with Stupid* sandwiched between two horizontal arrows. Teachers had long ago given up trying to make Scott wear school-appropriate clothing; they had to pick their battles, and T-shirts ranked at the bottom of their list. They were more concerned with Scott's total lack of interest in school and the constant disruptions he caused during class.

For reasons unknown, the school never actually called

Scott a bully. Instead, anecdotal records stated, "Student often displays aggressive and coercive behavior." According to Huber Hill, Scott McCormick was a bully of the worst kind, whose characteristics could only be defined with the vilest and most profane words.

To make matters worse, Scott and Huber shared five of seven classes.

CHAPTER 2

"HEY, BUTT FUNGUS, DIDJA eat dog poop for breakfast or something?" Scott asked Huber as he sat behind him in Mr. Morris's third period English class. A leftover smidgen of a chocolate Pop-Tart covered Huber's lower lip.

"Ya see that? He's been eatin' dog poo." Scott nudged the boy sitting next to him.

The boy looked at Huber. "You're right. It's all over his face. That's nasty, Puber."

Huber dabbed at his mouth with his shirt.

Laughs from nearby classmates followed. Did the kids join in because they genuinely believed Scott was funny or were they afraid of incurring his wrath if they didn't? Maybe both.

"Leave me alone," Huber mumbled.

"What's that, Puber? Speak up, will ya?"

"Leave me alone," he said more forcefully.

"Sure thing. Right after this."

Scott reached behind Huber's head and tugged on the hairs at the top of his neck. Huber winced but said nothing. Mr. Morris's wrinkled eyes squinted toward the back of the room. Thick white hair flounced about as he paced in front of the whiteboard. On the back of his head, a lick of hair stood up like a cockatoo.

"Hey, you boys, what's going on back there?"

"Nothin', teach. Just playin', aren't we, Huber?"

Huber brushed Scott's hand from his neck and remained silent. Confused eyes gazed through thick glasses before darting back to the board. Mr. Morris continued his boring lecture on Mark Twain. As soon as he did, Scott retrieved a black magic marker from his backpack. A vicelike grip clenched the back of Huber's neck. Felt brushed his skin. Huber deciphered the message as the tip moved up and down. PUBER STINKS. Snickers erupted from the back of the room. *Water off a duck's back*, he thought.

The most embarrassing thing that had happened to Huber that year transpired in the lunchroom, occurring just at the moment he had mustered the courage to saunter over and talk to the gorgeous Alison Harmon. He had barely opened his mouth when a cool breeze tickled his inner thigh. Peering down, Huber observed his Levis bunched up around his ankles. The spectacle of his tighty-whities were entertaining the large lunch crowd. Scott had cackled like a hyena. Immediately afterward, Alison had called Scott a jerk and surveyed Huber with sympathetic eyes. "Are you okay?" she'd asked. Red-faced and reeling inside, Huber had hoisted his pants up in a flash. "Yeah, fine," he'd said. *Water off a duck's back*. Her pity stung far worse than the collective laughter of the lunchroom.

As Mr. Morris's third period let out to lunch, Huber snuck to the bathroom to wash the writing off his neck the best he could and decided to skip lunch and roam the hallways instead. Experience had taught him to avoid the cafeteria on Hate Puber Day.

After school, Huber sprinted for the bus to get a front seat but arrived too late. Marching down the aisle, he passed his twin sister, Hannah, talking to a friend, decked out in her softball gear. Hannah, a vital part of Carbondale Middle School's softball team, spent her final period of the day practicing. She was the team's star pitcher. Though in the same grade, their schedules varied so that the only time he saw his sister occurred during lunch and on the bus. She eyed him, gave the slightest of smiles, and resumed her conversation. With a sigh, he ambled toward the back of the bus. Sitting in the last seat, grinning widely, sat the one and only Scott McCormick. The day wasn't over quite yet. Plopping down next to the redheaded monster, he waited. Seconds later, the familiar sting of neck hair being tugged returned. *Water off a duck's back*. The bus accelerated and took off.

"Puber, Puber, Puber," Scott breathed in a low voice, attempting to goad him into a confrontation.

The bus driver paid no attention. Scott pulled his hair harder, flicked his earlobes, and gave him a wet willy in both ears. After a couple minutes, Scott lost interest and let go, giving Huber's head one hard, final shove. Teachers and parents preached ignoring as the best plan of action. Huber had been ignoring Scott for many years now. Luckily, Scott got off one stop before Huber, granting him at least a few moments of reprieve before arriving home. The brakes of the bus screeched the vehicle to a halt.

"See ya tomorrow!" Scott bellowed as he went to get off. "By the way, Happy Hate Puber Day."

With Scott gone, Huber sunk back in his seat and absorbed the silence. Sometimes he wondered why Scott picked on him so much, but Huber realized he made a pretty easy target. Short, skinny, and weak, Huber posed no threat. Add this to the fact that Huber had no friends to rally around him, how could someone like Scott resist?

Two minutes later, he and his sister stepped off the bus in front of their house. Although home provided an escape from Scott's never-ending game of torture, Huber sometimes wondered if he'd rather be at school. For the past year, Huber's parents, Robert and Ellen, had fought almost every single night. They fought about what to eat for dinner and about how to handle Huber and his sister when they got in trouble. Most of all they fought about money. Ellen yelled at Robert for buying a new tool. Robert yelled at Ellen for buying new shoes when they were supposed to be paying off the credit card. The cycle usually ended up with plenty of yelling, crying, and hushed violent whispers muffled behind closed doors. During these confrontations, Huber hibernated in his room, headphones drowning out the noise, lost in his comics. Hannah preferred to go outside and play with their dog, Hobo.

"Think they'll fight tonight?" Hannah asked her brother as they walked toward the front door.

"Probably. Remember? Dad said he was gonna buy that new TV today."

"Oh yeah, I forgot. Think he'll really have the guts?"

"I doubt it. Mom said she'd take a hammer to the thing."

"Wanna make a bet?" Hannah said.

"Sure. I'll bet he chickened out," Huber replied.

"I think he did it just to get her goat."

"What do you wanna bet?"

"If he bought it, you hafta clean up after the dog in the

backyard. I think there's about a week's worth back there. I was supposed to do it a couple of days ago," Hannah said.

"Fine. If he didn't, you've gotta wash dishes on my week."

"Deal." They shook hands.

They tiptoed through the front door. As they entered, an enormous cardboard box immediately caught their gaze. Sitting defiantly in the middle of the front room, a plastic-y, fresh-from-the-factory smell emanated from the box. A bold picture of a 55-inch flat screen television was plastered on its side. Huber's dad had been pining for months over the thing, dreaming of watching sports in high definition. His wife, Ellen, was adamantly opposed to the idea. She hated TVs and video games in the house at all, claiming they only distracted the family from engaging in more worthwhile activities.

"Whoa, look at this!" Huber yelped as he imagined playing *Blood Wars* on the massive screen.

Ellen charged into the room. "Don't get used it! Your dad's sending it back tomorrow."

Apparently she had lost her nerve to destroy it with the hammer.

"C'mon, Mom. Why can't we keep it?" Huber whined as if his dad had brought home a cute puppy.

"If we can't afford to fix the carburetor in my car, then we can't afford this monstrosity!"

"I win," Hannah whispered triumphantly.

CHAPTER 3

"HOW WAS SCHOOL TODAY?" Robert asked his son at the dinner table. The cardboard box still sat in the adjacent room, unopened.

"Pretty good."

"How about you, Hannah?"

"It was okay."

"What'd you learn?" Ellen asked.

Huber responded first. "Mark Twain."

"Oh, I love *Huckleberry Finn*. Classic American literature," Ellen gushed.

"I learned more Spanish," Hannah butted in. *"Mi papá es un calvo."*

"What's that mean? Something about a potato?" Robert asked.

"Don't worry about it."

Her father laughed aloud. "I'm sure I don't want to know. Have softball practice today? How'd it go?"

"Good. Struck a few people out."

"That's my girl. Huber, maybe you oughta try baseball out."

"Robert . . ." Ellen raised her voice.

"I'm just saying. The boy spends all his time up there in

his room, reading comics, playing video games, and doing who knows what else. It'd be a great way to get out and make some new friends."

"Yeah, maybe," Huber said, sculpting a castle out of mashed potatoes.

"You do what you want to do, Huber," his mother added.

Robert's tone changed. "Y'know, maybe he'd try more things if you didn't give him an out all the time."

"I'm not forcing our son into anything he doesn't want to do."

"Ellen, you've got to stop babying him. The boy's in middle school, for crying out loud."

So it began. The nightly ritual. Huber didn't want to hear it again.

"I'll think about it," Huber muttered.

"Hey, that's all I ask." Robert threw his hands in the air. "When's your next game?" Robert asked his daughter.

"Next Wednesday at four. You guys coming?"

"Better believe it. So proud of you, honey," Robert replied while looking at Huber.

"We'll be there," Ellen echoed. "I saw one of your teachers at the grocery store this afternoon. Mrs. Shaw. Said you're doing an amazing job in science."

Hannah shrugged. Such compliments were nothing new. Teachers loved her wit and outgoingness. During every parent-teacher conference, she received glowing reviews.

A tug pulled on Huber's leg while his parents fawned over Hannah. Peering down below the tablecloth, Huber saw two large brown eyes begging for a taste of meatloaf. *Gladly*, Huber thought as he snuck a large piece into Hobo's mouth.

The family named the dog "Hobo" because of its origin from the pound. A mixture between a dachshund and a rat, the dog's coarse, black fur resembled a Brillo pad. It was a pitiful excuse for a dog. Even Huber had to admit, though, that because it was so ugly, it was kind of cute. The dog seemed to know when he was upset and would perform for him by sliding his behind across the lawn or chasing his tail. Other times, he nuzzled up to Huber, bringing him comfort when nothing else could.

"Huber, don't feed the dog," his mother said without so much as a glance in his direction. "Speaking of which, Hannah, did you clean up the poop in the backyard?"

"Huber's doing it for me."

"What? Why? Isn't it your week?"

"He lost a bet."

"What kind of a bet?"

The twins looked at each other, unsure of what to say.

"I . . . uh . . . I . . . ," Huber stammered.

"Huber bet that I wouldn't strike anyone out today."

"Should've known better, son." Robert winked at his daughter.

"Yeah, I guess so," he said distantly. His mashed potato masterpiece was nearly complete.

Ellen shook her head. "I don't care who does it, I just want it done tonight. Understand? If you two want to go to your grandpa's this weekend, you need to get your chores done."

"Dad, when I'm finished with the backyard, can we hook up the TV?" Huber asked.

A red color filled both parents' faces. An imaginary bell chimed above the table. Round one was about to begin.

CHAPTER 4

"SHOW 'EM," HANNAH SAID to Huber as they played blackjack with Grandpa Nick.

Huber flipped over his cards. "Twenty," he declared, full of hubris, showcasing a queen of hearts and a ten of diamonds.

"Bust," Hannah lamented as she displayed an eight of hearts, three of diamonds, six of spades, and a seven of diamonds. "I always hit too much. How 'bout you, Grandpa?"

Grandpa Nick raised his lips into the slightest of grins and laid down an ace of spades and a king of hearts, totaling twenty-one.

"Ahh man, how do you always win?" Huber complained.

On most weekends, Huber and Hannah visited their Grandpa Nick at his home a few miles east of town. Grandpa Nick, their mother's father and their only living grandparent, was adorned in his usual green scrub bottoms, a white T-shirt, and brown, fuzzy slippers. Mostly bald on top, he had a few wisps of white that danced in the breeze of the swamp cooler. On his wrinkled yet dignified face rested thick, retro-looking glasses, which magnified his bottomless blue eyes.

Grandpa Nick's small two-bedroom rambler was in shambles. Peering out the window, Huber observed a sea of weeds waving with the wind where once a healthy ten-acre alfalfa field prospered. Dilapidated, rotten fence posts ran parallel to the property line. Rusty barbed wire sagged in between.

The inside of the house contained scratched up hardwood floors and peeling, flowery wallpaper. Furnished with a lime green couch and brown armchair, the living room constituted a relic straight from the 1970s. A humid, musty climate enveloped visitors as they entered the hallway. Despite all its faults, this place was an oasis from the outside world for Huber.

Grandpa Nick rarely ventured beyond his bedroom. Orange, shaggy carpet, wood-paneled walls, and a small closet-like bathroom comprised his surroundings day after day, year after year. The smell of Vicks VapoRub and cherry cough drops hung heavy in his room.

He had battled lung cancer for years, and breathing on his own had become an impossibility. The sound of the ventilator, pushing air in and out of Grandpa Nick's lungs, accompanied the swamp cooler in perfect harmony. *Darth Vader*, a six-year-old Huber thought when he first saw the machine. Frightened yet fascinated, Huber didn't dare approach his grandpa for months. A blue tube traveled through Grandpa Nick's throat, connecting his lungs to the machine. To help him communicate, a mechanical larynx had been surgically implanted where his voice box used to be. Gyrations from his vocal chords traveled to the machine so that when he mouthed the words, the gadget verbalized them through an amplifier. Huber couldn't remember what his grandpa's actual voice sounded like.

Huber felt captivated as he listened in awe to tales of Grandpa Nick's many brushes with death as a marine during the Vietnam War. Huber imagined spending nights under starry skies in the middle of the jungle, so far from home. He heard the symphony of exotic birds and insects, sharing their music of the night and bringing a sense of calm to the chaos. He saw the peaceful, brilliant moon shining above the ocean of palm trees, its tranquility obscured by a cacophony of violent explosions. He experienced terror as Grandpa Nick described the day he stepped on a land mine and could not lift his foot from the object, lest it explode. As the men in his unit said their good-byes and took cover, Grandpa Nick had reluctantly released his foot from the mine . . . and nothing happened. A dud! "If it hadn't been, you wouldn't exist," Grandpa frequently reminded them. In Huber's eyes, Grandpa Nick embodied a hero in the fullest sense of the word.

As they continued playing blackjack, Huber became dealer. "Grandpa, hit or pass?"

"Pa . . . ," he tried to reply. His face contorted and turned scarlet as he wheezed and hacked, his body jolting upward with each cough.

"Maria!" Hannah panicked.

Maria rushed in the room and fiddled with something on the ventilator. Slowly, a normal color returned to Grandpa Nick's face.

"*Viejito*, you okay?" she asked in a thick Mexican accent.

"Fine," he replied coolly, collapsing backward. "Thank you."

"Don't want anything to happen to my sweet, little *viejito* now."

"What's a *viejito*?" Huber asked.

"Ornery old goat," she replied flatly.

Grandpa Nick shot a dramatized glare in her direction,

now regaining his composure. The twins struggled to suppress their laughter.

"Might be ornery, but I'm not old."

"Could have fooled me. You look in a mirror lately? Looks like you're around two hundred."

"All right, all right. How much abuse does an elder have to take?"

"Still, very handsome for a *viejito*," she added.

"Yes, yes. *Muchas gracias, señorita*."

"Time for lunch. Be right back."

Twenty-five years old with thick, beautiful black hair and olive skin, Maria had come to America two years earlier and was working on getting her citizenship. Huber flushed whenever she looked at him. Maria worked as a certified nurse's assistant for a home health agency that Grandpa Nick hired to help maintain his ventilator, prepare his food, wash his laundry, and perform daily chores.

Shortly afterward, Maria returned with sandwiches and fruit. Next to Grandpa Nick's bed, she hooked a small bag with cream-colored paste up onto a metal rod. The paste oozed toward the other end, which poked out of Grandpa Nick's stomach. Nourishment for his frail body. Huber couldn't help but feel guilty whenever he ate in front of him. Because of the tracheal tube, Grandpa Nick couldn't eat anything solid without choking. What would it be like, being unable to eat pizza, hamburgers, steak?

As they ate, Grandpa Nick posed a question. "How 'bout a story? Have I told you about the Dead Man's Treasure up 'round Mount Sopris?"

"No, no, no! Not again with your crazy stories. You get

too worked up!" Maria protested, monitoring Grandpa Nick's vitals. Throwing his arms up in the air, he dismissed her statement with the flick of his hand.

"Don't encourage him, you two," Maria warned Huber and Hannah as she exited the room.

"Ahh, don't listen to her. I'm fine . . . How 'bout it?" Grandpa Nick asked again.

"Sure, Grandpa," Huber replied.

"Yeah, tell us," Hannah seconded, even though they'd heard the story many times.

Grandpa Nick's deep blue eyes sparkled with renewed vigor.

"Okay. As you know, Escalante and Dominguez were the first white explorers in the area. They wrote about the beauty of these mountains in their journals," Grandpa Nick said, pointing outside the window at Mount Sopris jutting toward the sky in the distance. Grandpa Nick began to lecture like a college professor to a large group of students.

"When word got back to Spain about this continent with its riches and wildlife, more explorers flocked here. Spain, a vast and powerful empire, constantly needed more resources and wealth to fuel its expansion." He had to pause to catch his breath. "It was the mid 1500s, and Cortés had conquered Central America, Pizarro the south. Francisco Vasquez de Coronado hoped to earn the same fame in Europe as his fellow conquistadors by conquering the American Southwest. He and his men spent most of their time in Arizona and New Mexico among the Zuni, looking for the seven cities of Cibola—you know, cities supposedly made of pure gold. A fool's errand . . . a wild goose chase," he said, winking. "The cities of gold were just fiction, stories created by the Zuni to keep the Spanish on the move. While Coronado searched in vain, it was rumored that a branch of his men broke off from the main group and traveled north to mine the Rocky Mountains with great success. A seemingly infinite supply of gold ore existed right here around Mount Sopris. They named the mine *Tesoro de los Vivos*—Living Treasure!" Grandpa Nick's chest rose up and down as he got excited. He forced himself to slow down.

"Why'd they call it that, again?" Huber asked.

"Because the mine seemed to be alive, its veins flowing with gold. Anyways, they melted down the ore in smelters and molded the gold into *escudos,* gold doubloons bearing symbols of the Spanish empire. Loads were trekked to Mexico, then secretly shipped back to Spain. Coronado had no knowledge of this, of course. The local Ute Indians became concerned about the growing number of Spaniards coming onto the land. Skirmishes broke out between them, and the small band of Spaniards was forced out.

"The men agreed to keep the location of the mine a secret from Coronado, who would without doubt take the riches for himself and execute them for treason and betrayal. The men eventually returned to Spain, never breathing a word of the riches to anyone but their families.

"A hundred and fifty years later, at the beginning of the 1700s, the descendants of Coronado's defectors set out to find the mine they'd heard so much about from their fathers and grandfathers.

"They followed the maps to these mountains and were able to locate the Tesoro de los Vivos. It still held tons of gold within its veins. Once again, the Spaniards began to mint the gold and ship it back to Spain. Stories of the Spanish trespassers quickly reached the ears of the Ute tribal chief. Memories of the former Spanish invaders were still circulated among them. The attacks began anew. This time, however, the Spanish were better prepared, with more sophisticated weapons and armor. But what the Ute lacked in weapons, they made up for in sheer numbers.

"Out of necessity, the Spanish sent large garrisons to guard the mine and escort the transports that came from the mountains. Because of the risks transportation posed, large amounts of gold would be stockpiled—moved at one time—with a large number of men for protection.

"One day, before a large shipment was to be moved, the Utes made a plan to sabotage the Spanish. After weeks of waiting, the day of the attack finally arrived." Grandpa Nick was now wheezing, his words struggling to keep pace with his thoughts. "As the garrison traveled up the trail to pick up the enormous shipment of gold, they were ambushed just outside the mine by the Ute.

"Their numbers quickly dwindled until only a handful of them were left. Beleaguered and wounded, they were in no shape to move that gold from the mine. They would have to wait for reinforcements. The Spaniards, besieged on all sides, were continuously attacked and picked off until only one man was left standing. A group of twenty Ute surrounded him. Outnumbered, he threw off his armor, laid down his sword, and hung his head . . . ready to die. To his surprise, the Ute chief did not kill him. Instead the chief placed in his hand a single gold doubloon as a warning to never return. The Spaniard was forced to drag all thirteen of his comrades' bodies inside the mine. It became their tomb. As a finale, the Ute hollowed out several depressions above the mine entrance, causing the whole thing to resemble a skull. The survivor, a skilled mason, then sealed up the mine with a kind of booby trap and fled back to Spain. He renamed the place *Tesoro de los Muertos* or Dead Man's Treasure."

"I still don't get why they didn't kill him," Hannah interjected.

"They wanted him to carry on the story of what happened. The Ute hoped it would serve as a warning to others. After hearing the story from the lone survivor, the remaining Spaniards were so afraid of the Ute, they didn't dare venture around these parts again."

"Grandpa, I don't understand. Why didn't the Ute take the gold for themselves?" Huber asked.

"I suppose because they had no real use for it. Their economy was based more on bartering and trading. They believed money's influence could easily corrupt the soul. Maybe they were on to something."

"How do you know all this really happened, Grandpa?" Huber asked, somewhat skeptical. In his earlier years, Huber accepted everything his grandfather told him about the story as fact. At that time, he had also believed in the tooth fairy and the Easter bunny.

"Like I said, the man they allowed to survive spread the story."

"Yeah, but how do you know any of it is real? Maybe the guy never existed. If he did, maybe he just made the whole thing up."

Grandpa Nick looked hurt, and Huber regretted voicing his doubts.

Hannah glared at him. "Huber, if Grandpa says it's true, then it is."

"Just saying, some kinda proof would be nice."

"Proof, you say?" Grandpa Nick mumbled. "Well, I guess today's your lucky day."

"Huh?"

A sparkle lit up Grandpa Nick's eyes as he smiled wide. Opening a drawer next to his bed, the old man pulled out a weathered document and handed it to his grandkids to examine. Huber ran his finger along the smooth, glossy surface of the parchment, attempting to decipher the intricate, cursive lettering. The reverse side was decorated with elaborate calligraphy, symbols, and landmarks. Huber realized he was holding a map of some kind.

"What is this, Grandpa?" Hannah asked, puzzled.

"Buckskin parchment."

"Like deer skin?"

"That's exactly what it is, my dear. It lasts a lot longer than paper."

"What's it say?" asked Huber. "Is this Spanish?"

Grandpa Nick nodded slowly.

"I'm taking Spanish from Mr. Mendoza this year," Hannah remarked. "*Mi hermano tiene músculos como niña.*"

Confused, Huber remarked, "What's that supposed to mean?"

Grandpa Nick responded, "My brother has muscles like a little girl."

Stupefied, Huber and Hannah's jaws dropped.

"Grandpa, you know Spanish?" Hannah exclaimed.

Grandpa Nick continued to grin, "*Poquito* . . . little bit."

"How come you never spoke it before?"

"Guess the occasion never presented itself."

"How'd you learn?" Huber asked in amazement at yet another skill his grandpa possessed.

"I worked with a lot of guys who spoke only Spanish at the coal mine. I had to learn. I practice with Maria whenever I can. Like I said, it's not great—just enough to get by. Now, do you want to hear about this parchment or not?" he growled, growing impatient.

"Yes," they replied in unison.

"That in your hands is a letter and a map written by Pedro Salazar himself, the lone survivor of the Ute attack."

Huber and Hannah's jaws dropped as they realized what they held.

"No way!" Huber exclaimed, still clinging to his skepticism.

Grandpa Nick continued, "In this letter, he tells the story of his encounter in the green mountains across the sea, north of Santa Fe and east of California. He expresses his desire for his descendants to come to this place again to reclaim the lost treasure. Look at the back."

Turning the parchment over, they viewed the intricately drawn map with skulls, strange insignias, and phrases in Spanish. At the top, the map read, "*Mapa por mí—Pedro Salazar, 1747.*

"The map to Dead Man's Treasure, drawn by Pedro Salazar in 1747."

"How come you never showed this to us?" Huber demanded.

"Well, to be honest, I forgot all about the thing until Maria and I were going through some of my stuff. I'm trying to finalize my will for when I'm gone."

Huber hated when his grandpa talked like this. The thought of him vanishing from the earth was more than he could stomach. Emotion instantly welled up inside him. The fact that Grandpa Nick was sick and would soon die was no secret. But death was part of life. He'd heard it over and over again. Even though he understood the inevitability of death, he couldn't imagine not coming to visit Grandpa Nick anymore, not having an escape.

"Where'd you get it?" Hannah wondered in awe.

"Years ago, while fly-fishing up in Roaring Fork Canyon, I overheard a man cursing in Spanish off in the distance. He was yelling about not being able to find something—symbols of some kind. I followed the sound and found him staring up like an imbecile at some tree. '*No esta aqui! El tesoro no existe!*' he kept yelling."

"What's that mean?" Huber asked.

"'It's not here . . . the treasure doesn't exist.' I asked if I could help. He was surprised that I could speak Spanish. Told me that he had come all the way from Spain for nothing. He had wasted the whole summer looking for a treasure that wasn't real. He then smiled and handed me this map. He politely said *ciao*, then walked down toward the mouth of the canyon, muttering to himself. I didn't think much of it at the time. I folded the thing up, put it in my pocket, and went back to fishing. I decided to stop by the coffee shop that night. Lo and behold, I find my friend there, sitting all alone staring at the ceiling.

"I sat next to him and we became better acquainted. I asked him about the letter. He told me the story I told you just now. Said his name is Carlos Salazar and that he was a great descendant of Pedro Salazar, this man who survived the attack. His family was poor, and he had spent his life savings to travel to Carbondale and find this Dead Man's Treasure. He genuinely believed he was going to find the lost mine his father and grandfather had told him about. After his search, he was convinced the stories were nothing more than fairy tales." Grandpa Nick nodded toward Huber. "He returned to Spain a few days later. Have to admit that after our conversation, I found myself becoming more and more fascinated by the idea of old Spanish treasure right here in our own backyard. I started driving up to the mountain at least a couple of times a month to search . . . you know, just for fun. I read the letter, studied the map, and tried to follow the clues for many years. Of course, after so long, it's possible that the mine's collapsed or overgrown. Could've been right under my nose . . . I may not have known it. However, it wasn't all for nothing. I found a few things."

"Like what?"

"Fresh air . . . relaxation . . . peace."

Huber rolled his eyes. "You never found treasure, though."

"Maybe in some ways . . . I did."

Grandpa Nick looked wiped out from all the talking, sweat forming on his eyebrows.

"Whatever happened to Carlos?"

"Written him off and on over the years, keeping him up to date on my progress. Haven't heard from him in years. Wouldn't surprise me if he's kicked the bucket.

"I can't believe you never showed this to us," Hannah said, chagrined as she took the parchment from Huber. She then handed it to Grandpa Nick, who tucked it safely back in the drawer.

"Well, my dear . . . you forget so many things as you go through life. All your memories get put in some box and stored away in the attic. After a while . . . well . . . they just get . . . forgotten." Grandpa Nick stared wistfully at an old picture of Huber's grandmother placed atop the nightstand before breaking the heavy silence.

"Well, enough about that. Hannah . . . your deal."

CHAPTER 5

MONDAY ARRIVED TOO QUICKLY. To call it a terrible morning would be an understatement. The shirt Huber wore sported a big white crusty blob, the result of spilled milk during the car ride to school. Potholes. Carbondale was full of them. His stomach gnawed at him as he arrived to school late again. Today would be his fifth tardy in first period, and he knew what that meant. Carbondale Middle School has a strict policy about tardiness. If you get three, a call is made home by the teacher. If you get five, you get to visit with the principal. After seven, a suspension.

As much as Huber hated being late, he hated getting out of bed more. He couldn't help it if his brain turned on at night and refused to shut off until 2:00 a.m. How many tongue lashings had he endured from his mom and sister? The rub of it all was that Hannah didn't get in trouble at all. Her first period Spanish teacher, Mr. Mendoza, held a contrasting philosophy when compared with most teachers. Mr. Mendoza believed that if students were late to his class, it was his fault for not making school interesting enough. Mrs. Collins, on the other hand, viewed herself as a taskmaster, an enforcer of every jot and tittle of the school handbook.

Don't notice me, don't notice me, Huber prayed silently as

he lingered outside her classroom so he could sneak in unde-
tected.

Peering through the rectangular window on the door, he
observed Mrs. Collins trying to explain something on the
board. This was her second year as a teacher, and she seemed
intent on gaining a reputation as one of the meanest in the
school. She had smiled only twice the whole year. Twice. And
those smiles had only come when students were caught cheat-
ing on tests. Through the window, she appeared especially
sour today. The blonde ponytail of the tall, skinny woman
swished behind her lower back, her milky white skin camouflaged against the whiteboard. As she turned, her long nose
protruded sharply from her face. A festive blue vest with kit-
tens on it starkly contrasted her demeanor.

Mustering all the courage he could, Huber pushed open
the classroom door.

A scraping *creaaaaakkkk* echoed through the room as the
door slowly swung on its hinges. Then the handle slipped
from Huber's grasp. *Slam!* The heavy door crashed with a loud
bang, causing the class to jump in their seats. Huber cringed
and closed his eyes. Mrs. Collins stopped her lecture mid sentence. Like a turtle, he tucked his neck into his shoulders.
Dead quiet. Slowly opening his eyes, he beheld Mrs. Collins
glowering at him, hands on her hips, her thin wire-framed
glasses perching themselves upon her stately beak. Statuesque,
Huber remained stiff, his face expressionless. If he didn't say
or do anything, perhaps she'd allow him to journey the rest of
the way to his seat unscathed.

After what seemed like an eternity, Mrs. Collins barked,
"So glad you could join us, Mr. Hill. Do you have any idea

how distracting it is when you come into my room like that?"

Huber wrung his wrists together. "Sorry, Mrs. Collins. My sister slept in and—"

"Save it! How many tardies does that make this term? Five, I think? I believe that warrants a visit with the principal. Put down your backpack and get going. Chop, chop!"

Huber hated it when she said, "Chop, chop." He sauntered through the corridor toward the main office, taking as much time as possible to postpone the inevitable. The principal's office finally came into view. With each footstep, the door grew bigger and bigger until it seemed to tower a hundred feet above him. Holding his breath, he tapped lightly on the door.

"What is it!" a woman's voice screeched from the other side.

"Principal Harris, it's Huber Hill. Mrs. Collins sent me down here."

"Yes, she called me ten minutes ago. Where have you been?"

"Had to go to the bathroom," Huber lied, grimacing.

"Take a seat out there! I'll be with you in a minute."

Huber sat down in one of the vacant seats outside the office and wondered what tortures lay in store. Principal Harris possessed a reputation for tough love and making examples out of kids, especially first-time offenders like Huber, hoping a traumatic experience would keep them on the straight and narrow. Would this transgression go on his permanent record? Would he ever get into a good college or be able to obtain a decent job now?

All of these scenarios played out in his head as he wrung his sweaty palms. Finally, the door flew open. Principal

Harris's eyes burned into him, sizing him up. He felt like an ant beneath a magnifying glass. How could an old woman with permed, poofy, gray hair be so terrifying? A few wrinkles decorated her face, and it was obvious she drew her eyebrows on with a pencil. Her attire—a red button-up jacket with gold buttons and a black business skirt—demanded respect. To meet her gaze would be like trying to stare into the sun. With arms folded and one of her fake eyebrows tilted upward, Principal Harris chomped on a piece of gum. Wasn't gum against school policy? Adults never had to live with the same rules as students. After Principal Harris assessed him, she spoke.

"Get in here and shut the door behind you!"

Huber jumped out of the chair and dashed into the office, sure he'd never see the light of day again.

Ten minutes later, Huber exited the office, relieved. Not nearly as bad as he thought it'd be. "No excuses, no nonsense," she had told him. He told her he'd try harder to be on time. Not good enough. Either he'd be on time or not. Would he be willing to make a commitment? What choice did he have? A lecture followed his pledge. Take responsibility for your actions, get up earlier, and don't waste time. Two more tardies would result in a suspension. Did he understand? Yes, he did. Determined to keep his pledge, Huber marched back to class.

Back in the room, the class wrestled with a fractions assignment. Mrs. Collins, sitting at her desk, looked smug. Cautiously, he approached her throne to hand in the admit slip from the principal. Poring over the words with an incredulous

look, her lips turned inward. "Good thing I'm not the principal. You wouldn't have gotten off so easy. Go sit down."

Finding his seat quickly, he commenced his studies with
a renewed sense of vigor. Despite his hatred of Mrs. Collins,
Huber liked math. Each problem presented a puzzle waiting
to be solved. Most would think it strange, but more than anything else, Huber loved math tests. Test-taking time provided
peace and quiet—just man and equation. It was a battle in the
war of knowledge, and each problem, an enemy soldier. Solve
enough equations correctly and Huber would win the battle.

As he diligently prepared for the next battle, he peered
over at Alison Harmon, who studied just across from him.
He hadn't even thought about talking to her since the tighty-
whities fiasco. Now, caught watching her, Huber whipped his
eyes back toward his desk. From the corner of his eye, he stole
another look. A half smile. His heart sped up. Flushing, he
returned the gesture. Now, a full smile. Glancing down, he
covered the milk stain with his elbow, convinced she'd see
it. His mouth opened to say hello. *Smack!* Huber reached
around and felt a tiny, wet lump clinging to his neck—a Scott
McCormick–brand spit wad, obvious from its texture. Craning his neck, Huber turned to face his tormentor, who was sitting a few rows back, smirking deviously. His eyebrows flitted
up and down.

"Nice shot, dude," one of Scott's cronies whispered, slapping his hand.

Alison glared at Scott and shook her head. Scott turned
his palms outward as if to say, "What'd I do?"

Huber brushed the spit wad from his neck, wiped his
hand onto his pant leg, and tried to refocus. Another ruined

opportunity, courtesy of Scott McCormick. As he settled back into his rhythm, another sting followed, then another. Stifled laughter erupted from all around. He brushed it off. *Spit wads off a duck's back.* Huber wished he could shrink and disappear. Snakes slither into the ground, birds fly to their nests, turtles retreat into their shells, but in middle school, a boy has nowhere to hide his head.

Mrs. Collins stood up as she heard the giggling. She rapped her desk twice and looked at the group of students.

"Quiet! Get to *work*!"

All cowed at the command except Scott, who met the woman's gaze.

After four more spit wads and four more red welts, the excruciatingly long class ended.

During lunch, Huber sat alone, as usual, hastily trying to eat a peanut butter and jelly sandwich. No doubt, his dad had made the sandwich. Jelly dripped off the side and fingerprints indented the bread. *Nice, Dad,* he thought upon seeing the poorly constructed sandwich. After missing breakfast this morning, he'd have to settle. As he ripped into the sandwich, a force knocked him to one side. Scott McCormick plopped down next to him.

"Hey, moron, how'd ya like my spit wads today? Regular sharp shooter, ain't I?" he cackled, sliding his lunch tray next to Huber. School lunch today comprised of a rubbery chicken patty, soggy fries, and chocolate pudding for dessert.

"Go away," Huber stuttered.

Scott went on as if he hadn't heard, his mouth half full of fries. "Didn't see ya or your sister on the bus today. Man, she's hot. I's hoping that you were sick and didn't come to school, that way we coulda sat together during the ride home. Ya know . . . get to know each other better. No such luck, I s'pose."

Fingernails dug into Huber's palms as he clenched his fists. A tiny ball of hate materialized in the pit of his stomach.

"Don't talk about my sister."

"Can't help it if she's the hottest girl in school, Puber."

"Shut up."

"C'mon, Puber, just kiddin' 'round, man . . . She is pretty cute though!"

Huber took a deep breath to calm himself. The ball of hate grew larger, and in its center a tiny flame ignited.

Chomping away like a cow, Scott noticed Huber's shirt and pointed. "What's that on your shirt, dude? Ya puke all over yourself or somethin'?" Bending down, Scott sniffed the stain. "Whew, sure smells like it!" Waving his hand in front of his nose, he pretended to cough. Scott's cronies noticed and joined him at the table. Huber's stomach twisted in knots.

"Oh, man, that's terrible. Ya smell just like my baby cousin." Scott laughed, and the others followed suit. Huber stared at his food, no longer hungry. The flame intensified.

"Since you're already so messy and stinkin' up the place, ya won't mind if I do this, will ya?"

Scott raised the cup of pudding high above Huber's head. "Woops." The pudding oozed from the cup, splattered on Huber's head, and trickled over his eyebrows. A carousel of laughing faces encircled him. The cold, semi-solid mass flowed toward his mouth.

One small voice stood out amid the laughter. "Get away from my brother!" For Huber, the only thing more embarrassing than being picked on in front of everyone was to have your sister come to the rescue.

"Leave him alone, or I'll knock your teeth into the back of your throat," she shouted at Scott as she approached the table.

"Ya need your sister to protect cha? That's pathetic, dude."

"Get away from him!" she yelled as she approached Huber.

As she did, Scott shot his foot out in front of her. Sprawling forward, she stumbled and fell. A sickening thud filled the room as her mouth connected with the lunch bench. Crumpled on the floor and crying, Hannah held her hands to the bloody mess that was her mouth.

The blazing ball of hate erupted into a violent explosion. As if watching himself from a distance, Huber yanked Scott from the bench and onto the floor. Hatred coursed through his veins as he pummeled his tormentor for all he was worth. Taken aback by Huber's action, Scott had no chance to defend himself. Soggy fries, chicken patties, and milk showered the two boys. Teachers rushed to the scene attempting to pry them apart. Aghast, Hannah stopped crying and stood in shock as her brother's flailing arms continued to pound Scott to a bloody pulp.

Two adults finally brought calm to the chaos. Scott was now being detained by the janitor, Mr. Mason, and Mr. Mendoza's powerful arms held Huber securely in place. No point in struggling.

"Calm down, buddy. Just calm down now," Mr. Mendoza whispered in Huber's ear. Huber's breathing slowed as the adrenaline subsided. Mr. Mendoza eased his grip. "I bet that felt really good, didn't it, my man? I've been waiting for someone to clean that punk's clock all year." Flabbergasted, Huber twisted around to look at Hannah's Spanish teacher. Mr. Mendoza's wide mouth turned into a large grin, and just as quickly disappeared when Mrs. Collins barged into the lunchroom.

"What happened here?" she demanded in a shrill voice.

Mr. Mendoza acted angry as he clutched Huber's arm. In a gruff tone, he addressed Mrs. Collins. "I'll deal with this one, Mrs. Collins." He glared at Huber. "Let's take a trip to the principal's office, young man."

Mrs. Collins's lips pursed into an oval of satisfaction. Nodding her head, a hurrumph of air escaped from her nose.

On his way to the office, Huber eyed Mr. Mendoza. The grin had returned. Mr. Mason and Mr. Mendoza forced the boys outside of the principal's office. Mr. Mendoza rapped on the door.

"What!"

Huber observed Mr. Mendoza cower. He was actually nervous. "Principal Harris, Mr. Mendoza here . . . I've got two kids who were fighting in the lunchroom. They've made quite a mess of each other and the cafeteria, I'm afraid."

"Whooooo?"

"Scott McCormick."

"Big surprise. Aaaand?"

"And . . . Huber Hill," he gulped, looking at the boy as if he were a dead man.

A dramatic pause followed.

"Mr. Mendoza, get in here and shut the door behind you!"

An eternity passed as Huber waited outside of the principal's office for the second time that day. Consequences would surely be much more severe this time around. Tardiness was one thing, but fighting? Whatever leniency the principal granted him this morning surely had evaporated. Scott sulked beside him, holding an ice-filled Ziploc baggie to his swollen eye. Neither uttered a word. Pudding and blood caked their clothing. Standing guard across the way, Mr. Mason dared them to say something. Muffled sounds passed through the door as Principal Harris interrogated Mr. Mendoza. Every now and then, Huber made out an intelligible word. Hannah, propped up in the sick room adjacent to the office, held a wad of wet paper towels to her lip. Eyes round as saucers, she also heard the rumblings. Finally, the secretary returned with gloved hands and inspected her wounds. Mr. Mason was called back to the lunchroom to clean up the mess. Frowning toward the boys, he issued a warning that should there be any more fighting while he was gone, there'd be "h-e-double hockey sticks" to pay. In their isolation, the boys continued their silent treatment.

Scott finally spoke up. "Puber, I didn't mean for her to get hurt like that, honest."

"Yeah, right."

"I don't care if ya don't believe me. It's true, though." His split lip looked like it hurt. Moments later, Huber choked back a laugh as a ludicrous thought crossed his mind.

"What's so funny?" Scott scowled.

"Just thinking of something.

"What?"

"You ever seen the *Hunchback of Notre Dame?*"

"Yeah. So?"

"I was thinking you look like Quasimodo right now."

Scott drew his arm back as if he were about to throw a punch. Luckily, at that moment, the door to the principal's office flung open. Mr. Mendoza booked it out, surveying the two boys with a grave stare. "Whew, I'm glad that I'm not either of you."

Huber's eyes filled with fear. Scott sat impassively. Mr. Mendoza's face brightened considerably as he walked toward his classroom. "Best of luck guys. I'll look for your eulogies in the paper."

"Boys! My office, now! Shut the door behind you!" Not a shred of forgiveness in Principal Harris's voice.

Slowly, the boys arose from their seats. *Dead men walking.*

Seconds later, the grilling of a lifetime commenced. Not only had they violated the safe school policy but they had also damaged the school's image. How could they be so selfish? Huber felt guilty at the reprimand and let his eyes drift to the ground. Scott seemed to have heard it all before. Rolling his eyes toward the ceiling, he waited for the broken record to end.

The two boys listened on speakerphone as Principal Harris called their parents. The voices on the other side of the line assured her that there'd be consequences for their kids' actions. Upon hanging up, Principal Harris gave another short lecture about zero tolerance when it came to violence. Finally, she asked a question in a semicompassionate tone.

"Huber, why did you fight with Scott in the lunchroom today?"

Huber shrugged. "I dunno."

"Don't you dare pull that with me! Both of you already have detention after school today and ISS tomorrow."

ISS was the acronym for "In School Suspension." Based on the concept that kids might play video games and watch TV if at home, ISS made sure there'd be no fun. In ISS, you have nothing to do but watch the seconds tick by.

"If you refuse to answer, I will make it triple that. Want to reconsider your answer?"

"He dumped pudding on my head," Huber said flatly.

"And what compelled you to dump pudding on Huber's head, Scott?"

Scott stonewalled her.

"It's triple for you now, Scott. You want to keep playing this game? Answer me! Why did you dump pudding on his head?"

He glanced at Huber and then at Principal Harris with a rebellious glare. "Cuz I felt like it."

Principal Harris didn't take the bait. "I'm guessing this isn't the first encounter you two have had. Am I correct in that assumption?" she asked Huber.

He nodded.

"How long have you two been having trouble?"

Scott interrupted before Huber could answer. "A couple of years."

"That's a long time. Why am I just now becoming aware of it?"

"Cuz if he woulda said anything, I woulda made his life a livin' nightmare."

Huber interjected, "What did I ever do to you, anyway?"

"You were born," he said, chuckling and smiling. Neither Huber nor Principal Harris thought his comments funny. His smile soon faded.

"I think it's a valid question, Scott. Answer it, or I'll add three more days of ISS."

A full minute passed before he blurted out, "I tried to be friends with him when we were younger, but he always ignored me. Thought he was better than me. Thought I's just some white trash country kid."

Huber's jaw dropped to the ground.

"Huber?" the principal asked, observing the shock sprawled across his face. "Actually, let me ask Scott a question. Scott, how did you let Huber know you wanted to be his friend?"

"I dunno. Stuff that friends do."

"Such as?"

"I dunno."

"Huber, do you remember Scott trying to be friends?" Principal Harris asked.

"No."

"What do you remember from back then?"

"Yo' mama so fat jokes. Getting slugged and pushed around . . . pretty much like now."

Scott interjected. "It wasn't mean sluggin' and pushin'. It was friendly sluggin' and pushin'."

"Did you think of Scott's actions as 'friendly?'"

"No."

"Scott, did you ever stop to think that Huber may not have seen your actions as being friendly?"

Scott said nothing. He then turned to Huber and argued,

"I tried to invite ya to my house one day after school, and ya wouldn't even answer me."

"I figured it was just so you could get me alone and beat me up."

"I wasn't gonna beat ya up, Puber."

"Scott," Principal Harris warned. "Call him by his name."

"Sorry . . . *Huber*. Just wanted to hang out, dude. After that, figured ya musta thought that ya were better than me or somethin'."

"So you decided to make him pay, right?"

"I guess so." Scott shrugged.

"Huber, how do you feel toward Scott at this moment?"

"If he wanted to be friends, he had a funny way of showing it."

"Can you see yourself ever being friends with him?" Principal Harris asked.

"I just want him to leave me alone. Quit harassing me."

She looked at Scott. "Sounds fair to me. Scott, what do you think?"

"Fine. I'll leave 'im alone."

"I know you will. And, Huber, I know if Scott threatens you or doesn't leave you alone, you won't respond with violence anymore, will you? You'll talk to me about it."

"Yeah."

"Good. I'll be watching both of you. You're on my radar, and once you're on my radar, you don't get off of it." She smirked. "Now get to ISS."

On his way out of her office, Huber stopped and looked over his shoulder at Principal Harris. Smiling, she nodded her head at him. Even though he had to go to in school suspension and detention after school, it could've been a lot worse. Principal Harris was all right.

The remaining hours of the school day dwindled away within ISS. He'd have to stay in the same room with Scott for two more hours after school let out. With no bus ride today, he'd be walking home. The seconds, minutes, and hours crawled by, the unbearable boredom accentuated by each tick of the clock. No talking. No sleeping. No reading.

This has to be illegal, Huber thought. *Surely, something in the Geneva Convention banned such torture.* Before going home, Huber had to write a one-page reflection paper on how he'd change his actions if he could go back in time. Huber wrote something down that would please the ISS lady so he could leave, but deep down he regretted nothing.

CHAPTER
6

HUBER AND HANNAH'S moderately-sized, two-story home looked almost exactly like every other house on the street. They were truly "cookie cutter houses"—same size, same floor plan, just with different colored exteriors. As Huber tromped through the small front yard, he smirked at the plastic pink flamingo placed between their front two shrubs. His dad despised the thing. During the past two years, Robert had tossed the flamingo in the trash several times. Somehow, it always found its way back into the yard. Both parents possessed a stubborn tenacity when it came to giving in to the other.

Drained by the two-mile walk home, Huber neared the front door. As bad as his feet throbbed, it was nothing compared to his stomach, gnawing and gurgling after missing both breakfast and lunch. The memory of a leftover pizza slice in the fridge beckoned him forward. Huber's footsteps became heavy and slow, his breathing labored. He wrapped his clammy hand around the shiny gold doorknob. Slowly turning the knob counterclockwise, he heard the "click" of the latch, and the door inched open. Surely, the furious look of his mother's face awaited him on the other side. Bracing himself, he crept into the house, preparing for the tongue-lashing of a lifetime.

No one was there.

Huber heaved a sigh of relief and bounded into the kitchen, opening the refrigerator and snatching up the pizza. As he closed the refrigerator door, a vaporous figure materialized out of thin air. A flashing hand seized the pizza slice from his mouth and chucked it onto the counter. Ellen's angry gaze bore into him like a burning hot drill bit. His stomach groaned in disappointment.

"Hey, Mom. How was your day? Your hair looks nice."

Ellen's demeanor remained unchanged. Huber shrank beneath her ominous gaze.

"I am very disappointed in you. I never in my life expected you to do something like you did today," she said in a blend of anger and sadness.

Why couldn't she ground him or take away his video games? The word *disappointed* stung far worse than anything else. "But, Mom, Grandpa always says there's a time to talk, a time to walk, and a time for action! I couldn't just sit by and do nothing."

"Upstairs to your room. You'll be spending the rest of the evening up there contemplating your actions."

"But I'm starving!"

"Go! Now!"

Huber didn't think he could stand any more contemplating, but he tramped his way up to his room, stomach still growling. On his way up the stairway, he heard his mother babying Hannah, who had since walked through the back door.

"You poor thing. Let me see your mouth."

"Hmmm, pizza!" his sister exclaimed as she picked the

slice up off the counter and took a huge bite.

Huber glared at her from the top of the stairs. Grinning up at him, she tore another bite from the pizza and shrugged her shoulders. Huber retreated into his room, slamming the door.

Despite his hunger and fatigue, he somehow felt better than ever. Something deep inside had changed. A confidence he'd never felt before surged within him. He would call Grandpa Nick tonight to tell him what happened. He knew that his grandpa would understand even if his mom didn't.

Huber did his homework, then read a comic book about aliens that had come to earth thousands of years ago to lay their eggs underground. Hobo also kept him company. Most of the time, the dog just stared up at him absently or slept, but Huber appreciated his presence nonetheless. When he got tired of reading comics, Huber cranked up his music, performed a few push-ups, and then ripped off his shirt to admire himself in the mirror. He dimmed the lighting in his room and rubbed suntan oil all over his chest and biceps. He stood there, flexing as if he'd somehow grown tenfold in a day. He practiced the lines he'd say to people at school the next day. In the mirror, he imagined Alison Harmon. Hopefully, after today, forgotten were the memories of tighty-whities, spit wads, and everything else Puber.

Gawking into the mirror, he dramatized, "Yeah, no big deal. Just pushed me a little too far. Had to protect my sister. I'd do the same for you, you know."

At dinnertime, Hannah brought him some food. She knocked on the door, and he promptly put his shirt back on. He opened the door and saw that she held a plate of meat loaf and steamed vegetables. Huber normally hated meat loaf, but he was so hungry he could've eaten a horse. He snatched the plate and started wolfing it down.

"What you did today was so great!" she exclaimed. "I'm trying to convince Mom and Dad that you were only protecting me. I hope they'll go easier on you."

"What are they saying?"

"Dad's on your side. He said it's about time you stand up for yourself and do something. Mom says that violence is never the answer. They started fighting about it at the table, so I left and came up here. Maybe if they fight long enough, they'll forget about your punishment."

Hobo was wiggling back and forth, grunting, snorting, and whimpering while trying to scratch his back on the carpet floor.

"C'mere, boy, I'll scratch that itch for you," Huber said.

The dog ran to Huber's side and lay on his stomach. As Huber scratched his back, Hobo's lips receded back, and his back leg kicked wildly.

At ten o'clock, when everyone had gone to bed, Huber took out his cell and dialed his grandpa's number. Grandpa Nick told him he didn't really sleep through the night, so he could call anytime. Huber knew he'd be awake, probably watching old episodes of Perry Mason or Alfred Hitchcock.

"Hello," the mechanical voice said on the other end of the line.

"Grandpa, it's me. You won't believe what happened today."

Huber related the events of the day, sparing no details and

perhaps embellishing a little bit to make himself look better. He told his Grandpa how his words of wisdom about taking action came to mind.

"I'm proud of you," Grandpa Nick said. "You did what was right regardless of any negative personal consequences. You whipped him good, and I guarantee that he's going to be walking around like a dog with his tail between his legs for a while. You know what I always say, there's a time to talk, a time to walk, and a . . ."

"Time for action . . . I know. Unfortunately, my mom doesn't seem to get that."

"Bah! She'll come around."

"I wonder how things will change now," Huber said.

"Change always happens. As you get older, everything changes —your environment, your friends . . . and you change too, though you don't realize it. You can't control it, you can't escape it. The only thing you can control is how you deal with it. It's how we deal with change that shapes and shows us who we really are. Of course . . . I suppose some things don't change."

"Like what?"

"Well, you'll always be a member of your family, and they'll always love you."

"What else?"

"Like I said, people change a lot as they get older, but in some ways they stay the same. You're always going to be you."

"I guess that's true."

"Many friends will also come and go throughout your life. But the very strongest of friendships stand the test of time and don't ever really change. You can go years on end without speaking. Then when you see them, you just pick up the conversation right where it left off."

"I don't have any friends like that," Huber uttered.

"Give it time, my boy. You will. Then you'll wonder how you ever got by before. Look at that! It's a quarter to eleven. You'd better get to bed. I don't think your mom would like me keeping you up so late on a school night."

"Probably not. Can we still come to your house this weekend?"

"You're welcome anytime. Aren't you grounded, though?"

"Can't you tell my mom that you need me to do chores or something? It could be part of my punishment."

"I'll see what I can do. See you Saturday."

"Okay. Bye, Grandpa."

"*Adios, muchacho.*"

Huber was restless as he tried to sleep. The events of the day kept playing repeatedly in his mind. He wondered what life would be like at school the next day. Would people see him differently? Would Scott decide to get revenge? What would Alison Harmon think? Eventually he drifted off into a deep slumber.

A strange dream filled his mind. There was a dark tunnel, and he was running. Something was closing in on him from behind. In the distance up ahead, a bright light appeared. As he reached the light, a gentle nudge awoke him. Daylight crept in through the window and fell on his face. How could that be? It felt like he had barely fallen asleep. It was already time for school? His mother, sitting on his bedside, stroked his hair. A forlorn look crossed her face. Maybe she was sorry for the way she'd treated him the day before.

"Hey, Mom, something wrong?" Huber asked groggily.

Tears came to her eyes as she choked up. "Oh, Huber . . . ," she whispered. "Grandpa died in his sleep last night."

The day of the funeral, Huber stared at the casket, still in shock. He knew this day was bound to come sooner rather than later—he had imagined what it would be like numerous times—but he was completely unprepared for the barrage of emotions that filled his heart. There had been a viewing of the body the night before the funeral. The spectral image of his grandpa lying in the casket haunted him still. White, stiff, and cold. The man in the casket hadn't resembled Grandpa Nick at all. However, his respirator was absent, and Huber liked the idea that he was now free of the thing.

Ellen was taking the death of her father especially hard. It was one of the few times Huber saw his parents completely and utterly support each other. His parents held hands, hugged each other, and hadn't fought one bit since the passing. In an odd way, the tragedy seemed to bring everyone closer together.

Huber's father approached him and laid a hand on his shoulder. He wore a black suit with his favorite navy-colored tie. He definitely looked like a tax accountant.

"Huber, how are you doing, son?" he asked uncomfortably.

As Huber looked up into his dad's eyes, he wanted to scream out and unleash the flood of emotions damming up inside him. He couldn't do it though. He hadn't even cried since Grandpa Nick's death.

"Okay, Dad."

"That's good to hear," Robert slapped his son on the back.

As the officiator concluded his words, the family looked on as Grandpa Nick's casket slowly descended into the ground, next to his grandmother's grave. It was a surreal experience, thinking about Grandpa six feet underground. While his mom and sister sobbed, Huber felt empty. Tears still refused to come. The family stood around for a few minutes longer. Everyone took turns casting flowers into the grave. They landed with a soft thud onto the casket.

As Huber peered down, he tossed Grandpa's favorite flower, a red carnation, into the hole. *"Adios, muchacho."*

During the car ride home, it was just starting to get dark, and a light drizzle obscured the SUV's windshield. A few blocks from their house, Huber noticed something strange. A tall man, dressed in black, walked down the sidewalk. On his head rested a large, wide-brimmed hat. As the family's SUV passed him, he turned his head and made eye contact with Huber through the window. Huber gasped and sunk in his seat. He could've sworn that he'd just peered into the eyes of the devil himself.

CHAPTER
7

ON THE WEEKEND FOLLOWING the funeral, Huber found himself at Grandpa Nick's house with his parents and extended family. Hannah chose to stay home. She didn't want to come to the house without Grandpa Nick being there. In the living room, a guy in a suit droned on, informing the adults which possessions of Grandpa Nick's now belonged to them. Maria was there as well. Huber wandered through the house, relishing memories from years past. The place didn't quite feel the same anymore.

He opened the door to his grandpa's room and stepped inside. The outline of Grandpa Nick's body was still on the sheets and mattress as if he had just gotten out of bed. He walked over to the pillow and caressed it with his hand. On the nightstand lay cherry cough drops and Vicks VapoRub. The ventilator sat silently. Empty slippers awaited their masters toward the foot of the bed. Huber turned and surveyed the rest of the room. Sitting on a small table beneath the window were the board games and decks of cards Grandpa Nick had set out in anticipation of his upcoming visit. As he gazed around the room that longed for laughter and noise once again, Maria stepped inside. Gently, she put her hands on Huber's shoulder and asked him to join her in the kitchen for a drink. Looking back one last time, he shut the door.

As they had a soda at the kitchen table, Maria looked at Huber with melancholy, tear-filled eyes. "I loved your *abuelo* very much. He was like a father to me, you know."

Huber simply acknowledged her comment with a nod, then ventured, "Maria, I haven't even cried since Grandpa died. Does that mean I'm a bad person?"

"*Ay de mí*, sweetheart, no. Everyone grieves in their own way in their own time."

In the other room, they could hear the adults arguing over who was to receive Grandpa Nick's armoire since it wasn't specified in the will. Huber hated the idea of everyone taking things out of his grandpa's house.

"I know it is hard to watch all of this. Is difficult for me too. Your *abuelo* left something out of his will. Gave it to me a week ago. He told me to give it to you without telling anyone else after he passed." From under the table, she retrieved a large, bulging shoebox, tied around the top with bailing twine. "It's yours. When I give this to you, I am supposed to say that these were his most valued treasures and that he only trusts you and your sister with them."

Huber's heart raced as he began to pull at the twine. Maria stopped him, eying the adults. "Wait until you get home, *mi amor*. You should open it alone."

On the way home, his parents were so busy complaining about the selfishness of the other family members that they didn't even notice the box Huber held in his lap. When he got home, he raced to his bedroom and quickly slid the box under his bed. He couldn't wait to shut himself in his room that night and see what the box contained. He would wait until he was sure he'd be undisturbed.

That night, as the family ate dinner together, his parents were still going on about Uncle Carl and Aunt Bonnie thinking they had the right to take Grandpa Nick's old jukebox. The conversation sickened Huber. He ate quickly and then asked to be excused. He ran to his room, locked the door behind him, and pulled the box out from under his bed.

Retrieving some scissors, he gently cut the twine. His hands shook like leaves. His head swam with anticipation. His heart raced at the prospect of what lay inside. Grandpa Nick, it seemed, was giving him a gift from beyond the grave. His conscience tried to tell him to wait for Hannah, but he couldn't help himself. He tore open the box and grinned. Inside, bundled with rubber bands, were stacks of letters. Underneath the letters rested a stack of several journals, a black and white photo of Grandpa Nick in uniform, and an old cigar box. How many times had he heard stories about the war? His grandma? Now he had the source of the stories so they'd never be forgotten. What an honor to know that his grandpa entrusted them to him.

In his excitement to go through the materials, he hadn't initially noticed the sealed envelope that was stuck between two journals. Scrawled across the face of the envelope were his and Hannah's names. Huber tore through the seal of the envelope and ripped out the letter. At the top, the date caught his eye. *Tuesday, May 8*. Just days ago. Silently, Huber pored over the letter.

Dear Huber & Hannah,

If you are reading this, that means I've finally kicked the bucket. I don't know why I'm writing this now. It feels my time is almost up, so I figured I'd stop procrastinating and write this while I'm still able. Feels like I'm getting ready to go on some long journey, only I don't exactly know where I'm headed. That's part of the excitement, I suppose. I'm curious to see what lies in store.

Rest assured that this change will be a good thing for me. However, there are a few things I will miss greatly . . . our games on Saturday afternoons, having our long conversations, and watching you both grow up come to mind. Each day I spent with you was a gift, and I cannot adequately express my love for you. You're good kids, and I can't tell you how proud it makes me to call you family.

I am leaving my most valued possessions to you. Inside you'll find my personal letters and journals. It will be a way that we can still talk with each other.

Remember to be strong even when you're scared, and courageous in the face of change.

Adios,

Grandpa Nick

Smiling, Huber read it again and again. As he folded the letter to put it back inside the envelope, he almost missed the postscript on the back.

P.S. In case you ever get the itch to go treasure hunting, I've included all of my notes and clues about the Tesoro de los Muertos, including my map from Pedro Salazar. It's inside the cigar box. Good luck! One more thing . . . at the bottom of this box is a very special surprise. I've never shown it to a living soul until now. Show it to no one unless you trust them completely.

Excitedly, Huber dug through the box. Near the bottom, he found a blue, pocket-sized booklet, labeled "Prospecting Guide." He opened it up. Jotted notes, annotations, and crudely drawn maps that Grandpa Nick had created riddled the pages. Underneath the title, it read "1975–1980." He opened the battered cigar box, and sure enough, the folded, deerskin parchment from Pedro Salazar was resting on top. What was the surprise he mentioned? Huber continued to search through the contents of the box and found a small, velvet ring box hiding beneath some letters. Huber snapped open the box, and what he saw overwhelmed him. *It couldn't be! Could it?*

He snatched the object from the box and shoved it in his pocket. He tore out of his room, ran down the hall, and pounded on Hannah's door.

"What!"

"Hannah, open the door! I have to show you something!"

"Later," she called out, annoyed.

"Hannah! Open up!"

The door flung open. On the other side, stood a person Huber didn't recognize. She wore a towel around her head, and a green-looking goop plastered her entire face. Huber grimaced.

"What do you want?" Hannah yelled, plucking out her earbuds, hip-hop music blasting through them.

Huber took a step back. "What's all over your face?"

"Exfoliating cream, dummy. It unclogs your pores. Keeps

you from getting zits," she replied defensively. *Since when did Hannah care about zits?*

"You look like a zombie wearing a turban. You don't even have zits." This was the first time he had seen his sister do something so . . . girly.

"Because I use this stuff!" She glared. "What, you want some?" she asked sarcastically.

"No! Listen, you have to come to my room right now!"

"Like I said, I'm busy," she said, trying to close the door. Huber stuck his foot at the base.

"What's wrong with you?"

"Believe me, you'll wanna see this," he reiterated, grabbing her by the hand and pulling her out into the hallway.

"Fine, make it quick." She blew out a sigh and trudged along to his bedroom. Once inside, she noticed the pile of letters and journals.

"What's all this stuff?" she asked.

"Grandpa left this box for us. Maria gave it to me at the house today."

"You opened it without me!"

"I . . . um . . ."

"You jerk! You couldn't wait for me?"

"Here, just read this," Huber implored, trying to take the heat off. He handed his sister the letter their Grandpa had written them. As she read, tears streamed down her face, carving deep lines through the green gunk. If she were in a monster movie, she'd look truly terrifying. Turning the letter over, she observed the postscript.

"Where's the surprise?"

"This," Huber answered, fumbling through his pocket,

pulling out the object, and holding it up to the light. Between his thumb and forefinger, the solitary gold doubloon shimmered, etched and engraved with faded symbols on one side. A symmetrical cross decorated the other.

Jagged and worn edges vouched for the coin's authenticity. Hannah snatched the coin from his hand to examine it more closely. "Oh my gosh!" she gasped while turning it over in the palm of her hand.

After holding the coin for a few minutes, she looked over at her beaming brother and handed it back to him. "Here, you hold on to it for safe keeping." Her brother shot her a look of both disbelief and gratitude. "Wonder how he got this. Why didn't he ever show it to us?"

"I don't know, but you know what this means?

"What?"

"It's true. The Dead Man's Treasure is real."

CHAPTER 8

HUBER DIDN'T ATTEND SCHOOL the entire week after the funeral. When he returned, everyone seemed to have a newfound respect for him, maybe even a little fear. People were talking to him in the hallways and at lunch, laughing at his jokes, telling him again and again how great it was that he put Scott in his place. People sat next to him at lunch. Scott McCormick kept his distance and didn't utter so much as a word to Huber or Hannah at school or on the bus. When their gaze met from across the room, Scott would dart his eyes away. That week, there were no spit wads, wedgies, or put-downs. Eighth grade was starting to improve for Huber Hill.

Full of confidence, he'd actually managed to say "hi" to Alison Harmon, who returned the gesture with a brilliant smile. He'd thought about asking her to sit with him at lunch but quickly changed his mind. It was still too soon for such a drastic step.

Never in his life had so many people wanted to be his friend. What surprised him most was how much he hated it. Their words sounded hollow, their flattery disingenuous. These friends weren't really friends; they were just cronies, like those who used to flock around Scott but who had now abandoned him because he was no longer the alpha male. During classes, Scott slunk toward the back of the room, never making a peep. No smart-aleck remarks, no antagonistic comments. His teachers had no idea what to make of the blissful silence. One word now summed up Scott's existence . . . *nobody*.

Serves him right, a part of Huber thought. *Now he knows what it's like.* Huber also understood all too well the ache of being a nobody and empathized with his former enemy. But surely his passiveness wouldn't last. One day when Huber least expected it, his pants would fall or his head would get slammed into a locker. *Just a matter of time until the humiliated dog comes to reclaim his rightful place.*

Toward the end of his first week back, Huber was sitting in third period when a buzzing vibrated his pocket. Stealthily, he snuck the cell phone from his pocket and flipped open the cover. It was a text from Scott's number. Glancing over his shoulder, Scott was slumped in a desk against the back wall, a hoodie pulled over his head. *Here it comes.* His finger pressed the "read text" button. Huber stared, dumbfounded.

"SORRY BOUT YOUR G-PA."

Was it some kind of setup? Some kind of sick trick? Huber wasn't sure, but decided to let it play out. Thumbing a message back, he replied, "LUNCH?"

Moments passed. Another vibration. "OKAY."

In the lunchroom, Huber waited, surrounded by his fake friends. Hoodie still over his head, Scott edged through the crowd toward Huber's table. Silence swept over the entire cafeteria.

"They're gonna fight again! Rematch! Rematch! Scott's gonna tear his flippin' head off!" The whispers traveled like electricity from table to table instantaneously.

Students held their camera phones in the ready position. An eerie stillness overtook the place as Scott hovered behind Huber.

Huber glanced behind him, then turned to the boy sitting to his left. "Move over."

Bewildered, the boy slid down the bench as Huber motioned for Scott to join him.

The whispers and texts resumed. "No way! Are they actually sitting together? Are they friends or something now?" Disappointed spectators slipped off to other tables.

"So, we good now?" Huber asked after a five-minute silence.

"Sure, Puber, we're good," Scott replied.

After lunch, the two boys wandered onto the field and talked. All eyes followed them, longing for another entertaining scuffle. During their conversation, the two realized they held more in common than they previously thought. They both loved sci-fi comics and video games. And then Huber did something that would have been unfathomable just weeks before.

"Wanna come by my house today? My dad got this new TV, and I've been playing *Blood Wars* on it. It's pretty sweet."

"Puber, are you serious? I didn't know you were into BW."

"Yeah. You played it?"

"Just at Walmart. My dad says we might get it for Christmas, but I doubt it."

"So how about it?"

"Yeah, dude, count me in."

As the school year came to an end over the next couple of weeks, the two boys continued their association. Hannah watched the relationship cautiously but eventually came to believe that Scott was not out to get her brother or her. Every day—even weekends—the boys were together. The friendship acted as a balm to Huber's aching soul. Summer vacation arrived, the most blessed time of the year. The inseparable friends made the most of each day.

One rainy afternoon, the boys lounged in Huber's living room, playing video games. After killing each other scores of times, the game grew boring. Huber decided it was time to let Scott in on the secret. While he wasn't ready to show him the gold coin just yet, he revealed Grandpa Nick's prospecting guide and the map drawn up by Pedro Salazar, leading to *Tesoro de los Muertos.*

"You kiddin' me, Puber? We gotta find this thing!" Scott almost yelled upon examining the map. Turning it over, he studied the words written in Spanish. "What's it say?"

Huber relayed the story with almost as much enthusiasm as his grandfather had.

The same look of shock that crossed Huber's face when he first held the map now covered Scott's.

"I can't believe ya been holdin' out on me all this time. We gotta find this Dead Guy's Treasure."

"I wouldn't even know where to start," Huber replied.

"We can use your Grandpa's notes, dude. The mouth of the canyon ain't too far from here. Just a few miles. We can camp out!"

There was a long pause.

"Never really camped out before," Huber admitted sheep-ishly.

"Never camped out before? Ya realize we live in the mountains, don't cha?"

Huber nodded, ashamed.

"Aw, that don't matter. Been in Scouts all my life. I can teach ya everything I know. We've gotta try. Just imagine if we actually found it!"

"It'd be pretty cool, I admit. The booklet says *Tesoro de los Muertos* is deep inside a mine though. It's probably collapsed by now. My grandpa even said so," Huber related, trying to bridle his own excitement.

"Then we'll dig it out. C'mon, Puber, we gotta try."

"My mom and dad would never go for it."

"C'mon, Puber. What's the point of havin' all this stuff if ya ain't gonna use it?"

Huber opened his mouth for a rebuttal, but a knock came to the door.

"Huber, will you get it?" Ellen yelled from the kitchen downstairs.

The two boys flew down the stairs together and flung the door open to observe a man, about six feet tall, dressed in a long, white-sleeved shirt rolled up to his elbows. Covering the shirt was a black, intricately lined vest. The vest had silver stitching that created a dazzling, symmetrical design upon the breastwork.

Mesmerized by its appearance, Huber's eyes gradually climbed upward, until they locked on the man's face. He tried to mute an audible gasp. Gaunt cheeks concaved into the man's mouth. But what held him spellbound were the man's eyes. The left one, a bluish white color, bulged out grotesquely. A long, thick scar traveled vertically from his upper lip, over the discolored eye, and ended just above the eyebrow. Pale, almost translucent skin struggled to stick to the bony face. A wide-brimmed, black leather hat curved around the man's forehead. Black, oily hair dangled in a ponytail. Tight, black jeans with a leather belt hugged the man's skinny legs, and thick, steel-toed boots covered his feet.

As the boys gazed upon their visitor, the man removed his hat, held it in his hands, and bowed slightly. A strand of stringy hair tumbled toward his chin. Huber thought he recognized the man from somewhere. When he spoke, his voice carried a thick Spanish accent. He extended his right hand. A tattoo of a black serpent winding its way around the man's arm caught Huber's attention. When Huber took the man's hand, the snake's mouth enveloped his own.

"*Buenas tardes, muchachos.* My name is Juan Hernán Salazar."

CHAPTER 9

SALAZAR? HUBER STARED AT the man in the doorway. *As in Pedro Salazar?*

"*Jóvenes*, are either of you a relative of Nicholas Eldredge?" the man asked through two rows of rotten, yellow teeth. His atrocious breath carried death's decay. The smell caused Huber to become light-headed.

"What the heck's a *joven*?" Scott piped up, struggling to decipher the man's accent.

"*Ho-ven*," the man corrected his pronunciation. "I apologize. Often I forget that not everyone speaks in my native tongue. Especially those of . . . limited capacity," he said, motioning toward Scott. "It means 'young one.'"

"Yeah, well, 'round here, we don't get too many wannabe Zorro types . . ."

The stranger leveled a vicious stare in Scott's direction.

"You should mind your tongue, *joven*," the man whispered.

"Um, Nicholas Eldredge was my grandpa," Huber replied reluctantly.

Salazar's eyes darted from Scott to Huber. A smile lit up his face. "Wonderful news. I have traveled all the way here from Salamanca, Spain. May I enter?" the man asked politely, never letting his eyes leave Huber's.

"Um, one sec. Let me get my mom first," Huber replied, and he and Scott retreated into the house to find his mother.

Huber's mom hummed in the kitchen, slicing up a cucumber for a dinner salad.

"Hey, Mom, there's this creepy looking Zorro guy from Spain at the door."

Huber's mom shot him a look of confusion and frustration at being interrupted. "What? A guy from Spain? What's he selling? Whatever it is, we already have enough."

"No, he's not selling anything. Says he knew Grandpa or something."

Bewildered, Ellen put down the knife and wiped her hands on a towel. She brushed by Huber, who followed her. In the meantime, the man had invited himself in and stood in the foyer, smiling broadly. There was something about the way he looked at them that made Huber feel ill at ease.

Startled by the ghastly appearance of the tall Spaniard, Ellen gasped. "Oh, my goodness. May I help you?"

"My apologies, *señora*, I did not mean to frighten you. I do believe you can assist me. Is it okay that we sit down?" the man asked, pointing to the couch and love seat in the living room.

"Sure, why don't we," suggested Ellen, obviously uncomfortable.

As the man walked to the living room ahead of the group, Ellen shot Huber a chastising look for allowing the stranger inside. Huber could only shake his head and shrug his shoulders.

The man sat down on the love seat while the others sat on the couch across from him.

"I didn't catch your name," Ellen hesitated.

"*Gracias, señora*, for allowing me into your beautiful home. As I told the children, my name is Juan Hernán Salazar. I have traveled here from Salamanca, Spain, looking for relatives of Nicholas Eldredge," the man repeated as the boys fixated on his discolored eye. The man noticed their stares.

Ellen nudged her son and whispered, "Don't. It's impolite."

"Is okay," the man said. He then pointed to his blue, scarred eye. "I know it looks strange. I am mostly blind in this eye. An injury sustained in my youth."

"I am so sorry. It's really none of our business," Huber's mom continued. "I'm Ellen Hill. Nicholas Eldredge was my father."

"Oh, *querida*," the man in black moaned in faux sympathy. "I am very sorry for your loss. Your father was acquainted with my father, Carlos. They met one day in these mountains and became friends. I'm sure he has told you about this," the man said, pointing toward the mountains through the front window. "Word came to Spain recently about his passing. My father was very sad to hear of his death. He told me of their friendship all of my life."

"I appreciate your condolences, sir, but I'm wondering why you come all the way here to convey them," Ellen stated flatly.

"I do confess that there is another reason I am here. I believe your father was in possession of something that's very important to my family."

Huber remembered that Carlos was the name of Grandpa Nick's Spanish friend and that Carlos had given Grandpa Nick the map. This man was his son?

"What is it you're looking for, Mr. Salazar?"

"It is a letter written by an ancestor of mine. It contains information that is . . . how do I say? . . . very sentimental. My father gave this . . . letter to your father many years ago."

The two boys exchanged glances and then stared back at the stranger, knowing exactly what he was talking about. The stranger seemed to take note of the exchange.

"I don't know anything about that," Ellen answered. "I vaguely remember him talking about a man from Spain who he met in the mountains one day. I don't recall anything about a letter."

Salazar's tone transformed. "I know your father possessed this letter! I want it returned to me immediately!" The shroud of politeness had fallen.

Ellen, rattled by the stranger's angry tone, asked, "Why did your father not come himself?"

"He is very ill and unable to travel. He sent me here to retrieve this letter in his stead," the man replied defensively. "I need that letter!"

"Like I said, I haven't the slightest clue what you're talking about, Mr. Salazar, but please allow me to take down your information. I will look through his things and contact you if I find this letter. If I do, perhaps I can mail it to you in Spain."

The man glared at her for a split second before his features softened. "*Gracias, querida*, I will be most grateful. I would feel much better if I had the letter in my possession before I return to my country. I will be here for the next couple of weeks. Allow me to leave the number of where I stay. I am at the Roaring Fork Lodge. Please let me know if you find this letter."

The man then wrote down the number of the motel along with his room number and left the house. As he walked through the door onto the porch, he replaced the hat on his head, turned around, and eyed the two boys, who stood in the doorway. His mouth curled into a snaky smile. "Take care, *jóvenes*. Stay out of . . . trouble."

Huber closed the door and locked it behind him. They all went to the window and watched the man stand on their porch. With hands on his hips, the stranger surveyed the house and slowly walked away.

"Why did you let that creep inside our house?" Ellen demanded. "You know better than that!"

"I didn't let him in, Mom! He just walked inside when I came to get you."

"True, Mrs. H.," Scott said, backing him up. Ellen leveled Scott a look that conveyed her annoyance at his interruption.

"I'll be quiet now," Scott said.

Ellen's features relaxed. "It's all right. I just don't like strangers in our house. That guy gave me the willies. I have no idea what he was talking about. I don't remember Dad talking about any Spanish letter. Do you?"

Huber shrugged his shoulders as if he had no idea what she was talking about either. The two boys then flew upstairs to Huber's room.

"What was that?" Scott asked in disbelief.

"I dunno. I don't trust that guy, though."

"There was something about him, wasn't there? Did you see his tattoo?"

"No way I was gonna give him the map."

"Your mom doesn't know about it?"

"No. My grandpa only told me and Hannah. I don't want anyone else to know about it besides you."

"No problema, Puber. I can keep m'mouth shut," he garbled as he ate a handful of potato chips.

"Yeah . . . evidently not."

"Ya realize what this means, though?"

"What?"

"Other people are looking for it. Don't ya think we should find it before some other yahoo like him does?"

Huber twisted the blinds open to his bedroom window. The man in black—Salazar—was nowhere to be seen, yet Huber had the distinct feeling of being watched. "Yeah . . . maybe."

That same night, Huber sat in his room preparing to read his latest comic about computers becoming self-aware and enslaving humans to do their bidding when he heard his parents yelling at each other downstairs. They were fighting about the budget again. Would they never stop? In that instant, Huber made a decision and grabbed his cell phone. He dialed Scott's number. The phone rang twice before he answered.

"Puber, what's goin' on, man?"

"Pack your stuff. We're going to the mountains this weekend to find it."

"Now we're talking, dude. I'll come over tomorrow so we can work out the details."

"Yeah," Huber muttered through the phone. "See you tomorrow."

As soon as he hung up the phone, Huber looked up to see Hannah's face staring angrily at him through the doorway.

"I'm coming too, or I'll tell Mom and Dad what you're up to."

"Eavesdropping, eh? Go ahead, tell them. They can't stop me."

"C'mon, Huber. Grandpa Nick left those things for both of us. It's only fair that I get to come. I don't want to be left here all alone with Mom and Dad."

In his heart, Huber empathized with his sister, understanding all too well what she was feeling. However, he hated the idea of his sister tagging along on a guys' camping trip. Huber also had no doubt that Hannah would tell on him if he refused her request. What alternative did he have?

"Fine, you can go, but don't breathe a word to anyone."

"What are we going to tell Mom and Dad? If we just leave, they'll have the police out looking for us. They'll think we ran away or something."

"I know. I was just thinking about that."

"Tell Mom and Dad that you're going to spend the weekend with Scott and his dad. Tell 'em you guys are going to Six Flags in Denver. You're staying two nights so you won't be back until Sunday afternoon. I'll tell Mom that I'm going with my friend Alyssa to the Sarah Sprite concert down there too."

Huber agreed. "But what if they want to talk to the parents before we go?"

Hannah's eyes got big as she thought about the question. She acted like she was going to answer but stopped short.

"We'll have to think of something," she finally replied.

Huber called Scott again once Hannah was out of earshot. "Hey, we've got a problem. My dumb sister is coming along."

A groan echoed from the other end of the line.

CHAPTER •10•

THE NEXT DAY, A CALL came to the Hill household. Ellen looked at the caller ID and answered.

"Hello."

"Hello, Mrs. Hill, this is Brad McCormick, Scott's father. How are you?"

"I'm fine, Brad. How are you doing?"

"Great, thanks. Hey, the reason I'm calling is that I would like to take the boys to Denver this weekend. Scott and I were planning on going out to Six Flags Friday and Saturday."

Located just two miles north of Denver, Six Flags, Elitch Gardens, was the state's biggest amusement park. Huber and Hannah loved going every year, but their parents hated it. Huber felt sure his mom would jump at the chance of having someone else take him.

"Scott really wants to take Huber with us. We'll be staying at my sister's place in the city and we're planning on seeing some of the sites as well. We're leaving tomorrow morning and will be back on Sunday afternoon."

Ellen thought a moment. "Well, I guess that'd be all right. I'm sure he'd love to go. Are you sure there's enough room and that he's not a bother?"

"Absolutely not. There's plenty of room, and the boys will both enjoy it."

"Okay, that sounds wonderful. Thank you, Brad. I'll let Huber know that he's allowed to go. I'll bring him over in the morning."

"We look forward to it."

"Okay, bye," Ellen said.

"See ya," Scott McCormick said and hung up the phone, removing the voice changer from his mouth. He had received the magnificent gift for his birthday last year. He gave Huber the thumbs up sign. "She bought it, dude."

"That thing is so cool," Huber said, snatching the device.

The contraption could make his voice sound like an old man or a little girl. They had been playing with it for hours, laughing their heads off with all of the different sounds they could create. Scott had practiced what he would say to Huber's mom for the last half hour and was relieved that it was now over. Hannah repeated the procedure later that day, playing the part of Huber's mom as she called Scott's dad and then called her own mom, playing the part of Alyssa's mom. She took the bait again, hook, line, and sinker. It was all working out beautifully.

The next morning, the two Hill kids convinced their parents to let them ride their bikes to their respective friends' houses. Their backpacks were packed extra tight. Mom said something about making sure they had enough socks and underwear packed for their trips. The two smiled at each other when she wasn't looking. Huber felt alive and invigorated, even if a bit deceptive.

"It worked out kind of strange that you're both going to

Denver on the same weekend," Ellen said nonchalantly.

"Yeah, that is kinda weird. It's gonna be a lot more fun riding the sidewinder than watching stupid Sarah Sprite prance around all night though," Huber joked convincingly.

"You're just jealous you're not going," Hannah played along.

Mom laughed and asked, "Sure you don't want a ride? It's going to be hard riding your bikes while lugging those backpacks."

The two siblings assured her they were fine and could handle it.

"Fine, have a good time. Give me a kiss and hug good-bye."

Guiltily, they kissed their mother good-bye and went in separate directions on their bikes. They would meet up at Scott's house shortly thereafter. Scott's dad was at work, under the assumption that his son was going with the Hills for the weekend.

Twenty minutes later, the two siblings regrouped and cycled toward Scott's house. When they arrived, Scott was sprawled out on the front lawn, three orange trail packs alongside him. Each pack contained a sleeping bag and a large pouch full of food and supplies. On top of Scott's pack rested a rolled up tent. As they approached, Scott looked up, smiled, and asked, "Ya'll ready to go find some gold?"

"Oh yeah!" Huber exclaimed. He threw down his bike and started unloading the contents of his backpack into the trail pack.

"Is that tent big enough for all three of us?"

"Definitely. It's a two-room tent. There's a big area where

two people can sleep and an extra room on the side for *that one*," Scott answered smugly, glancing toward Hannah.

She returned the hostile stare but was relieved to know she'd have her own compartment. Thinking about staying in a tent with boys made her feel uncomfortable. She hadn't been sure how to bring it up. Now she wouldn't have to. Of course, Scott probably just didn't want her around when he and Huber were talking about guy things and having fart contests.

They finished packing their bags and checked to make sure they had everything they needed for the excursion. The group had a tent, sleeping bags, two days' change of clothes, a full jar of peanut butter, a loaf of bread, water-filled canteens, trail mix, rope, matches, a fishing pole, and a can of pink spray paint.

"Why do we need spray paint?" Hannah asked curiously.

"Just in case we need to leave markers for ourselves. Handy if ya get lost," Scott replied, annoyed at her question.

"Looks like we have everything," Huber said proudly as he checked the time on his cell phone.

"Why ya bringin' that?" Scott asked.

"Why not?"

"Ain't no reception up there."

"I can use it as a watch."

"Here, take somethin' useful." Scott tossed Huber a black lighter with two chrome dice engraved on it.

"Whoa! Thanks," he said, flipping the top off and on, admiring the tall flame as he sparked the fuel.

"It's yours. I have another just like it. It's always a good idea to have a lighter with ya when ya go campin'." Huber stuffed the lighter in his pocket, next to the gold coin he had brought along. The morning sun showered golden rays upon the scene—a perfect morning for hiking. The temperature hovered in the mid-seventies. The sky was a blue, cloudless ocean. They ditched their bikes in Scott's backyard behind some shrubs. They placed their arms through their trail packs and began walking down Euclid Avenue toward highway 133. Mount Sopris loomed ten miles to the south.

At a safe distance, a light blue sedan rolled down the road. Behind the wheel, a tall man in a white, long-sleeved shirt and a black vest shadowed their every step.

CHAPTER
11

THE TRIO PRESENTED QUITE a sight, slogging down the road with huge fluorescent packs on their backs. They didn't get far before deciding to stay off the main thoroughfare. Side streets would be the way to go until they reached the 122. If word got back to any of their parents about what they were up to, there'd be dire consequences.

A half mile outside of town, Huber's legs were on fire. Each step seemed like a dagger dug through his thighs and out his hamstrings.

"Ugh. I need a breather."

Scott and Hannah rolled their eyes and plopped down on the curb.

"How far from here?" Huber inquired, struggling to catch his breath.

"'Bout nine more miles," Scott replied.

"What! Nine miles?"

"C'mon, Huber, we haven't even started to go uphill yet," Hannah chided him.

Chagrined by his sister's superior physicality, he retorted, "My pack is heavier than yours. I'm carrying more stuff."

"No, you're not. They're the same."

"I did put most of the food in his pack," Scott said, trying to diminish his friend's embarrassment.

After a few moments' rest, the group resumed their trek southward toward the highway. Huber's legs continued to burn as he walked along the pothole-riddled road that led to Roaring Fork Canyon. As he marched forward, the pain in his legs subsided somewhat. Huber had heard someone refer to this process as "getting your second wind." Still, the mountain looked so far away. *Chasing a mirage.* As they trudged along, sweat dripping from their eyebrows, an old 1978 Chevy pickup truck pulled up alongside them. The rusty vehicle sputtered and jumped before stopping. Scott instantly recognized the driver. A junior in high school, Barry McCormick rolled down his window. Bleached blond hair curled out around his grimy baseball cap. His small, brown eyes evaluated the crew. Hannah thought he was cute in a roughneck sort of way.

"Well, ah'll be. What up, little cuz? Whatcha doin' all the way out 'ere? Y'all runnin' away or somethin'?"

"Hey Barry," Scott answered in an annoyed tone.

"So where y'all headed, young'uns?"

"Campin' up at Sopris."

"I see. That your girlfriend there?" He motioned with his chin toward Hannah.

Scott shot him an insulted look. "No, she ain't my girlfriend!"

"Hey, don't get lippy. I's just askin'. She's cute. I wouldn't be so quick to deny it." Barry winked at Hannah.

Hannah blushed and grinned. Huber's fists clenched.

"Uncle Brad know 'bout your lil campin trip?"

"No, and I wanna keep it that way."

"I guess I kin keep my mouth shut, dependin' . . ."

"On what?"

"Gimme a new fuel pump from your dad's shop . . . and put it on for me."

"Fine," Scott said spitefully. "Hey, if I'm gonna do that, how 'bout ya give us a ride up to the mouth of the canyon?"

"I guess I kin do that, dependin' . . ."

"What now?"

"How much money y'all got?"

The three kids looked at each other, exasperated at Barry's request. Hannah no longer thought he looked very cute. When Scott didn't answer, Barry started the engine and revved it as if he were about to drive away.

"Hold up a sec, Barry," Scott yelled as the three huddled together.

"I say we do it. I don't want to walk all the way up there. It'll save us a ton of time," Huber whispered.

Scott turned toward his cousin. "How much for the ride?"

"I'd say fifteen dollars'll just about cover it."

"What! It's not that far. It'll only cost you a few bucks in gas!"

"My time's valuable, little cuz. Time's money, ya know? Suit yourselves. Have fun walkin' 'nother ten miles or so." He revved the truck forward.

"No, wait! Just wait a sec," Scott implored as they all huddled together again.

"I've got a five and three ones." Scott pulled the money out of his billfold. "How much do you guys have?"

Huber took out a ten and exchanged it for Scott's five. Hannah had seven ones. They gave Barry the ten and five ones.

"All right, hop in back. If y'all see a cop, duck down. If I git pulled over, you're payin' the ticket."

"Fine, whatever," Scott replied, annoyed at his cousin's greediness.

The three jumped in back as Barry slammed the truck into gear and gunned it. They all fell toward the tailgate. Huber felt taken advantage of, giving away that much money, but relief washed over him as his legs got to rest. Ten minutes later, Mount Sopris stood in full view. Sagebrush and cedar trees lined both sides of the highway, giving off a wild, earthy aroma—the smells of summer. The scent filled Huber's nostrils, and, despite the mucus building up in his sinuses, he loved it!

Up ahead about a quarter mile lay a lonely gas station. The last beacon of civilization before the three descended into pure wilderness. Completely constructed of dark, treated timbers, the gas station appeared more like an abandoned log cabin. Vintage gas pumps, hailing from an era long ago, rusted out front. Hoisted upon two tall corroded poles, a sun-bleached, metal sign read, "Thomas Family Mercantile, est. 1956." Barry stopped the truck in front of the store.

"All right, y'all get out here," he demanded.

"Hey, the canyon is still a couple of miles up," Scott complained.

"I ain't takin' y'all the way up there. Look at that road! You know what that'd do to the shocks on m'truck. This is as far as y'all go."

The three jumped out of the pickup truck and slid their packs back on. Ready to venture off, Barry called toward his cousin again.

"Hey, Scott. Ya said ya didn't want Uncle Brad to know

where ya are, eh? To keep that kinda secret, I'm gonna need another five bucks."

"We already gave ya what ya asked for. Ya ain't gettin' no more outta us."

Barry glared and let out a slow drawl, "Well . . . guess I'd better head straight to Uncle Brad's shop and let 'im know your whereabouts."

"Fine, you moneygrubbin' shark!" Scott yelled.

"Huber, give me the five," Scott demanded.

"No."

"Do it, or we're caught for sure."

"Fine," he bristled as he parted with the last of his money.

Scott threw the bill through the driver-side window.

"Much obliged, lil cuz. Have fun with your girlfriend there." Barry laughed and peeled away out of sight.

As Barry drove back toward town, he passed a light blue sedan. As was customary in this part of the country, drivers would wave to each other with the flick of their index finger from the top of the steering column. Barry waved at the strange looking driver, who waved back.

The trio decided to visit the mercantile and buy some provisions with what little money they had left.

"Let's get some water so we can save our canteens," Scott suggested.

"Why can't we just fill 'em up in the river?" Huber asked.

"Parasites and bugs. Animals pee and poop in there. It'll make ya sick."

"Isn't it diluted though?"

"Still, I wouldn't risk it. I didn't bring any iodine tablets either."

Hannah had to admit that Scott was a knowledgeable Scout. He had brought enough water, trail mix, beef jerky, peanut butter, and other victuals to last them for at least five days. He had also brought his fishing pole, and with any luck they'd be eating a fat trout cooked over a roaring campfire for dinner. As the three kids approached the door to the mercantile, they came upon an old Ute man sitting in a wicker chair next to the ice cooler. Sporting a sweat-stained cowboy hat, the man rocked back and forth. Two long, grayish-black braids flowed from the sides of his head and rested on his chest. As the man looked up, his face revealed a lifetime of age and experience. Etched around his eyes and forehead ran thousands of tiny wrinkles and age spots. Hidden behind the layers of sagging skin, two sparkling eyes shone like stars in the night.

The man was humming something softly in his native tongue, and Huber stood mesmerized. Huber had heard similar songs at local powwow ceremonies. His family visited them almost every year to observe Ute culture, as members of the tribe played drums, sang, and danced for days at a time. As Huber approached the door, he peered briefly into the man's twinkling eyes. When he did so, the man stopped singing, nodded in his direction, and then looked away before resuming his song.

Stepping into the mercantile transported them all into a different era. Time must've forgotten this place. Ancient-looking Coca-Cola ads and old trinkets gathered dust. The gouged floors begged for a treatment. Thick, musty air, produced by

82

years of age and mold, made it difficult to breathe. An old, bald man with bushy eyebrows stood behind the counter, lazily sweeping the floor. Dense glasses magnified his blood-shot eyes. He had to be over eighty years old. A stained white apron covered his torso, and his face reminded Huber of an ornery bullfrog. Eying them suspiciously, his throat bulged in and out as they walked past the counter. All in all, the store reflected the qualities of its owner—both falling apart and desperately clinging to memories of better days.

"Can I help you?" the storekeeper asked in a low, raspy voice.

"Just pickin' up a few things," Scott replied.

"Uh-huh. And where might your parents be?" the old man asked suspiciously, resting the broom against the counter and putting his hands on his hips.

Huber's mind panicked. They were caught! Why had they decided to stop here in the first place?

"Meeting us up in the mountains. Dropped us off here and drove up ahead of us. Told us we needed to get some exercise," Scott tried to lie.

"Uh-huh." The owner nodded his head before asking dubiously, "Do I look like I was born yesterday?"

Scott assessed the man from head to toe, examining his wrinkles and liver spots. "No, sir. Not at all."

"Danged right I wasn't. Don't try to sell me a load of manure and tell me it's honey. I'm sure you kids are into some kinda mischief, but, fortunately for you, I don't care as long as you buy *somethin'*," the man said tersely.

"We will," Huber quickly replied, and the three of them huddled together to pool their remaining resources.

They had enough to buy three cokes, a pack of Skittles, and three packs of chocolate Hostess CupCakes with three cents left over. Scott dropped the pennies in an ashtray by the register. "Keep the change." The old man turned up his nose and resumed sweeping.

"Think he'll tell on us?" Hannah asked as they exited the store.

"I don't think so," Huber replied. He then mocked the store owner's voice and froglike demeanor. "After all, we bought *somethin'*." The gesture earned him a hearty laugh from the other two.

The old Indian man was still sitting by the cooler, singing softly. The group walked a few steps past him before his voice startled them.

"You kids goin' up through that canyon?"

The three looked back at the man, no one willing to answer. Finally, Huber spoke up.

"Yeah."

"Goin' up to find Dead Man's Treasure, eh?"

How did he know? Did he have some kind of sixth sense or something? Flabbergasted, Huber didn't reply.

"Naw, just campin' out," Scott answered in his stead.

"Lotsa people try to find it. They never do. Hidden too good."

"But we're not—" Scott was unable to finish his sentence before the old man interrupted.

"If by some chance you did—and you won't—but if you did, stay out . . . That mine's cursed."

"We're just camping," Hannah repeated, visibly shaken by his comments.

"Stay outta that mine . . . it's filled with evil spirits," the man repeated before starting to sing again.

"Yeah, sure thing." Scott rolled his eyes and started down the road. Hannah turned around with him. Huber continued to stare at the old man, ruminating over what he just told them. This was the first time he had heard anything about the mine being cursed. Scott turned back around and nudged Huber in the shoulder, jolting him out of his trance.

"C'mon, dude. Don't let that old man scare ya."

"Sorry. I'm coming."

As they resumed their journey, the softness of the paved road morphed into a rocky, dusty, washboard that led to the mouth of Roaring Fork canyon. The peak of Mt. Sopris hung high in the air.

"You think that's true what he said?" Huber asked as they trudged along.

"What who said?" Scott asked.

"The old Indian man—about the mine being cursed?"

"C'mon, Puber. I quit believin' in ghost stories in second grade."

"It's weird how he knew where we were going . . ." Hannah commented.

"Why is that weird? Ya think we're the first people to go looking for the Dead Guy's Treasure? I bet he lives up here. Prob'ly sees people hunt for the dang place all the time. He's just tryin' to scare us off."

"Maybe," Huber admitted.

"Ya guys should know this by now . . . adults just make up ghost stories to scare kids. It's how they get their kicks and giggles."

Huber outwardly agreed with Scott but couldn't shake the shiver that had crawled down his spine upon hearing the old man's dire warning.

Finally, the trio arrived at the mouth of Roaring Fork Canyon a little bit after noon. To Huber, his feet felt as if they had been walking for days, but the pain ebbed away at the spectacular scene that lay before him. At the entrance of the canyon arose two massive sentinels: foreboding walls of sharp, gleaming, white limestone cliffs. Beyond the mouth of the canyon, a thick, forested landscape—full of pines, alders, aspens, and precipitous bluffs—beckoned to be explored. Beneath the towers of stone, a panorama of sweeping escarpments—made up of gravel and loose rock, obliterated by countless years of erosion—crept toward the canyon floor. The Roaring Fork River carved a divide through the middle of it all. The river gushed, roared, and foamed with fury, reminding Huber of a boiling pot of hot water as whitecaps burst high into the air. *No wonder the Spanish were attracted to this place.*

"Good feelin' up here, ain't it?" Scott admitted. "Good to get away."

"It's amazing," Huber agreed.

So taken with the scene, nobody noticed the light blue sedan parked a half mile from their position. Inside the driver's seat, Juan Hernán Salazar watched their every movement through a pair of binoculars. Lips curling slowly around his teeth, Salazar grinned wickedly as he caught a glimpse of what looked like a weathered document in Huber's hands. His suspicions had been correct. How convenient that they'd led him up here in the isolated mountains. No one would hear their screams.

CHAPTER
12

HUBER EXTRACTED HIS grandpa's prospecting guide
and compared it with the map. The guide, yellowed with moisture and age, barely held together. Dates, notes, and thoughts,
often skipping months at a time, were littered throughout.
Each page displayed a date along with a passage, detailing the
events of the day. Most pages simply read, "Prospected all day.
Nothing." Many passages contained footnotes, half drawn
diagrams, arrows, and notes inserted after the original passage
had been written. Deciphering all the cryptic messages would
be almost impossible. Curiously, the last page of the journal
seemed to have been ripped out.

"How are ya even supposed to read this thing?" Scott asked.

"I've gone through it a little bit. A lot of it doesn't make
sense, but here and there, some longer passages do. Let me
find one—just give me a sec." Huber opened the journal and
thumbed through the first few pages before stopping. "Okay,
here it is," he said before starting to read out loud:

> September 15, 1975
> On the map Carlos gave me, I can make out the
> entrance to Roaring Fork Canyon. At the mouth of the
> canyon, the river flows into the Thomas Lakes. I believe

that the Spanish must've entered through here and gone north. I'll follow that route today. The map is nowhere near to scale. Probably better to go by the written instructions rather than the map itself. The directions say, "Siga el serpiente hasta que coma la tierra. Cruza allí y sube la escalera de vidrio." **Translation**: *"Follow the* **serpent** *until it* **eats the earth**. *Cross there and climb the* **glass staircase**." *Not sure what that means but hopefully will find out soon.*

Later same day:

Found the crossing! Tried to climb the glass staircase but didn't have enough time. Will have to come back another day.

Huber closed the journal and delicately placed it back into his bag.

"Huh?" Scott asked, bewildered. "Follow the serpent? Glass staircase?"

"How do we know what any of that means?" Hannah wondered aloud.

"I dunno. Hopefully we'll figure it out as we go."

"Just walk blindly through the wilderness and hope we figure it out. That's smart," Hannah chided.

"Not blindly. We're supposed to go north, we know that."

"What if we get off track? How do we even know which direction is which?"

"Gotcha covered. I figured neither one of ya would bring one of these," Scott said and pulled out an old, beat-up looking object. Encased in wood, a glass lens covered the top of the object.

"A compass?" Huber asked.

"Does that thing even work?" Hannah eyed the compass skeptically.

"Hey, don't judge a book by its cover. This thing is as reliable as they come."

"It looks like a piece of junk,"

"It was my dad's when he was in Scouts, and he gave it to me. So yeah, it's old, but it still works like a charm."

"If we get lost, we might as well just dig ourselves an early grave trying to use that."

"If it comes to that, don't worry. I'll dig yours for ya."

Hannah stuck out her tongue, then said, "I think a storm might be coming in. I can feel it."

"That's not what the weather report said," Huber argued.

Off in the distance, a few clouds drifted lazily overhead, but otherwise the skies were clear as a bell.

"Bet you your Hostess that it don't rain all day," Scott chimed in.

"You got it. I'm gonna enjoy eating those cupcakes right in front of your fat face."

"C'mon, let's just get going," Huber prompted, slightly irritated at the interaction between his sister and Scott.

As they passed the white rocky cliffs at the canyon's entrance, they entered a vast world, disconnected from all civilization. Huber flipped open his phone. The bars disappeared one by one until the screen read, "No service." No contact with the outside world now. "This place is awesome!" Huber said, still mesmerized by the mountains.

"Pretty incredible, ain't it?" Scott asked. "My dad and I come up here once in a while. Can't believe you two've never been here. How come you've never camped out before, Puber?"

"Our dad isn't the biggest camping fan. Says that only an idiot goes and sleeps on the ground when he can sleep in a nice, soft bed."

"My mom always tries to get him to go, but he won't budge," Hannah interrupted. "I've been camping and stuff with friends a few times though."

"Fascinating," Scott said flatly. "Don't think anyone was talkin' to *you*, though."

She glowered at him and choked back a disparaging comment.

An hour later, as the trio slogged alongside the river, the love affair between Huber and the mountains started to wear off. The mud acted like suction cups, tugging on his feet. Huber's legs burned in agony as he slowly fell behind his fellow travelers. Gnats and mosquitoes swarmed around his head relentlessly, searching for a place to nest. It was enough to drive a person mad.

"Why aren't they bugging you?" Huber yelled in frustration toward Scott and Hannah.

"You put on hair spray this morning, didn't you?" his sister quipped.

"So?"

"Gnats love hair spray. Attracts 'em by the hundreds," Scott added, laughing.

"Why didn't you tell me that?" Huber demanded of his sister, whose head was safely tucked beneath a New York Yankees baseball cap.

"I know you like to look good," she laughed. "Just dunk your head inside that river there."

"I'll dunk your head in the river," Huber replied contemptuously.

In his misery, he began to wonder why he came on this trip, but then he pictured his Grandpa Nick trudging along this same path in his younger, healthier days. The image gave Huber the will to carry on. He clasped the gold doubloon in his pants pocket and rubbed it again and again, drawing strength from the coin.

Up ahead, Scott and Hannah moved as if this route were a walk in the park. He couldn't hear what they were saying but could see they were laughing. *What in the world? Were they friends now?* Twenty minutes ago, they had been fighting like cats and dogs. This was supposed to be a guys' trip. Couldn't she at least give him this? She had her outings; she had friends. Finally Huber caught up to his companions, who waited impatiently.

"Hey, you can put some of your stuff in my pack if you want," Scott offered.

Huber was tempted but also insulted. "I can do it!"

"Hey, just tryin' to help a brother out, Puber."

The pity party gave Huber a much-needed burst of energy as he pushed himself to his feet. He refused to be pitied. "C'mon, let's go."

The next mile, Huber pushed through the pain and told his aching muscles to "shut up." When Scott and Hannah pulled ahead of him, he willed his body to continue until he caught up to them. An hour and a half later, they stopped to assess their progress. Huber felt proud, strong, and exhausted as he plopped on the dirt for a much-needed rest. Glancing at his phone, he gazed at the time: 3:28 p.m.

"Ain't seen no serpent yet. You?" Scott asked.

"Can't say I have," Huber heaved as he took out the map. Examining it closely, he tried to decipher the faded symbols and lines. "Gibberish. Can't understand a dang thing on this map."

"What'd the letter say again?" Hannah asked.

"Something about crossing where the serpent eats the earth, then climbing a glass staircase."

"Why couldn't he just say what it is?"

"That'd be too easy," Huber replied as he handed his sister the parchment and climbed up a small embankment.

Scott and Hannah pored over the map, bickering about what the riddle meant.

Huber scanned his surroundings and sighed. Then he saw it. "The river!" he barked.

"Huh?" Scott said.

"Come up here! Look!"

Scott and Hannah ran up the bank and looked in the direction of his finger. The river snaked and twisted, curving up and down. Ahead in the distance, the river split in two as it crashed upon a rocky outcrop.

"The river is the serpent!" Huber exclaimed. "Look where the river forks. It looks like it swallowed that little island. That's where we cross! Where the serpent eats the earth!"

"Nice eyes," Scott complimented him. "Could be."

Hannah nodded and grinned. "Nice work, brother. I think you may be right."

The revelation invigorated the group as they raced toward the island. Within a few minutes, they arrived. The river was shallow but wide. Across the water, a wall of scree, or shards of loose rock, sloped infinitely upward. After resting for a minute more, the group readied themselves to cross the water.

"The river is sandy and shallow here. Take off your shoes," Scott advised them.

"What? Are you crazy?" Huber protested.

"Huber, if you get your shoes wet, you might as well turn back. Your feet will never dry and you'll be miserable the rest of the day," Hannah said as though she were an expert and he some kind of moron. She was getting more annoying all the time.

"Fine," he muttered.

They ripped off their shoes and rolled up their pant legs. Scott went first and howled as he dangled his foot in the rushing, cold water. Hannah followed suit and screeched loud enough for the entire mountain to hear. Their reaction made Huber feel a bit of trepidation as he dipped his foot into the river. A thousand icy needles pierced his skin and shot straight through the bone. The cold dealt such a shock that he almost keeled over. Screaming at the top of his lungs, his pitch exceeded that of his sister. More than once Huber almost lost his balance in the rushing water. His brain sent an extra boost to his equilibrium as he imagined how cold the river would feel if he fell in and became completely immersed.

The riverbed was a blanket of silt that completely enveloped his feet. At times, it took all he had to pull his foot up out of the river mire and put it in front of his other. Polished, smooth river rocks hid beneath the silt and tried to trip him up. Huber and his companions enjoyed a brief rest as they crossed the dry island. Ten agonizing minutes later, Huber stepped out of the frigid water and onto the other side, his feet a bluish hue. Falling onto the grassy bank, he feverishly rubbed them until they turned pink. A steep slope loomed overhead just to the southwest. The hillside had several tiny ledges, which were buried by millions of obsidian shards.

"What'd it say to do next?" Scott asked.

Huber flipped through the prospecting guide and surveyed the map.

"Climb the glass staircase . . ."

Scott approached the base of the slope, picked up a piece of jagged obsidian scree and craned his neck upward toward the ascending slope. "Dang! These rocks are as sharp as—"

"Glass," Hannah finished his sentence. "Obsidian is a form of volcanic glass. There must've been a lava flow here a long time ago."

Huber eyed the extremely steep escarpment looming overhead and heaved a sigh. "I think we've found our glass staircase. Gimme a minute before we head up."

"Sure thing, Puber. Mind if I take a look at that map?"

Hannah and Scott studied the map a little longer. Huber mentally prepared himself for the climb ahead.

"Man, I'm thirsty," he complained more to himself than the others. "My throat feels like I've been gulping sand all day."

Scott and Hannah, engaged in debate about what to do after ascending the glass staircase, didn't hear. Wandering to the edge of the river, he bent down close to the water's edge. A wavy face gazed up at him. Cupping his hands, he dipped them in the liquid. The temptation to drink overcame him. Scooping the refreshment in his mouth, Huber gulped the coldness. Scott turned and noticed Huber drinking from the river.

"Puber, ya idiot! Don't drink river water!" Scott yelled as he jetted toward him and slapped Huber's hands away from his mouth.

Huber jumped to his feet, scathing. "It's hot! I'm thirsty!"

"Dude, I told ya. There're bugs in the water. Parasites! You're gonna get the squirts big time now. I know from experience."

Hannah roared, "Hope you packed lots of toilet paper, brother."

Scott became more serious. "I hope you didn't drink too much. You'll get all dehydrated and sick. I'll have to carry ya back home. That'll put an end to our trip real quick."

Huber's face filled with fear. "I only drank a handful, I swear."

"Aw, ya should be all right. Like I said, probably'll get just a little bit of diarrhea. Ya packed extra underwear, right?"

Huber's face was on fire. "Yes, I packed extra underwear, *Mom*."

"Well, ya live and learn," Scott said with a smile. "Hopefully, ya won't need 'em."

"Let's get going. It's getting late," Hannah suggested.

Reluctantly, Huber forced himself to his feet and braced himself for the next struggle on his journey.

Just beyond the entrance of the canyon, Juan Hernán Salazar carried a trail pack of his own, following three sets of footprints left by the muddy riverside.

"Oh, *jóvenes*, you are making this too easy," he chuckled.

CHAPTER 13

SCALING THE OBSIDIAN SCREE, which layered the ascending slope, was like trying to walk uphill on a million shattered dishes. Huber continually lost his footing and slid backward. Clinging with his hands and feet to the edge of the hill, the entire mountain seemed to slide down with him. Grappling onto tiny shrubs and trees, he struggled to keep his balance as the sharp, jagged rocks cut the skin on his hands and he slithered downward. Step after painstaking step, the group tramped their way up the slope.

After an hour of ascending the rocky face, Scott and Hannah neared the top. A collective sigh of relief arose from them as they gasped for breath and looked forward to a much-needed rest.

"We made it!" Scott blew out as he and Hannah collapsed on their backs, inhaling the air. After a few moments, they peered over the edge and witnessed Huber at a distance, still scurrying up the slippery escarpment.

"C'mon, Puber!" Scott yelled down to him. Huber, glued to a spot on the slope thirty feet below, struggled to maintain his foothold. He didn't dare move as he glanced below to watch obsidian shards tumble all the way down to the river.

"I'm stuck! Can't move!"

"Yes, you can!" Hannah encouraged him.

"Hey, open my pack, and hand me that rope."

Hannah fished through the pack and found a long, skinny rope. Scott grabbed one end of it and threw it toward Huber, landing ten feet in front of his position.

"Just go a little further and grab the rope, dude. We'll pull ya up. Look how far you've come. Ya just need to gut it out a little more."

Huber stared below and felt dizzy as he imagined falling to his doom. These razor-sharp rocks would tear him to ribbons. The impact along the way would knock him unconscious, and finally he would plunge into the water and drown. He shakily put one foot in front of the other. Hannah looked nervously on.

Extending himself on his belly as far as possible, the tips of his fingers tickled the end of the rope. Grunting and stretching even further, Huber finally grasped the end, wrapping it around his scraped up hand. Scott wrapped the rope around his waist as both he and Hannah pulled on their end. The rope burned Huber's skin a little, but the help of his companions made the going much easier. Upon reaching the top, Huber gasped for breath and muttered a brief "thanks" before collapsing in a heap on the ground.

Shortly afterward, Huber pulled himself up and the three gazed at the distant river below, meandering through the trees and rock. Huber's cuts and rope burns on his hands stung something fierce. However, elation overpowered the pain. Like David slew Goliath, Huber had defeated the "glass staircase." A month earlier, he would've never attempted such a daring feat.

"What time is it?" Scott asked.

Huber pulled out his cell phone. One tiny bar of reception flickered in and out. "5:34."

"Better find us a place to camp 'fore long. It'll start gettin' dark round 7:30."

"Which way do we go?" Huber asked as he stared at the dense forest ahead.

"Not sure. Let's take a look," Hannah said, and Huber took out the blue guide and map. He flipped a few pages and found the next entry.

> *September 30, 1975*
>
> *Climbed the glass staircase today. From here, Pedro writes, "Continúa a través del laberinto de arboles. El ojo de Dios te guía a las aguas de vida."* **Translation:** *"Continue through the **forest maze**. The **eye of God** guides you to the **waters of life**." I am at a loss.*
>
> *Later same day:*
>
> *Wandered all day through the trees. Nothing. What is the eye of God?*

"That's it?" Scott asked.

"Wait!" Hannah said, taking the guide and flipping through the yellowed pages. "Just wait, there's more."

A few pages later, she read:

> *May 27, 1976*
>
> *Found the waters of life! The eye of God guided me right to it. How did I not see before?*

"Are ya kiddin' me? That's all it says?" Scott moaned.

"Grandpa Nick wrote this guide for himself. He knew what it meant. He didn't have to explain it," Huber said.

"He may as well've just left it in *español*," Scott muttered.

"We'll figure it out as we go," Huber said, snatching the guide back from his sister.

"I guess ya figured out that whole serpent thing. Don't worry, I got the next one." Scott grinned.

"What's wrong, Scotty? Don't like being shown up by my brother?"

"Don't call me that!"

"Why not, Scotty?"

"Cuz I don't like it, that's why!"

"Huber, do you like being called Puber?"

"Not really, no."

Hannah turned back toward Scott. "Are you going to stop calling him that?"

"No."

"Why not?"

"Cuz I don't want to. That's his name."

"And your name is Scotty."

Scott cocked his head back and forth, trying to come up with a rebuttal, but he couldn't. Huber smiled at his friend's annoyance but felt unnerved by the playfulness in his sister's voice.

"Wanna make another wager, Scotty?"

"I'm listenin'."

"Whoever figures out what this 'forest maze' and 'eye of God' means gets the other's Coke tonight."

Scott thought it over a few minutes. "I think you're gonna be pretty sad when ya lose your coke *and* your cupcakes. Haven't seen any rain yet, have you?"

"Just wait."

Again, Huber noticed that their eyes locked for just a second too long.

"Eye of God . . . ," Scott said to himself as he ambled ahead of the others. "Huber, lemme see the map again."

Huber handed Scott the parchment.

"I don't know if I'm lookin' at this right, but I think we should go further north."

"Looks that way," Hannah agreed. "Guess it's a good thing you brought that rattletrap compass of yours."

Scott flipped open his compass and was taken aback.

"What's wrong?" Huber asked.

Scott held up the compass for him to see. The needle spun in fast circles counterclockwise.

"Told you that thing wouldn't work," Hannah gloated.

"I don't understand. It's always worked before."

"Why do you think the map labels this place the forest maze?" Huber said.

"Because in a maze . . . you get lost." Hannah answered.

"There must be something going on in this area with magnetism. Compasses won't work."

"The eye of God guides you," Hannah repeated. "That's how we get un-lost."

For the next half hour or so, the group walked onward, unsure of which direction, all the time thinking about what Grandpa Nick's journal meant. *Eye of God?* Hannah instinctively looked up toward a smattering of silver clouds, outlined by the sun behind them. In that moment, a realization hit her like a brick.

"Hold on! Social studies. Ancient Egypt."

"Huh?" Scott said.

"The sun god, Amun-Ra."

"What about him?"

"Just made me think. Lots of ancient cultures thought the sun was God watching over them. Look at the eye on the map! It's an Egyptian hieroglyph!"

"Nice work, sis. I see what you're getting at," Huber said.

"Gettin' at what?" Scott asked.

Hannah took over. "The sun sets in the west. We need to go in that direction until we find our way out of here and to the waters of life."

"So simple. *God's eye guides you.* I'm going to enjoy that Coke." Scott smiled.

The group looked upward and followed the sun's path as it made its journey toward the western horizon. As they tromped west, the sun became enshrouded in clouds until they could no longer see it. Faint splatters of water began to land on their heads. Scott looked up in the sky as a big, fat raindrop hit him square in the eye.

"Aw, dang it," he cried out, rubbing his eye. "So much for following the sun."

"Those cupcakes are gonna taste soooo good with my Coke," Hannah gloated.

"Ain't really a storm yet. More of a sprinkle," Scott argued. "Doesn't count."

"Give it a few more minutes," she replied, sure of herself.

A small clearing opened up among the trees fifty feet

ahead of them. Next to the clearing, a small stream fed into a tiny pond. Huber sheltered the map, trying to keep it from getting wet.

"Hey, do ya think these are the 'waters of life'?" Scott asked.

"I don't know—looks pretty puny," Huber answered. "Plus on the map, there's a waterfall."

"Yeah, this probably ain't it," Scott conceded. "We may as well set up camp since we can't follow the sun anymore. It'll be gettin' dark 'fore long anyhow."

A loud clap of thunder rang through their ears before he could finish his sentence. At a frantic pace, the group shed their packs and started to pitch their tent. Scott shoved the poles every which way, quickly assembling the framework. As they worked, the sky tore open and heavy rain poured in hard, thick sheets. The three hollered at each other to hurry as water and dust hurled up into their mouths and nostrils.

Juan Hernán Salazar had climbed halfway up the face of the glass staircase when the thunderstorm hit. As the obsidian scree became wet, he lost his footing and slid backward down the slope, ripping his right pant leg and receiving a large gash above his right eyebrow. With a renewed sense of determination mingled with anger, he ascended again, eventually reaching the top, his face a bloody, soaking mess.

He observed a craggy overhang thirty feet to the west, and ran to it, seeking protection from the storm. Stewing in his spot, Salazar retrieved his large, eight-inch combat knife and balanced it between two rocks, using it as a mirror to examine his wound. It was deeper than he thought. Taking out a small fishing hook from his pack along with some black thread, the man winced as he applied pressure and pushed the hook through the top of his eyebrow. The pain momentarily took his breath away. Salazar continued stitching up the gash in a diagonal fashion until the wound completely closed. Tying the thread, he cut off the slack with the knife. The man retrieved a small cloth from his bag, then soaked it with some whiskey he had brought along. Placing the cloth on the wound and applying pressure, he cried out in anguish.

After finishing his self-surgery, he realized that he had no clue which way his prey had traveled. The rain had swept away any signs of their path. Dejected, he sat in his rocky alcove, twirling the knife around in the dirt, glowering at the thick forest ahead of him.

Huber and Scott argued about how to thread the final pole through the tent.

"We've got to hurry or all of our packs are gonna get soaked," Hannah said, panicking.

"Throw 'em in!" Huber yelled through the roaring thunder and lightning. Quickly, she tossed the packs inside as they finished setting up.

Scott and Huber hurled themselves inside and zipped up the outer door. However, the damage had been done. All three huddled together, now soaked to the bone and shivering. A flash of white blinded them momentarily. Thunder shook the ground like an earthquake. Listening in awe to the fury of Mother Nature, they all huddled even closer, Huber purposely positioning himself in the middle of the group.

"Scott, do you think we're safe here? Remember that story about the man and woman who were struck by lightning and died a couple of years ago?" Huber asked.

"Yeah, I remember that. It was kind of a freak accident. Your odds of being hit are like a million to one."

"Unless you're standing outside like an idiot holding up a metal rod or standing under a tree. Then you're just asking for it. Rubber shoes don't actually do anything to protect you either," Hannah added with an air of academic superiority.

"True," Scott agreed as they exchanged glances, again for too long.

"I'm freezing my butt off," Huber remarked as the rain continued to pour outside.

"Huber, you complain way too much," Hannah sniped.

"Why don't you just shut up? Can you do that? Shut up for more than two seconds? I honestly don't think you can. Maybe we should make a wager and see. I bet ten million dollars you can't be quiet for two seconds. How 'bout it? You know, maybe I *complain* so much cuz you're always around. You ruin everything."

Hannah's eyes went from hurt to rage. Huber pressed on.

"You're always a know-it-all, trying to show everyone how smart you are. Why can't you just *shut up*?" Huber instantly regretted his words.

Incensed, Hannah shot back. "You know what? You're weak, Huber! It's pathetic!"

"Whoa, now! Come on, ya guys. Take it easy!" Scott said.

"Huber, you don't want me here? Fine! I'm leaving! I know *you* don't want me here either!" she yelled at Scott.

"Hey, I didn't say nothin'."

"Earlier, you did. Remember? You didn't want me to come. You told my brother that."

"Well . . . maybe. But I'm okay with it now."

"Believe me, once you say anything about her, she'll never forget. She'll hold it over your head till you die!" Huber sneered, trying to agitate her further.

"As soon as the rain stops, I'm outta here! I've got better things to do than hang out with two losers. Careful when you go to sleep tonight, Scotty. Hubey wet the bed until he was nine and probably still does when he gets *sc-air-wed*," she mocked.

Without thinking, Huber lunged toward his sister, intent on pummeling her. As they rolled around and punched each other for all they were worth, the tent became a chaotic madhouse. In the commotion, one of the bodies collided with a supporting pole, causing the roof to collapse. Somehow, Scott ended up in the middle of the two, trying to break up the fight.

"Stop it! Knock this stuff off! What's wrong with you?" Scott yelled, sounding like Hannah and Huber's father. "We can't waste energy fightin' like this. Look what ya did to the tent," he complained, holding the roof above their heads with his hands.

The rain suddenly stopped. That was the thing about rocky mountain thundershowers; they were so fierce that they usually blew themselves out within a few minutes.

The two siblings fumed and refused to look each other in the eye.

"Hey, come on. Ya both said some stupid stuff," Scott said in a conciliatory tone.

"I shouldn't have come. I'm going home," Hannah said before she picked her pack up off the floor, unzipped the door, and bounded out.

"C'mon, Hannah," Scott pleaded.

As she disappeared from the tent, Huber followed her outside. "C'mon, sis, you're crazy. You realize how far away from home you are? It's getting dark; you'll get lost. At least wait till tomorrow."

"I'm leaving now!" she uttered defiantly, walking in the direction they had come.

Scott stepped through the tent door, wanting to stop her, but Huber constrained him.

"She's my sister. I know her. She just needs to blow off some steam. She'll come back. She's not dumb enough to try and hike back home alone in the dark."

"You were out of line dude . . . ," Scott said and went back to fix the tent. Huber knew he was right as he watched his twin sister disappear beyond the maze of trees ahead.

After the rain had stopped, Juan Hernán Salazar wandered aimlessly in the woods. He was on the verge of giving up for the night when he heard the sound of footsteps coming his way.

CHAPTER
14

HANNAH LOVED THE SMELL of the forest right after it rained. The therapeutic aroma throttled down her anger. As she walked back toward the way they'd come, she thought of how slick those shards along the glass staircase would be, if she even made it there without getting lost. With each step, her determination to return home waned.

"I'm such an idiot!" she screamed out loud to herself. "What is he going to think of me now?"

Huber's comments had caused her to lose the ability to think rationally. Why was she so worried about what Scott thought of her anyway? He was a bully and a smart aleck who almost knocked her tooth out only a month earlier. However, underneath all the exterior bravado, a smart, funny, and interesting guy existed. If it wasn't for her brother, they might actually be able to become friends. Huber didn't have many friends though. He needed Scott more than she did. A spasm of shame coursed through her mind as she thought about what she had done.

"Really, Hannah? You told Scott about your brother's bed-wetting problem? Was that necessary? Why do you always say things without thinking?" she asked herself aloud. The sun was just beginning to set. "Better hurry and get back to camp before it gets dark." She turned around and began to double back, leaves and pine needles swishing beneath her feet. Light was quickly diminishing. "Didn't even bring a flashlight? Such an idiot!"

A sound came from behind. Darting her head around, she saw something. It was a shape moving among the trees. Facing forward, she sprinted toward the camp as fast as her legs would carry her.

When Hannah arrived back at the camp, relief and a sense of security washed through her. The two boys had fixed the tent and started a fire with some red pine needles and a small amount of dry wood they'd managed to scavenge. Huber sat on a log by the fire, staring absent-mindedly into the flickering orange flames, drying himself. The smoky fragrance of the fire infused her soul with comfort. At the small pond, Scott was fishing. The clouds had cleared, revealing a stunning array of reds, oranges, and yellows, which reflected and shimmered off the rippling pond water. The mesmerizing effect of twilight instantly dispelled any animosity Hannah felt toward her brother. Next to Huber sat two empty, rotted out logs. They had known she'd come back. She approached the fire and sat down on the log closest to her brother, saying nothing.

"Glad you came back, sis."

"Me too," Hannah replied. "I think some kind of animal was following me on my way back. I caught a glimpse of it moving around in the trees."

"Probably just a deer or something."

"Yeah, maybe. I didn't like being out there all alone."

"Hey, I didn't mean what I said. I was just ticked off."

"I know. It's been a long day. Sorry for telling Scott about . . . you know . . . wetting the bed."

"Yeah, wish you wouldn't have done that . . . ," Huber trailed off. "Let's just forget about it."

As they enjoyed the peaceful moment, Huber's eyes suddenly bulged out of his head. He leapt to his feet and ran for a distant thicket of pines. Confused, Hannah yelled after him, "Where're you going? What's the matter?"

Huber didn't reply as he disappeared behind the trees.

She heard Scott laughing next to the pond, and he began to sing, "*When you're slidin' into home and your pants are full of foam, diarrhea, diarrhea!* I told 'im not to drink that river water."

Hannah began to crack up as well. "You okay, brother?"

"Will be in a minute," Huber yelled, concealed behind the trees. "Will one of you get in my pack and bring me some toilet paper, please?"

"He's your brother. *You* take it to him," Scott said.

"No way! That image will scar me for life."

Scott reeled up his fishing pole and walked toward the fire, holding up two large, wriggling, rainbow trout, lashed together with rope he'd slid between their gills. "Fine, I'll take it to 'im if ya gut the fish," he said, tossing them onto her lap.

Startled, she pushed the fish into the dirt. Despite her love of the outdoors, Hannah had never liked the slimy feel or smell of fish.

"C'mon, somebody. Please . . . ," Huber moaned in the background.

"I'm comin', I'm comin' . . . keep your britches on—though it's too late for that, I guess," Scott yelled back as he pulled a roll of toilet paper out of his pack. Hannah flopped alongside the fish on the ground, rolling with laughter.

A half hour later, the three sat around the blazing fire, eating the freshly caught fish. Scott taught the two how to cook the trout "Scotty style." Huber and Hannah watched in amazement as he began to assemble all sorts of culinary items from his pack. Set out before them was a roll of aluminum foil, a bag of salt and pepper, imitation spray butter, and a plastic, lemon-shaped container. He started by cutting a piece of the aluminum foil twice the length of the fish and a little wider than the body. On top of the filet, he added a pinch of salt, pepper, and a few sprays of butter. To complete the recipe, he drizzled a few drops of lemon juice over the top. Folding the foil over the fish, Scott sealed each side so that none of the steamy flavor could escape as the fish simmered within the coals of the fire. Within a few minutes, Huber, who normally didn't like fish, was enjoying the best-tasting meal he'd ever had, complimented by the sweet taste of the fizzy cola.

"Glad I saved my Coke till now," Scott said as he untwisted the cap.

"I think you're forgetting something," Hannah interrupted before Scott could drink.

"Oh, c'mon . . . were you really serious about that?"

"As a heart attack."

"Fine, take it," Scott replied as he took a big swig and wiped his lips. "Sure ya still want it?"

"I'm not afraid of cooties anymore," she answered, snagging the bottle from his hand.

After the main dish, the group sat around the fire, stomachs full, laughing about the events of the day. For dessert, they pulled out their packages of Hostess CupCakes. Cracked and smashed, they'd taste delicious just the same.

After the three tore open their packages, Scott was about to take a bite when Hannah stopped him. "What do you think you're doing?"

Scott's melancholy eyes reminded her of Hobo, begging for a leftover piece of hamburger.

"Hoped you'd forgot," he lamented.

"Not a chance. Hand it over."

Scott hesitated momentarily and then tossed the cupcakes onto her lap.

"Come on, sis, he did cook us dinner. You already drank his coke. Have a heart," Huber said in Scott's defense.

"Then give him some of yours. Scotty, the fish was amazing, but what kind of person would I be if I went back on my word? I just couldn't do that and feel good about myself."

"You're a very cruel person, ya know that?"

"I was going to leave you a few bites till you said that," she replied with a wide smile. Hannah shoved Scott's entire cupcake into her mouth and closed her eyes. "Mmm, mmm, this is soooo good," she exaggerated, licking the remnants of chocolate cake off of her fingers. Scott's stomach growled in envy.

After seeing the look on his face, she had pity and chucked him the uneaten cupcakes she had purchased for herself.

"Pathetic. I can't take the look on your face. Just like my dog."

"Smell like him too I bet!" he replied, taking a whiff of his armpits. He ran at her, trying to put them in her face.

"You're so sick! Don't make me gag!" she yelled as they struggled together and fell to the ground laughing.

Huber wanted to gag himself as he witnessed the interaction. After a few moments of wrestling, the two went to sit back down on their logs. Huber darted to the log in the middle, forcing them to sit on opposite ends.

The group finished eating their cupcakes and was soon sucked back into the hypnotic dance of the fire. Huber broke the solemnity.

"What do you think our parents are up to?"

"Probably celebratin' that we're gone," Scott replied cynically.

"Hey, what happened to your mom?" Hannah asked cautiously.

There was a long pause.

"Come on, sis, that's none of our business," Huber reprimanded her.

"It's okay. I'll tell ya. One night 'bout three years ago, my mom and dad were goin' at it real bad 'bout some stupid thing. I was flunkin' a couple of my classes, and I think they were fightin' about who should make me do my homework. My dad was yellin' at my mom, sayin' that he had to do everything— make dinner, do laundry, wash dishes, and pay the bills— while she was always out with her friends partyin' or doin' who knows what. They didn't know I was listenin' through the heater vents. My dad called my mom a lousy excuse for a mother. They swore at each other a few times, and then I heard some screamin'. There were some loud crashes and then the front door slammed. I found out later that she had thrown a vase at my dad's head. After that, I guess my mom got in her car and just drove off. She came back a couple days later when I was at school and packed up all her stuff and left. She wrote me a letter sayin' how sorry she was and that she still loved me . . . blah, blah, blah. She sends postcards from Vegas once in a while sayin' that I should come visit her for a weekend, but she don't really mean it. Whenever I get her postcards, I go to the backyard and set 'em on fire."

"Wow, sounds pretty harsh," Huber said after a subdued silence.

"And I thought *our* parents had problems," Hannah said with sympathy in her voice.

"Y'all are the Brady Bunch compared to my family. I'm startin' to get past it now though. I figure that life ain't fair. Bad things happen to good people. Good things happen to bad people. My dad says that no matter how bad you think ya got it, somebody else's got it worse. He says if you have a roof o'er your head, food to eat, and at least one person who gives a hoot about cha, then you should count yourself pretty lucky."

"I guess that's true," Huber admitted.

The fire crackled and popped, amplifying the somber tone of the conversation. Huber never realized that Scott had been through so much. After a few more minutes of staring into the glowing embers, Scott changed the subject and asked a question.

"Do ya think the Dead Guy's Treasure really exists?"

"Yeah, I know it's real," Huber replied.

"Yeah, but ya don't *really* know for sure."

Huber gripped the gold coin in his pocket. He knew that his Grandpa Nick had told him to be very careful about who he showed it to, but he felt in his heart that his grandpa would approve of Scott. Reluctantly, he pulled the doubloon from his pocket and handed it to him.

"What's this thing?" Scott asked, eyeing the coin. A baffled look crossed his face. "No way. Is this what I think it is?"

"Proof," Huber replied proudly.

The gold coin shimmered and reflected as the light of the fire bounced off the metallic surface.

"Huber, where in the heck did ya get this?" Scott yelled in excitement.

"It was with the stuff that Grandpa Nick left me."

"Us!" Hannah reprimanded him.

"Huh?"

"He left it to *us*," she reminded him coolly.

"Yeah, to us, I mean."

"Why didn't you ever show it to me?" he asked, sounding a bit hurt.

"I was waiting for the right time. Grandpa's letter told us not to show it to anyone, but we trust you."

He turned the coin over and over and held it up to the light, still unable to believe his eyes.

"Did you ever find out what the symbols on the coin stand for?" Hannah asked.

"It's the coat of arms of the Spanish monarch. Symbolizes the strength of the Spanish kingdom with all of its different regions," Huber answered as if he were teaching a history class.

"What's the cross on the other side?"

"Tribute to the Church, I'm guessing. It was basically part of their government," Huber went on. "At least that's what I read on the Internet."

"Where did your grandpa find it?"

A look of disappointment crossed Huber's face. "I dunno. He didn't ever say."

"He never said anything about it?"

"Nope. Nothing. Just left it in the box with the other stuff."

After studying the coin, Scott reverently handed it back to Huber, who thrust it back into his pocket. "Well, better hit the hay, got a long day ahead of us tomorrow," Scott reminded them as they watched the flames die down. The trio began cleaning up for the night. "Don't leave any food out. It'll attract animals. The last thing we want is some bear comin' into our camp."

Huber and Scott unzipped their tent and retrieved their sleeping bags from their trail packs. They rolled them out and got ready to settle in for the night. Hannah, still staring at the glowing coals, was lost in thought. Huber stuck his head out of the tent. "Hey, sis, will you put out the fire?"

"Huh? Oh, yeah."

Hannah kicked dirt over the flames and coals. As the last of the flames struggled to stay alive, she saw movement from the corner of her eye. The fire's last flicker of light illuminated something in the distance. Panicked, she gasped and bolted into the tent.

"Scott! Huber!"

"Hey!" the two boys shouted because they were undressing to get into their bags.

"Sorry! Sorry!" she yelled and covered her eyes.

"What's wrong?" Huber asked.

"In the trees," she stammered, out of breath. "Putting the fire out . . . I saw it! I saw it! I know I saw it!"

"Saw what?" Scott asked.

"A face! A human face!"

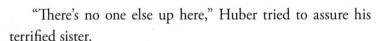

"There's no one else up here," Huber tried to assure his terrified sister.

"Are ya sure ya saw somethin'?" Scott asked skeptically.

"It was just for a second, but yeah, I'm sure it was a person." Hannah's voice shook.

"Sometimes your mind'll play tricks on ya in the dark, especially out in the woods," Scott tried to explain. "Happens to everybody . . . like when you're home alone in your house."

Hannah said nothing as she continued to stare in the direction where she had seen the face.

"C'mon, Huber. Let's get our flashlights and go take a quick look see just to be sure."

"Scott, no! Don't go out there!"

"Aww, we'll be fine. It's more just to put your mind at ease, is all."

A knot developed in Huber's stomach. The last thing he wanted was to venture off alone in the pitch black of night to face something unknown. Trying to sound fearless, he replied, "Sure, let's do it."

The two boys grabbed their flashlights and went off in the direction Hannah had pointed. She tried again to stop them, but Scott persisted. Sitting back in the tent, she watched the two boys fade away into the blackness. Occasionally she'd see their beams of light skip around the tree trunks.

"See anything?" Scott yelled to Huber off in the distance.

"Nothing," Huber responded.

The boys soon came back into view.

"Nothin' out there," Scott shouted as he approached the camp.

"Maybe I was just seeing things," Hannah said, trying to convince herself, but she still felt unsure.

"Try to forget about it. I can't tell you how many weird things I've seen and heard when I've been campin' out."

"Stop worrying about it. Let's just go to sleep," Huber suggested.

"Okay . . . see you guys in the morning." She zipped up her compartment.

Huber and Scott lay side by side in their sleeping bags within the larger room of the tent. Nothing had ever felt so comfortable and warm to Huber. His aching legs and back thanked him for the rest and shut down for the night.

In the adjoining room, Hannah lay in her bag, feeling a bit isolated, but grateful for her privacy, still shaken from what she was sure she'd seen. After twenty minutes or so, the adrenaline had run its course. She finally felt calm. Through the nylon zippered wall, she could hear the boys' muffled voices and sure enough, farting sounds followed by loud laughter. After a while, she heard the conversation take on a more serious tone. She inched closer to the wall in order to hear more clearly.

"You like my sister?" she heard Huber whisper as a statement of fact more than a question. Hannah's eyes widened. Her heart raced. A long silence followed.

"What if I do?"

"I dunno. It'd be kinda weird, I guess."

Another long pause. Hannah pressed her ear even closer to the nylon.

"Don't worry, Puber. I don't," Scott replied.

It was like someone slugged her in the gut. She fell backward into her sleeping bag. She struggled to hold back tears as she fell into a fitful asleep.

"Puber, wake up, dude!" Scott whispered frantically.

"What? What time is it?" Huber opened his groggy eyes.

"I dunno."

Huber withdrew his cell phone. No bars, the battery half dead. 2:11 a.m.

"Why did you wake me up?" he groaned.

"Shhh, somethin's outside. Quiet, just listen."

Huber lay motionless, holding his breath and listening for whatever it was Scott had heard. Thousands of crickets sung their song of the night, accompanied by his fast-beating heart, which reverberated through his ears. Minutes passed. Slowly his heartbeat decelerated.

"I don't hear any—"

Out of nowhere it came. A low, hissing sound he guessed was about ten feet away from their tent. It reminded Huber of the sound a lawn mower made when pulling on the cord to start the engine.

Huber spoke softly, "It sounds like . . ."

"A cat," Scott finished the sentence. "A cougar," he trembled.

Huber's eyes closed and his hands began to quiver as he

visualized the massive predator prowling just feet from where they lay. A memory flashed through his mind about a fourth grade report on cougars. The cougar, or "mountain lion" typically weighed around 130 pounds and stretched six to eight feet long, nose to tail. The hind legs of a cougar were built to spring up to twenty feet toward its target. The large, muscular cat stalked its prey, waiting until it caught them off guard, and then jumped from its hiding place to maul its victim. As the wounded prey lay prostrate on the ground, the cougar began feasting by burying its white, sharp teeth in the neck. As the cougar ripped out the jugular vein, its prey would quickly bleed to death, allowing full access to the carcass without a struggle. In his report, Huber posted pictures of the cat taking down deer, elk, and other forest mammals.

Huber imagined the glowing eyes locked on their tent wondering what tasty morsel lay inside. *Sardines in a can.* Those eyes must've been the ones Hannah saw in the fire- light. Huber had never thought of himself as being food for an animal. Any thought of the Dead Man's Treasure vanished as he silently prayed for the cougar to move on and let them survive. His prayers were in vain.

The hissing and purring grew louder and closer to Huber, who was frozen stiff with fear. Hannah snored on in the adja- cent room, oblivious to the danger. Huber desperately wanted to unzip the door separating them and tell her to be quiet so they didn't die. The outline of the cougar materialized as it pressed its body against the tent and circled them. Huber's eyes, having adjusted to the dark, locked on the bulge. No doubt the cougar was salivating at their scent, anticipating its savory meal. Paralyzed with terror, neither boy made any kind of motion.

All of a sudden, the bulge stopped near the door of the tent. The air turned so quiet, a person could've heard a pin drop. The purring sound grew louder. All of the muscles in Huber's body instantly turned to Jell-O.

The two pale-faced boys looked dreadfully at each other for what they were sure would be the last time. During that moment of trepidation, illumination entered Huber's mind—a snippet of his report called, "What to do if you encounter a cougar." Huber unzipped his sleeping bag and pulled himself up on his knees.

"What the heck are ya doin'?" Scott whispered in disbelief.

Huber belted out the words, "JOHN JACOB JINGLE-HEIMER SCHMIDT!" Huber turned to Scott. "Start singing with me! Trust me!"

Scott hesitated but joined in.

"THAT'S MY NAME TOO!"

By the time they got to "THE PEOPLE ALWAYS SHOUT," the shape had backed away from the tent. The purring faded in the distance until it was quiet again.

"It left!" Scott said in amazement.

"Will you two shut up!" Hannah's irritated voice shot through the nylon wall. "What are you doing?"

"Nothing. Sorry. Go back to sleep," Huber responded.

"Were you guys just singing? In the middle of the night?"

"Nope. You musta been dreamin'," Scott answered.

"Yeah, whatever. Please just shut up so I can sleep."

"Sure thing."

Hannah released a loud groan as she buried her face in her pillow.

The two boys, fearful the cat would return, sat on alert for a few more minutes. As the silence continued, the fear slowly ebbed away. Relief filled the boys, and the duo slunk down to the ground, grateful they were still in one piece. Snores echoed again through the nylon wall.

"How'd ya know to sing like that, Puber?"

"A report on cougars I did. If you make yourself seem big and loud, the cougar thinks it won't be worth the fight and runs away."

"Glad ya thought of it. Thought we were goners for sure," Scott said as he unzipped his pack sitting next to him.

"What are you doing," Huber asked, confused.

Scott looked at him shamefully. "Pee'd m'britches. Gotta change my underwear."

"Are you serious?" Huber asked, suppressing a mirthful glee.

"Promise me ya won't tell your sister."

Scott the bully peed his pants! Months earlier, Huber would have gladly given his life savings to possess this kind of black-mail material. However, the pleading in Scott's eyes struck a chord of compassion within Huber. After all, Scott hadn't said anything to him about his own problem Hannah had revealed earlier. Never in his life had he seen Scott so vulnerable.

"It'll stay between us."

"Thanks, man," Scott said, clicking off the flashlight. A few minutes later, he was snoring softly. How could he sleep so soon after what had just taken place?

Another hour passed before the adrenaline subsided from Huber's system. As it did, he quickly fell into a deep slumber and dreamed of the cougar. Glowing green eyes stalked him in the darkness, and ivory white teeth eagerly waited to devour him. The big cat chased him through a pitch black tunnel. The darkness extended its inky fingers, scraping his face and clutching his arms as he tried to escape. All the while the cougar gained. In the distance, a glimmer of white light pierced through the darkness. Pushing and pumping his legs, the light grew brighter. A silhouette in the shape of a man materialized. He tore through the darkness, the cougar right on his heels. The light turned blinding as he approached. He tripped, falling at the feet of the man. The brilliance obscured his vision. Huber couldn't see the man's face. The cougar stopped in its tracks as the man bent toward him. He woke up in a cold sweat. He pressed a button on his cell phone: 5:04 a.m. One hour until dawn.

HUBER TOSSED AND TURNED until 7:00 a.m. Finally, he mustered the strength to rise from his sleeping bag. Sunlight slowly filtered through the green nylon of the tent and onto his eyelids. He heard Scott and Hannah arguing animatedly outside. Hannah was launching into one of her classic diatribes. Huber's body stiffened and ached as he tried to move his legs from their locked position. He moaned and yelled out, "I can't move my legs."

"Ya need to stretch out, dude," Scott yelled from outside. "Reach down and touch your toes." The squabble outside the tent promptly resumed.

Huber reached toward his feet, his face contorting in excruciation as the taut muscles and tendons slowly loosened. His hair stuck up all over. He changed into a new set of clothes and then unzipped the tent, finding Scott and his sister sitting on the logs outside. Hannah pointed toward the ground near her brother's feet. Dropping his gaze, he noticed several large paw prints that circled the tent. Hannah walked toward Huber and belted him hard in the shoulder.

"Ouch! What was that for?" he scathed.

"Why didn't you tell me there was a cougar prowling around our tent last night?"

"Wouldn't have done any good to tell you," he retorted while rubbing his aching shoulder.

"What if that thing had ripped into my side of the tent and drug me off in the woods for a snack?"

"We were afraid that if we woke ya up, you'd just start screamin' like girls do," Scott jumped in.

"I'm not talking to either of you," she said in anger and walked back to her log.

"Promise?" Scott replied.

After sitting for a couple of minutes, glaring in silence, Hannah half grinned, looked up, and said, "Actually, maybe it was better I slept through the whole thing. I probably would've peed my pants."

Huber grinned at Scott, who once again silently pleaded for Huber to stay quiet.

The three ate some beef jerky and trail mix for breakfast. As soon as they finished eating, the three collapsed their tent and folded it back into its bag. Scott tied the tent to the top of his pack, agreeing to haul it again for the day. Huber retrieved his grandpa's journal along with the faded, yellow map.

"Where do we go from here, boss?" Scott asked.

"Still gotta find *Aguas de Vida*. After we get there, we'll figure out the next part."

"It can't be too much further," Hannah commented.

"Terrain looks pretty flat. Shouldn't be nearly as hard as yesterday," Scott added.

"Let's hope not," Huber said. "Sure you don't have to pee before we go, Scott?"

Scott said nothing but glared at Huber so hard, Huber thought Scott's eyes would burn a hole right through him.

Huber got the message loud and clear but enjoyed watching his old nemesis squirm. He'd never say anything, but the threat of doing so brought immense pleasure.

Scott pulled out his compass. The needle ticked back and forth like a pendulum. "It's still not working."

"Surprise, surprise," Hannah said.

Huber pulled out the map and surveyed it, then pointed at the sun, peeking just above the tree line. "The sun rises in the east. We just halfta head in the opposite direction to go west. *Aguas de Vida* can't be too far."

"Sounds like a plan." Scott snapped his compass shut.

"I hope you're right," Hannah said as she slid her baseball cap back on.

The going was much more flat and manageable as they traversed the forest. Huber even managed to keep pace with his two companions. The group trudged along the forest, laughing and telling jokes. Twice they walked upon some deer, which spooked and bolted upon sight of the threesome. One, rubbing its small fuzzy antlers on a tree, had looked straight at Huber for several moments. The two large eyes observed him with curiosity, probably the first time they'd ever seen a human being. Shortly afterward, its instincts kicked in, and it had bounced away like a spring.

The sun drifted lazily across the sky and was quite warm now. Huber glanced at his phone: 11:22 a.m. The sun was nearly overhead now. Sweat trickled from his forehead. Like old friends, the gnats and mosquitoes returned. Welts and bumps covered his entire body, and they itched terribly. He'd take mountain lions over mosquitoes. He flailed his arms about, trying to shoo the pests away from his head and face, but to no avail. The prick of a mosquito punctured his neck, and he slapped it hard, resulting in a bloody explosion. Hannah and Scott slogged on, seemingly immune to the bugs.

"Why are they still just bugging me?"

Hannah looked back and noticed his misery. She stopped, took off her pack, retrieved a small green can, and tossed it in his direction. Huber picked up the spray can labeled, "Off!"

"You had this the whole time and didn't give me any?" he yelled angrily.

"Remember that time a couple of years ago when Dad took you to McDonald's cuz you told him you cleaned the garage, when it was really me?"

"Are you for real? That was like two years ago!" he complained while dousing himself with the repellent.

"Now, we're even," she said, satisfied.

"I can't believe this. You guys had repellent the whole time?"

"It was the one thing I forgot to bring," Scott answered. "Your sister'd only share if I promised not to tell ya she had any."

"Like I said, now we're even." She smiled.

The three trudged westward until 1:30 p.m., now walking in line with the sun, when they emerged from the forest and came upon a wide clearing with rolling grasses, dotted throughout with bluebells and purple wildflowers. Standing in the middle of it all was a small, crystal blue lake. It was a lush paradise. A rushing waterfall flowed from a rocky ledge, towering above the basin. Near the falls, four deer peacefully drank.

"How far have we come?" Huber asked.

"I'd say about two miles." Scott gazed at the deer drinking from the basin. "Hey . . . do you think this place . . . ? Yeah, it has to be. These must be the waters of life! Look at that waterfall!"

They surveyed their surroundings—grasses, flowers, trees, animals, and water.

"I think you might be right," Hannah said. "There hasn't been any other place like this so far."

"This is it!" Huber nodded.

"It's awesome!" Hannah ran toward the lakeshore. "Never seen anything so beautiful. Look at the deer! They're so cute! Don't you think so, Scotty?"

"They'd be cuter as jerky."

Hannah slugged him in the shoulder.

The three found a nice grassy spot and took off their packs to begin eating peanut butter sandwiches. Huber couldn't believe how hungry he always felt up here. His body incessantly begged for more fuel to keep going. The three ate their sandwiches with potato chips. The chips had been crushed in their packs, so Huber and Hannah sprinkled them between their bread slices.

"Chips on your sandwich? C'mon, that's messed up."

"What's so bad about chips on your sandwich? It all ends up in your stomach anyway," Hannah replied.

"It's just weird."

"You ever tried it?" Huber asked.

"Naw, and I don't plan to."

"Well, don't knock it until you try it," Hannah said with a hint of flirtation.

There they go again, Huber thought. He quickly scooted

between them and tried to steer the conversation elsewhere.

"So where do we go from here?" Hannah asked excitedly.

Huber pulled out the map along with the blue prospecting guide.

June 2, 1979

Made it to the waters of life today. The map says, "Continúa al noreste, sube la concha de la tortuga, y camina oeste hasta que conozcas a mis hermanos." **Translation:** *"Continue to the northeast, **scale the turtle's shell**, and head west, until you **meet my brothers**."*

"Wonder what the turtle's shell means?" Scott said.

"No clue. What's all that about meeting his brothers?"

"No idea, but good thing I brought my binocs."

"Your what?" Hannah asked.

"Binoculars. Good for spyin' on people too."

"Gross. What are you, some kind of Peeping Tom?"

"A Peeping Scott." He flitted his eyebrows up and down.

Huber took the binoculars and looked at the deer drinking by the waterfall.

"So we have to head northeast until we find the turtle shell thing," Huber said, happy with the progress they'd made. He dropped the binoculars next to his pack.

After they finished eating, the group lounged on the ground.

"So what are ya gonna do with your share of the money?" Scott asked.

Hannah answered first. "Use it to go to college."

"Are ya kiddin' me? What's the point of goin' to college if ya already got money?"

"Oh, I don't know . . . how about to learn! To do something with your life! You think all it takes is money to be happy?"

"Absolutely."

"Then you're a moron."

"Hey, I'll be a rich moron, livin' it up, doin' whatever I want when I want. How 'bout you, Puber?"

"Haven't really thought about it."

"Really?"

"Guess the first thing I'll do is buy some bug spray and sunburn cream."

"Don't forget toilet paper," Hannah said, laughing.

"And some deodorant, man. Ya smell like three-day-old tacos that've been sittin' out in the sun," Scott said.

"Thanks for the suggestions." Huber rolled his eyes as he looked at his cell phone and saw it was 2:30 p.m. "Hey, we've been sitting here for almost an hour. Better get going."

"Come on, we've got time. Can't we just stay here a little bit longer?" Hannah yawned, then sprawled out on the ground to smell some flowers. "It's so nice up here."

"Fine, but just for a few more minutes," Huber relented.

The two boys followed Hannah's lead and decided to lie on the ground too. From the air, their bodies formed a "Y" shape, with their heads coming together in the middle. They looked up at the sky and watched billowy white clouds float by. Warm sunlight rained down and splashed onto their faces, infusing them all with a warm and drowsy feeling.

"Well, we'd better go," Scott said unconvincingly.

"I don't wanna get up. Can't we just take a teeny, tiny, little nap?" Hannah yawned, scooting her head closer to Scott's.

Huber yawned too. "Gotta keep moving if we want to make it there today." However, he did not stir from his position.

Hannah looked at her brother, scratching the large red welts on his sunburned neck. A pang of guilt coursed through her mind for withholding the bug spray for so long. A minute later, his eyes were closed, and he was snoring softly. She looked at Scott. His baseball cap covered his eyes. Mustering all her courage, she laid her head so it was touching his shoulder. She wasn't sure if he was awake or not, but he didn't stir. Her own eyes began to droop as the distant sound of the waterfall lulled her to sleep.

Off in the distance, Juan Hernán Salazar pulled his binoculars from his eyes. It was time to strike.

CHAPTER
• 16 •

STARTLED AWAKE BY THE SOUND of a cracking branch and a shrieking bird, Hannah jolted awake. Lifting her head from Scott's shoulder, she noticed the two boys snoring away. How long had they been asleep? She looked at her watch and saw it was 4:24 p.m. They had been sleeping for two hours! Struggling to her feet, she stretched and yawned. Taking in the meadow around her, Hannah gasped as she saw a giant moose showering its head within the waterfall off in the distance. Forgetting about the time, she swiped the binoculars Scott had loaned Huber earlier and zoomed in on the majestic creature.

"Huber, Scott, wake up!"

"What time is it?" Scott asked foggily.

"It's after four. We've gotta get moving. But before we go, I want to show you something."

"What? After four! We gotta go!" Scott jumped to his feet.

Huber didn't stir.

Scott was now on his feet. "I'll get 'im up in a minute. What'd ya wanna show us?"

"It's by the waterfall. C'mon, let's get a closer look." Hannah took his hand, noticing the warmth of his skin, and began to guide him toward the lake. As they peered at the waterfall, she pointed out the moose and handed him the bin-oculars.

"Whoa, awesome! That's a huge bull!"

"Bull? It's a moose."

Scott looked at her condescendingly. "A male moose is called a bull. A female is a cow."

"Oh, I didn't know."

"That's surprisin'. I thought ya knew everything."

Hannah punched him in the shoulder as he laughed.

"Man, I wish it was huntin' season."

Hannah looked hurt. "You would actually shoot that wonderful animal?"

"How couldn't I? Its head would look so cool hangin' in our livin' room."

"I can't believe you, Scotty. Have you ever shot an animal?"

"Got my hunter's safety permit a couple of years ago. Shot some small stuff like rabbits and prairie dogs. But last fall, my dad took me deer huntin'. We hunted for three days and didn't see anything. Then on the last day, just 'fore it got dark, I found and shot this nice four-point buck." His excitement waned at the look of mortification covering Hannah's face.

"I can't believe you!" she pushed away from him. "I knew you were coldhearted, but I never thought you were a killer."

"A hunter ain't a killer."

"You killed the defenseless thing, didn't you?"

"Yeah."

"Well, that's makes you a killer."

"Hannah, there's a difference, ya know. A killer is some-one who just kills for fun. A hunter respects the animal. He eats what he kills. Guess ya wouldn't understand."

"Did you eat the deer?"

"Of course. Where do ya think I got all that jerky you've been eatin' this whole trip?"

"Oh . . . I didn't think about where it came from."

"Nobody ever does."

"You didn't feel bad after you shot him?"

"Naw, not really. Shot him in the neck. He died real quick-like, so he didn't suffer. Guess I feel bad 'bout shootin' those prairie dogs and rabbits cuz I never ate 'em. Now I just shoot what I'm gonna eat."

"Can't you just go to the grocery store and buy meat?"

"How is that any different from huntin'? Someone still has to do the killin'. It's just easier cuz you don't have to see it."

"I never thought of it that way, I guess. Maybe I'll become a vegetarian," she replied.

"Yeah, ya do that, but don't get all high and mighty till then. Look, he heard us," he said, pointing to the moose.

Hannah looked through the binoculars and saw the bull looking directly at them with its large brown eyes. "Oh, he looks so sweet."

"Oh, so you've eaten moose before?"

She gave Scott an evil eye and hit him on the shoulder again.

The bull continued to survey them a bit longer before deciding to play it safe and run away. "Oh no, he's leaving," she said sadly.

"Yep, must not like ya very much."

Hannah shot him a wry look. "Actually, I think he caught wind of you. I know that'd make me run away too."

Scott smiled.

"Let's go see the waterfall," she suggested in a bubbly fashion.

"What 'bout your brother?" he asked nervously.

"He's not going anywhere. He won't even realize we're gone."

"Okay, but just for a few minutes. We've gotta get goin' soon." They made their way toward the falls. Walking shoulder to shoulder, each nudged the other flirtatiously now that Huber wasn't around. Intermingled with the grass grew wild mint and berries.

After a few more minutes, they arrived at the western wall of the meadow from which the water fell. The cascade seemed much larger when they were up close.

"Wow, this is so pretty," Hannah said.

As the two sat by the basin, enjoying the cool mist that bathed their faces, they could see their reflections in the water as well as several large trout swimming against the current. "Oh man, I shoulda brought my fishin' pole. Wait here. Be right back."

As he got up to leave, Hannah grabbed him by the back of his shirt and pulled him back. Grinning, she said, "Wait! It looks like there's a little cave behind the waterfall. Let's go check it out."

Last night, Scott had told Huber he didn't like Hannah. But what Huber didn't know wouldn't hurt him. Standing beneath the waterfall, he had to admit that Hannah looked amazing with her sandy blonde hair and large, brown eyes. The sun's rays reflected off and filtered through the mist, highlighting her features. His heart pounded faster. Inching behind the waterfall and being careful not to slip on the muddy rocks, they found themselves in opaque isolation. The small grotto retreated about five feet behind the falls. Scott took out his lighter and flicked the device until it turned into a small orange flame. Hannah's face looked even prettier as she smiled in the firelight. Water cascaded in front of them, providing a wavy window to the outside world. Inside, they felt totally alone and secure. The lighter revealed they were not the first people to step foot inside this place. Etched along the back wall, names and symbols dotted the surface. "Jamie and Scott forever, 1996," encased within a heart shape and "Rick + Brianna, 1975," were just two pairs of names among the twenty or so.

"Lotsa people been in here o'er the years," Scott's voice reverberated throughout the small niche. The waterfall was loud, but not deafening.

"I know. I wonder how many of them are still together."

"Not many, I bet," he said cynically at the thought of his own parents.

"I bet they were really in love when they were in here though," Hannah commented, and Scott's legs turned to mush. His hands started to shake.

"Are you cold, Scotty?"

"Naw, I'm all right." His voice cracked.

She stood in front of him and gazed into his eyes. Slowly, she reached with her lips toward his.

"Hey, wait! 'Fore we—" but before Scott could finish his sentence, their lips touched. A floating sensation washed over both of them.

Scott's stomach lurched up and down as his hands trembled with excitement. Her lips tasted like mint. Their lips stayed locked for a couple more seconds before finally breaking apart. Hovering like a balloon while the world spun in circles, Scott feared he might pass out. They both smiled and laughed awkwardly, hands still quaking.

"Wanna know somethin'?"

"What?" she asked softly.

"That was the first time I've kissed a girl," he said, embarrassed. "Hope it wasn't too bad."

"Guess I wouldn't know. It was my first kiss too."

They chuckled awkwardly. Scott took out his pocketknife and added their names to the cave wall. They sat in silence, staring up at the graffiti.

"I knew you liked me," Hannah broke the silence.

"Does this mean we're boyfriend/girlfriend now?" he asked.

"I guess."

"What does that mean exactly?"

"Not really sure. I think it means you have to be nice to me and buy me stuff," she said with a grin.

"Wait a sec, I didn't know that was part of the deal."

"Well, too late now unless you wanna break up, Scotty."

"Hey, just hold on a sec. I think we can work somethin' out. What about your brother though? He'll freak when he finds out."

"We'll have to keep it a secret for now."

A duplicitous feeling settled in Scott's gut. "I guess that's probably best, at least till we're finished with our trip. I don't think he'd take this all too well up here."

"I don't think so either. We'd better get back. He might be awake by now."

"If he is, what do we tell him?"

"The truth . . . well, half the truth. We saw a moose by the waterfall and went to get a closer look."

"Yeah, all right. Let's go. We've gotta get a move on if we wanna find the mine tonight."

The two sauntered through the meadow, their hands brushing together, bringing the familiar light-headedness. When they came within sight of their gear, their eyes couldn't register what they were seeing.

A shredded trail of material laced the ground. Their trail packs, supplies, and tent lay in ruins. Clinging like snow to nearby trees and grass, stuffing from their sleeping bags waved in the soft breeze. Scott knelt down on the ground, next to his dad's shattered compass.

In shock, Hannah couldn't get a word out. As she continued to survey the carnage, a dawning realization settled upon her.

"Where's Huber?" she panicked.

Scott snapped out of his own world of sadness and looked at her in alarm.

"Huber!" they both shouted.

"Scott! Look!" Hannah ran toward the spot where Huber had been sleeping. A circle of crimson soaked the ground. Distinct bloody handprints stamped the nearby trees and rocks, appearing as if the hands had been grasping for the objects while being drug away. Hannah dropped to her knees, hands trembling. "Oh no! Oh no!" she said, rocking back and forth.

Through a vacant stare, Scott whispered, "What happened here?"

CHAPTER 17

(THIRTY MINUTES EARLIER)

Huber was dreaming again. Running through the blackness, he panted heavily as the animal closed in from behind. The light shone ahead and preemptively, he knew he was going to trip before reaching it. When he did, he hoped this time he'd see the face of the ethereal being waiting in the light. To his disappointment, he again woke up a moment too soon. Hazily, he opened his eyes and looked around. It took a moment to realize he was alone. Hannah and Scott were gone. Their packs and gear still sat where they'd left them. A hot flash of anger washed through him as he came to the conclusion that they had snuck off somewhere while he was sleeping. *Where'd they go? What were they up to?*

"Hannah! Scott!" he bellowed angrily through the open air.

No response. Frustrated, he sat down on an old tree stump and kicked the dirt. He wasn't about to venture off into the woods by himself and get lost looking for his stupid friend and sister. As he sat brooding on a stump, his senses heightened. It felt as though he was being watched. Holding his breath, Huber surveyed his surroundings. Suddenly, a jolt with the force of a freight train struck him from behind. In an instant, his face slammed into the dirt. A large, bony arm wrapped itself around his neck and pulled him up into a headlock. He struggled and tried to yell, but the pressure on his windpipe made it impossible for any sound to escape. A whiff of body odor wafted into his nostrils. Then he saw the tattoo of a snake cover the arm that held him bound.

A voice from behind whispered in his ear, "Shhh, calm now, little *joven*. Do not struggle. Do not scream. It will do you no good. I will not hurt you unless you give me reason." The man's rancid breath reeked of decay. A long, shiny knife appeared in front of Huber's face. A look of fear and impending doom reflected up from its surface. On the tip of the knife, Huber noticed spots of dried blood. *Scott. Hannah.*

"You have something that belongs to me. Hand over that map of yours, and I won't hurt you," Salazar whispered softly.

Panic swept through Huber as he imagined his companions tied up somewhere or worse.

"I am going to release you now, *joven*. When I do, you will give it to me," Salazar seethed and eased the headlock, pushing Huber back onto the ground. "Do not try to run or do anything foolish. If you do, I will chase you down and gut you like a pig."

Terrified, Huber reached into his bag and retrieved the map. Salazar hovered above with an angry grimace on his face. In that moment, Huber had no doubt in his mind that the man would live up to his word. His sharklike eyes held no feeling, no remorse, no pity. Shaking, Huber held up the map and struggled to his feet. Salazar's eyes glimmered with excitement as he relished the sight of the document.

"All of this could have been avoided if you had just given me the map in the first place, *joven*," Salazar said wryly. "You had the chance."

Huber, still catching his breath, didn't speak. He had to think of something fast. Above all else, he had to try to save Hannah and Scott if they were still alive. Grandpa Nick's voice came into mind. *A time to talk.* Just then, he remembered the lighter in his pocket that Scott gave him. He swiftly removed it and sparked it. The flame licked the air just inches below the parchment.

"I'll do it! I'll set it on fire," Huber threatened.

"Bad decision, *joven.* Yoo-ber, isn't it? Now, don't be hasty," Salazar stated, attempting to hide his anxiety.

"I'll do it unless you tell me where my friend and sister are!"

"Yoober, I will tell you when you give me the map. I swear to you that I have not harmed them."

"I don't believe you. Tell me where they are and then I'll give it to you."

"Yoober . . . I think you should just give me the map or you will never see them again, *joven.*"

Huber faltered at the comment. Reluctantly, he extinguished the flame. Against his better judgment, he crept toward Salazar, who towered above him with one hand outstretched and open, the other wielding the bloodstained knife.

He placed the map within Salazar's palm. The man's eyes closed in relief, and he began to chuckle, his rotten teeth jolting up and down. His bony fingers caressed the document. His beady eyes pored over it carefully. Jubilantly, Salazar folded it up and placed it inside his front shirt pocket.

"Now, tell me where they are!" Huber tried to sound tough but couldn't hide the frailty in his voice.

"Who?" Salazar laughed, now in a world of his own.

"You know who! Where are they?"

Salazar laughed violently, *"Joven,* I have no idea where they are. But when I do find them, I assure you, they will share your fate." Salazar lunged with surprising speed toward Huber and pinned him to the ground with one hand as he sat on Huber's chest.

"Yoober, Yoober, you should have given this to me when I asked for it the first time, *joven.* However, since you did not, you will pay. Your friend will pay . . . your sister will pay," he spat.

Salazar drew his knife, tossed it up, and watched it spin in the air before catching it in his free hand just above Huber's face. He lowered it toward the boy's chest. Huber lay in shock, consumed with fear as he saw his life flash before his eyes. He'd never see his family or loved ones again: no more scary movies on Halloween night, no more Christmas mornings, and no more long talks with Hannah out on the back porch during warm summer nights. His parents had no idea where he was and would likely never find his body. How had they all been so stupid to come into the mountains alone? Images of his mother, father, and sister continued to filter through his mind. Remorse racked his soul for all the times he was rude or mean to people. He would never be able to tell them sorry. He thought of Hobo at home, sitting and waiting for his master that would never arrive. One comforting thought came to his mind; he hoped to see his Grandpa Nick soon. The thought brought a sense of serenity to his mind.

He steeled himself and looked into the eyes of his murderer. If he was going to die, he was going to do it bravely.

Salazar momentarily looked puzzled, taken aback by the boy's calm demeanor. He hesitated. "You understand, I have no choice, *joven*? I cannot let you go now. I promise to make it quick. Relatively painless."

"You won't find it." Illumination suddenly entered Huber's consciousness as he concocted a plan to get out of his predicament. "People have spent their entire lives looking for Dead Man's Treasure and have never found it . . . even with maps."

"I will find it, I assure you. *I* am not those people."

Huber noted a hint of doubt in his voice.

"Maybe you're right. But don't you think you should have some kind of insurance just in case?"

"What do you speak of? Insurance?"

"My parents would pay a lot of money. When my grandpa died, he left them a huge check."

Huber saw Salazar's eyes dart back and forth as he rolled the thought around within his scheming brain.

"*Cuánto*? How much?"

"500,000 dollars," Huber lied. "You can take me with you. When you find the treasure, you can just take my shoes and go. You'll be long gone before I ever find my way out to tell anyone."

The morbid smile returned to Salazar's face. Huber waited, unsure of what would happen. Seconds passed like hours. Finally, he spoke.

"I like the way you think, *joven*. You will join me. If I do not find *Tesoro de los Muertos*, I will hold you for ransom. However, know this, Yoober, if your parents do not pay, you will die. I will send them one finger at a time."

Salazar hoisted Huber up to his feet. He positioned the boy in front of him and jabbed the knife tip to his spinal cord.

"Don't try . . . *anything*."

"I won't."

"I won't . . . sir!" Salazar hissed.

"What?"

"Say it! I won't, *sir*. Show me some respect."

"I won't, sir," Huber uttered.

Salazar smiled at his hostage as he led him toward a large pine tree. "That is better. Do as I ask, and you may just make it out of here alive. Now, hug the tree," he demanded.

Huber complied, and Salazar lashed his wrists together with a thin rope. Huber had never been held captive before. A helpless feeling engulfed him. At least he was still alive. He wondered where Scott and Hannah were. Was Salazar telling the truth? He had no way to know.

"Your friends will return here soon. When they do, they will come looking for you, unless . . ."

"Unless what?"

"Unless they think you are already dead."

With his face pressed against the tree, Huber could only listen as Salazar took his knife to all of their camping gear, furiously ripping through their sleeping bags, tent, and trail packs. He scattered their food and dumped out their water. He heard the snap of Scott's prized fishing pole. When he was finished with the destruction, Salazar took off his hat and plopped down next to the tree, catching his breath.

"Just one more thing that must be done."

Huber nervously inquired with his eyes.

"There must be blood."

Huber's eyes widened as Salazar stood and pressed the cold knife to his cheek. His chest heaved in and out. There was nothing Huber could do. *Water off a duck's back*, he told himself. His lip quivered as he tried his best not to scream out.

Salazar inched his face next to his, gazed straight into the boy's terrified eyes, and whispered, "Don't worry, Yoober. It won't hurt a bit."

He traced the knife's tip along Huber's face slowly. It made a tickling sensation.

"Do you really want to know how I got this?" Salazar asked, running the knife tip along the scar that ran from his eye to his lip.

Huber said nothing. His chest continued heaving in and out.

"You see, Yoober, I wasn't completely honest with you before when I claimed that Carlos was my father. He was my uncle who took me in. My father was a very mean man. A *borracho*. Always came home drunk. When he drank, he became angry. When he became angry, he became violent. One night he came home, drunk as usual. I was only a few years younger than you are now. As he walked through the door, he tripped on my shoes. I had left them in front of the door by mistake. I heard him fall to the floor, but then he got up and screamed my name. My brother locked the door, and we hid under the bed together, hoping he would not find us. He tromped throughout the house, went to his closet, and grabbed his army knife. He then came toward my room. My mother clung to him, pleading for him to stop, but he did not. When he reached the door to my room, I heard him throw my mother against the wall. She made no more sound. When he realized my door was locked, he became angrier."

He paused and drew even closer to Huber's face.

"*Boom! Boom! Boom!*" Salazar shouted, accentuating

each word with a flick of his fingers. Huber flinched at each instance. Salazar continued his story.

"The door flew open, and from underneath my bed, we saw his feet. Beyond them, I saw my mother's eyes staring at me, but her eyes did not blink. My father walked toward the bed. His hand shot underneath and drug me out by my hair. He threw me on top of the bed. I saw the knife in his hand and screamed, *¡Socorro! ¡Socorro!*

"I yelled for my mother, but she still made no sound. My father looked at her and ran to her side. He dropped the knife and started crying, yelling that *I* had killed her! *Me!* If I had not made him angry, this would not have happened, he told me. My father went mad.

"He picked up the knife and came at me, repeating that I had killed my mother and needed to be punished. He took the knife and carved this line in my face so I would never forget what I had done. All the while, my little brother sobbed beneath the bed. The neighbors heard the screams and came. They pulled my father off me and took me to the *médico* and him to the *policía*. My brother and I were separated and put in orphanages. A few months later, an uncle I'd never met came and took me into his home. My father went to prison and I never saw him again. I never saw my brother again either. My uncle claimed he had been adopted before he could find him." Salazar snorted. "You see, my father's punishment went far beyond these scars."

A part of Huber felt pity for the man, but more than anything, he felt terrified at what the man might do next.

"When I returned to my home a few days later to gather my things, the knife still rested beneath my bed. I picked it up and hid it in my suitcase. I've kept it with me ever since. Difficult to believe that such a small thing could cause so much pain," Salazar said reverently as he caressed the blade with his fingertips. "You see, Yoober, it is better to feel pain than nothing at all."

Salazar inched the knife away from Huber's face and gripped the blade within the palm of his left hand. Huber watched in horror as blood flowed through his fingers. Salazar's eyes closed almost in pleasure. Walking over to where Huber had been sleeping, he sprinkled blood over the ground and spread it on some nearby rocks and tree trunks. When he was finished, he wrapped up his hand with a piece of cloth.

The scene did appear as if some wild animal had ransacked their camp, feasted upon the poor sleeping boy, and dragged his carcass off into the woods somewhere, never to be found.

Satisfied with his work, Salazar placed his black hat back upon his head, loosened Huber from the tree, and rebound his wrists in front of his torso. Salazar retrieved a compass from his pocket along with the map. *"Continúa al noreste, sube la concha de la tortuga, y camina oeste hasta que conozes a mis hermanos.* Come, *joven,* we go we northeast, up and around the falls until we find the turtle's shell."

As they departed, Huber remembered that he had stuffed his pockets earlier in the day. While Salazar wasn't looking, he quickly slid his fingers into his pocket and fished around until he found a small round candy piece. Silently, he dropped the brightly colored, neon Skittle. Salazar hadn't noticed. It was a desperate attempt, but maybe Scott and Hannah would find the colorful trail before an animal did.

CHAPTER
•18•

HUBER AND HANNAH'S FATHER strolled down the toiletry aisle at the Carbondale grocery store. As Robert continued to travel down the aisle, he deliberated which toilet paper to buy. The Charmin two-ply was a good dollar more than the one-ply. "What the heck," he said to himself. "I'll splurge for the good stuff." He threw the package in the cart and moved on.

"Good call," said another man who was coming down the aisle. He was wearing overalls smudged with black grease. He had short red hair and a light, stubbly beard. On his overalls, within a small white oval, the name *Brad* jumped out in red cursive stitching. "Ya won't regret it. That stuff's worth the extra dough, in my opinion," he added, pointing to the toilet paper as he moved along.

Robert laughed and collected the rest of his items. A few minutes later, he stood in line to check out. Two people waited in front of him. At the register was an older lady, taking out coins one at a time and arguing with the clerk about a coupon that had expired months ago for cottage cheese.

"Looks like we'll be here awhile," a voice echoed from behind him.

Robert looked behind him and recognized the same man

from the toilet paper aisle, also waiting impatiently.

"Brad, is it?" he asked, pointing at the red stitching. The name sounded familiar somehow.

"Yes, sir. Brad McCormick," the man replied, and they shook hands.

"Robert Hill. Nice to meet you."

"What do ya do around here, Bob?"

Robert chuckled. Not many people called him Bob. "I run my own tax accounting business. Hill Accounting. The building's on Main Street. Blue and white sign. How about you?"

"Oh, yeah, I've seen your place. I'm a business owner m'self. McCormick Auto Body and Repair."

Robert's brow furrowed as he struggled to recollect where he had heard this man's name before. The two men looked at each other for a moment longer, and a dawning realization came upon both of them simultaneously. "Hold on a minute! You said Brad McCormick? Don't our kids run around together?"

"Sure, yeah," the man responded.

A puzzled look covered both their faces.

"Isn't my son supposed to be with you in Denver this weekend?" Robert asked.

"No, Scott said he was goin' with y'all," Brad replied with a befuddled look.

"Didn't you call and talk to my wife about it a couple of days ago?"

"No, sir. Your wife called *me* and said your family was goin' up to Denver."

"Something here isn't right. I get the feeling that we've

both had the wool pulled over our eyes."

"I think ya might be right about that. I'm gonna bust that kid's butt so hard when I see 'im."

A couple of hours and many phone calls later, the two parents realized that their kids were missing and no one had a clue where they were. The worst part was that the kids had been gone for more than twenty-four hours. Their parents felt a mixture of fear and red-hot anger toward their children. They called the police, who put out the word. Brad called Robert and reported that all of their outdoor gear was missing.

Later in the day, the phone rang at the Hill household. Ellen answered.

"Mrs. Hill, Sheriff Brady. I think we may have some information on the whereabouts of your kids."

"Oh, thank you, sheriff. Where are they?" she asked, waving over her husband as she conversed.

"Well, we don't know exactly. After we put out the alert, Gary Thomas, the owner of Thomas Family Mercantile up on highway 122, called in. He reported that three kids came into his store yesterday and bought some snacks. Said it looked like they were fully decked out with camping gear and headed up toward the mountains."

"Do we know where in the mountains?" Ellen asked. Fear returned to her face.

"No, ma'am, we don't know exactly where in the mountains they were headed, but it looks like they were going up Roaring Fork Canyon, up toward Sopris. It'll be dark soon, so it won't do much good to look for them tonight. Since there aren't any signs of abduction, we can't rule this as a missing persons case, and I can't spare any men to look for them. If they're not back by tomorrow night, let me know."

"We appreciate you finding out where they went. Thank you, sheriff," Ellen said, exasperation returning to her voice as she hung up the phone.

"Camping?" Robert asked. "Why would they go up there without telling us?"

"I don't know. It doesn't make any sense. I just hope they're all right. We need to find them, Robert. Do you have any idea what could happen to them in the woods? If they got lost, they could . . ." Ellen couldn't finish her sentence.

Brad McCormick, who was sitting at the kitchen table drinking a glass of water, felt compelled to try to comfort the woman. "Ellen, it is kinda scary thinkin' of them kids up there all alone. But if it's any consolation, m'boy knows how to survive in the woods. He's been in Scouts ever since he was a little guy, and I've taught him everything I know too, so I'm guessin' they're just fine. What I dunno is why they'd do this without lettin' us know."

The words brought some relief to the room.

"Brad and I will head up there at first light. Ellen, you can stay here in case there are any new calls or updates," Robert said.

Wiping tears from her eyes, Ellen implored her husband, "Please, just find them."

CHAPTER 19

"WHAT DO WE DO NOW?" Hannah trembled.

"We go get help."

"What if my brother is still out there somewhere? By the time we get help, it'll be too late. What happened here?"

"No idea. Bears don't usually go through the trouble of tearin' everything up like this."

"What are you saying? You think it was a person?"

Scott shrugged. "I dunno. Coulda been."

Hannah thought of the face she saw the night before. "Then we have to look for him. He might not have much time."

The Boy Scout in Scott told him to go get help, but he knew Hannah made a good point. It would take hours to climb down the mountain and come back with help. Most likely, they wouldn't be able to come back until the morning. If Huber was alive in the woods, they needed to find him quickly.

"Maybe you're right."

The two scavenged the area around the bloody scene. They couldn't really tell which direction Huber had been taken. Then Hannah saw it. A fainting ray of sunlight filtered through the treetops and shone on something that didn't quite belong among the browns and yellows of the forest floor. It was a small, bright blue object. She walked over to it, reached down, and picked up the Skittle. She looked ten feet ahead and saw another vividly colored piece of candy. She dashed forward and picked up a red one.

"Scott, I think Huber might've left us a trail!"

Scott caught up to her and scanned twenty feet or so ahead of them and saw a bright green Skittle.

"Ya know, I think he might've."

"C'mon then! Let's go!"

"Hold on a sec."

"What? Why? We've got to help my brother."

"We can't go unprepared. It's gettin' late, and we might be out there all night. We need to scavenge as much as we can."

"Hurry up then!"

Scott rummaged through the ruins, searching for anything usable. It seemed that whatever monster had entered their camp had taken its time to make sure everything was destroyed. Minutes later, Scott had collected a few socks, the can of spray paint, fishing line, and some scattered nuts, half buried in the dirt. Off in the distance, between two shrubs, Scott saw something glimmer in the twilight. He ran and picked up the object.

"Hannah, look!" he yelled as he clicked their flashlight on and off. They wouldn't have to wander in the dark.

"Okay, great. Let's go!"

They followed the trail Huber left behind. He seemed to be dropping Skittles further and further apart. Searching the perimeter of the area turned difficult as light dissipated. After the fourth Skittle, they picked up the direction the trail was heading, making it easier to find the next one. They had found twenty-one pieces when the sun disappeared over the mountain and daylight evaporated. Finding a Skittle in the dark would be like trying to find a needle in a haystack. Scott clicked on the flashlight. They searched for the next piece of candy in vain. A half hour later it was almost completely dark.

"This is gonna be impossible. We ain't gonna find nothin' out 'ere."

"We're not waiting until tomorrow, Scott. It's my brother. Who knows what's happening to him. We can't wait and just hope he's okay. I'll get on my hands and knees and crawl around on the ground all night if I have to. Keep shining that light around and look!"

Scott haphazardly swung the light ahead of him. The light glinted off something metallic. "Hey, look!"

Hannah ran to the object and held it up in the light. She gasped. A gold coin with the emblem of a faded cross stared her in the face.

CHAPTER 20

HUBER HAD RUN OUT of Skittles. He had no choice but to drop one of the last two things in his pocket: his grandfather's gold doubloon or the lighter. In his current predicament, the lighter seemed to hold more value. Holding back tears, he had begrudgingly released the treasured piece from his hand when Salazar's head was turned. What now? He had nothing else to leave behind. Probably didn't matter anyway. Chances were that no one would ever find the trail to begin with. Why would anyone even bother to look?

The two continued to walk for a half-mile or so before stopping. Salazar threw his pack in front of Huber and told him to open it. The knife poked him softly in the back. Exhausted, Huber stooped to his knees and struggled to unzip the pack. Inside, he observed a bloody, torn up shirt, a small, battery-powered lantern, beef jerky, a can of pork and beans, a bottle of whiskey, and a small green oxygen tank. Did Salazar have asthma or something? He didn't dare ask.

"Turn on the lantern. Give it to me."

Huber did as he was told. Bizarre, demented shadows danced all around the forest as a million crickets chirped away in the background. Visible above the treetops, stars splattered across a black canvas. A long strip of white streaked across the great expanse. He had never been able to see the Milky Way within the city limits. There had always been too much light pollution. They continued their march in the dark. Would they walk all night? Would Salazar ever get tired? He showed no signs of slowing as he prodded Huber along, holding the lantern in one hand, the knife in the other. Huber was coming down from the adrenaline rush he had experienced earlier. Parting with his grandfather's coin had also taken a toll.

"*Qué tal, joven*? You look like death is at your door. Are you not happy that I was gracious enough to spare your life?"

"I was just thinking about my grandpa . . . sir"

"Hmmm. Nicholas Eldredge?"

"Yeah."

"My uncle always talked highly of him—said he was an honorable man, unlike my uncle."

"Yes, sir."

"There are not many people like that, you know? People with honor."

"I know, sir."

Salazar slowed his steps, stopped, and turned Huber to face him. "My mother was one of those people. Know this, Yoober . . . life is unfair. It steals away the good people and leaves behind those like me." Salazar whispered, "In the end, everyone leaves you—your friends, your family. Everyone betrays you. You must rely on yourself and no one else. Trust no one. You must live only for yourself."

In a strange way, Salazar made perfect sense. Life had been unfair in so many ways. Grandpa Nick had been taken from him. Salazar's mother had been killed in front of his very own eyes. What would this man be like if he had grown up with a loving mother? Why did so many unfair things have to happen to people?

They walked a hundred yards more. Huber's legs wobbled and refused to go any further. He stumbled and fell to the earth. Expecting Salazar to kick him and tell him to get up, he braced himself. Instead Salazar looked at the boy with a softened gaze.

"Well, that's enough for tonight. Let us rest. What do you say?"

"Thank you, sir."

For the next few minutes, Huber lay on his back looking up into infinity as Salazar created a circle of rocks. He gathered some dry wood nearby and threw it in the center of the circle. Huber, too worn out to even think about trying to run, could barely move. Besides, where would he go? It wouldn't do much good to run blindly in the darkness.

In minutes, a fire raged a few feet from where Huber lay. Salazar sat across from him. In the firelight, only his twisted lips were visible beneath his wide brimmed hat. He rifled through his pack, searching for something. At last, he pulled out the jerky and the can of pork and beans. He placed the aluminum can within the crackling fire. The can made a sizzling sound. Before long, it bulged in and out like it was breathing. Salazar retrieved a pair of pliers from his bag and lifted it out of the flames. The insides of the can calmed as it cooled. Slowly peeling back the aluminum top, the sweet smell of pork and beans filled Huber's olfactory senses. Normally, Huber would be repulsed by such a dinner. After all, it looked like dog food. Tonight, however, it smelled better than turkey on Thanksgiving Day. His body craved any kind of protein after its grueling ordeal. Huber's stomach moaned and gurgled as Salazar retrieved a plastic spoon and started shoving the stuff into his mouth. After a couple of spoonfuls, the Spaniard noticed Huber's hungry eyes.

"*Patético.*" He laughed and shoveled another spoonful into his mouth, shaking his head. After doing so, he scooted around to where Huber sat. He took out his knife. Huber winced and shut his eyes. He felt the cold blade tickle his forearm and then, all of a sudden, his hands were free. Huber opened his eyes and looked at his raw wrists. He rubbed them and eyed his abductor, who now slid back to his original position. Adjacent to where Huber sat, a half full can of pork and beans steamed upward. Without thinking, Huber snatched the spoon and began piling the ecstasy into his mouth. Salazar's face remained expressionless as he watched his captive eat.

"Thank you for the food, sir," Huber uttered. He burped and glanced up at Salazar.

Salazar said nothing. His enigmatic face held no clues as to what he thought or felt. Huber looked at the ground as the man's emotionless eyes stared through him.

Finally, the Spaniard broke the silence. "I see you are finally learning respect."

"Yes, sir."

"Will you not even thank me for cutting your bonds?"

"Thank you, sir."

"I trust you will not run away. It will do you no good out here in the dark, you know?"

"I know, sir."

"*Qué bueno, joven. Qué bueno.*" A few moments of silence

passed as Salazar threw some beef jerky Huber's way. He wolfed it down in seconds. "Your mother and father must be worried about you."

"They don't even know I'm up here. Even if they did, my dad wouldn't care. He'd probably be happy that I'm gone . . . sir." Huber immediately realized how stupid he'd been to share this information.

Salazar smirked. "Fathers . . . who needs them, eh?"

Salazar raised his right arm over his head and took off his hat. His long, dark hair fell in front of his temples. As he did so, he winced and held his arm. He rolled up his sleeve. Deep, scabbed-over gashes covered his left forearm. Blackish blue bruises surrounded the cuts. Huber also observed the stitched cut above his eyebrow.

"What happened?"

Salazar looked up sharply with a threatening glance.

"I mean, what happened to your arm, sir?"

Salazar glared for a second longer and then looked back at his arm. "None of your concern, *joven*."

"It just looks like—"

"None of your concern!" he said sharply.

Huber took the hint and piped down. He would ask no more questions.

The two said nothing more. Huber's eyes kept closing as he stared at the flickering flames. He would jerk himself awake, afraid to fall asleep. He glanced over at Salazar, who was also struggling. If he could just stay awake longer than Salazar, maybe he could get the knife.

"I know what you're thinking, *joven*. Wait until I fall asleep . . . slit my throat. Know this: I sleep with one eye open.

You come anywhere near me, make any kind of noise, I will hear. I trust you will not be stupid?"

"No, sir."

"*Qué bueno, joven.* Try anything, know that I will kill you without hesitation. Now, let us rest. I give you my word, I will not harm you while you sleep. I always keep my word. I always keep my honor."

"Yes, sir."

Crickets continued singing as the fire died down.

"What does this name mean—Yoober?"

"I don't know what it means. It was like my great-great-grandpa's name or something. It got passed down to me, sir."

"Was he an honorable man?"

"Yes. From what I hear, sir."

"Then it is a good name. Yoober, you may call me Juan. Let us sleep now."

Sleep overtook Huber within minutes. The dream happened as it always did. Running through a dark tunnel. The breath of the creature warmed his neck. Huber didn't dare turn around to see what chased him. He knew where he'd trip. This time, there was no one standing in the light toward the end of the tunnel. The creature's teeth sank into his leg, and sharp pain followed. It started dragging him back into the darkness. The light at the end of the tunnel flashed and then disappeared, flashed again, and then disappeared.

A flash of red, then black. Another flash of red, then black. Tiny purple veins became visible behind Huber's eyelids. Groggily, he opened them to a blinding white flash, then a reddish darkness. What in the world? Lifting his head slowly, he took in the scene around him. The coals of the fire smoldered a deep volcanic crimson. Salazar lay by the fire pit, his face covered by his hat. Huber scanned the perimeter of the forest. His eyes returned to their original position. A flash of white light blinded him and then disappeared. His eyes adjusted to the darkness. Off twenty feet or so, he made out two figures, two faces. *Scott! Hannah! Could it be?*

"Psst, Huber," Hannah whispered through the darkness, shining the light on his face.

Huber brought his finger to his lips and glanced over at Salazar, whose chest moved up and down evenly. He didn't stir.

"Huber, c'mon, dude. Let's get outta here," Scott beckoned.

Huber shook his head no. His paralyzed body refused to move an inch.

"What's he doing?" Hannah asked.

"I dunno. Maybe he's tied up or something?" Scott asked.

A million thoughts traveled through Huber's head. More than anything, he wanted to sprint away, but he didn't dare move. Scott and Hannah inched closer. To their surprise, Huber wasn't bound.

"Huber, what's wrong? Let's go," Hannah whispered again.

"Shhh. Get outta here," Huber whispered back, sure the noise had awoken Salazar. Huber observed the man. His chest still heaved in and out.

"We're not leavin' ya here, dude."

"Too dangerous . . . just go. Get help. I'll be okay."

"No way! C'mon, what are you waiting for?"

Huber looked at Salazar, took a deep breath and nodded. Stealthily, he inched up into a sitting position. With all the caution he could muster, he extended his knees until they locked in place. Salazar snored softly adjacent to the burning coals. Huber stepped over the log he was using as a pillow. He cringed as dried foliage crunched under foot. Salazar's bandaged hand flinched. Huber brought his other foot over the log, causing another rustling sound. Salazar's body squirmed.

Huber cautiously crept toward his companions in the darkness. Looking back every few steps, Salazar still dozed fitfully. Each step brought more trepidation. Salazar would surely wake. Huber approached Scott, now only feet away.

"Y'okay?"

"Yeah."

"Did he do anything to you?" Hannah asked, worried.

"No . . . not really."

"Let's get the heck outta here." Scott said.

Hannah shone the light through the darkness. "Which way?"

"Anywhere but here," Scott insisted.

They snuck light-footed through the forest. A few hundred feet into the forest, an ear-piercing yell penetrated the still night air.

"Yoober! Yoober!" the voice shouted.

The trio hit the ground and turned off the flashlight.

"Yoober!" Salazar wailed again.

Huber's guts wrenched within him as he hyperventilated. They all lay on the ground, straining to see through the trees.

Barely visible in the distance, Salazar swung his lantern in all directions, yelling for the boy. His voice sounded hurt and almost sad. Just as quickly, the man's apparent sorrow turned to unfettered rage. He shrieked toward the forest.

"I'll find you, Yoober! Hear me! I'll find you! *Te mataré!* Our deal is off, *joven*! You are dead! Hear me! *Muerto!*"

The three jumped to their feet and ran blindly through the darkness. Any stiffness in Huber's legs was now overcome by the will to survive. Branches smacked them in the face; rocks tripped them up. Never did they look back to see if Salazar followed them. The threats hurled in their direction soon drifted further and further away until they could hear them no more. The trio continued to run for what must've been an hour, changing directions every so often, just in case Salazar was trailing them.

Once they felt safe, the three of them collapsed on the forest floor and heaved in exhaustion. Clouds briefly parted overhead, revealing brilliant stars, oblivious to any earthly concerns. After resting for five minutes without speaking, they all began to realize their predicament. In their flight to escape the clutches of the madman, they had dashed into the woods without any direction. They were lost. At least they were safe for now. Huber grasped Scott's shoulder.

"Thanks."

"Don't thank me, Puber. Your sister found the trail. When I saw all that blood and stuff, I was too scared to do anything."

Huber gave his sister a thankful look. She simply nodded as a silent understanding passed between brother and sister. She took his hand.

"Here, you dropped this."

Cold metal struck his palm.

He instantly choked up. "Thanks," he barely got out. "How'd you find me?"

"We were just wanderin' around after we followed your trail and then we smelled somethin'."

"Smelled like hot dogs," Hannah added.

"We followed the smell and then we saw your fire," Scott continued.

"Pork and beans."

"Huh?" Scott looked puzzled.

"It was pork and beans you smelled."

"Oh. Well, after that we just kinda hid and waited around till it was safe to come getcha."

"I wonder where we are," Hannah said.

"Come daylight, we'll find our way outta 'ere," Scott reassured her.

"The map is gone. He took it," Huber said dejectedly.

"It's okay, dude. Right now we just gotta get outta the woods and get to the cops."

"Grandpa Nick trusted me with it. I'll never get it back." Huber strained to hold back tears. "Where were you two, anyway?"

Hannah and Scott looked at each other, shamefaced.

Scott looked at Hannah. He opened his mouth to speak, but Hannah beat him to it.

"We saw a moose down by the waterfall. We wanted to show you, but you looked so tired, we didn't want to wake you up. When we came back, all we saw was a bloody mess. We didn't know what had happened. I knew you were alive, though. I felt it. I saw the Skittle and knew you left it on purpose." Hannah felt a little guilty for not telling the whole truth, but now was hardly the time or place to tell Huber that they were kissing while he was being assaulted.

"It's good you guys weren't there. We all may've been goners," Huber remarked solemnly.

"It was that Spanish guy, wasn't it?" Scott asked. "The one that came to your house."

"Yeah. Salazar."

"The guy you told me about . . . the one that said his dad was friends with Grandpa Nick?" Hannah asked.

"Yeah. That was a lie. Actually, his dad's in prison for murdering his mom."

"C'mon, we've been through a lotta garbage these last few hours. Let's just settle down for the night. Talk about things tomorrow," Scott suggested.

"Where? Here?"

"We don't wanna keep wanderin' in the dark, that's for sure. We'll just get more lost. Let's hunker down for the rest of the night. In the morning, we'll try to find our way out."

"You mean just stay out here in the open? We need to start a fire or we'll all get hypothermia," Hannah protested.

"We have our lighters. We can start a fire," Scott said.

"What if Salazar sees it?" Huber said.

"I don't think he will. This forest is too dense. You'd have to be really close, and I don't think he is, but it's up to y'all too."

"Do it," Huber said.

"All right," Hannah said, shivering from the cold.

The group gathered some red pine needles and small logs. Scott ignited the pine needles with his lighter and blew on them. A few minutes later, a small fire erupted. Soon the three were huddled around it, attempting to fend off the creeping chill of nocturnal air. Their stomachs ached with hunger as they reminisced about the fish they ate the night before. Had it really been only twenty-four hours? Last night, they were all happy, confident, and excited. Tonight, they were hungry, cold, and scared for their lives.

The fire slowly died and morphed into smoldering ash as a vespertine fog settled upon them. The three lay down together as close to the coals as they safely could, covering themselves with pine branches for blankets. The threesome attempted to sleep as best they could. The wind periodically blew, gusting up dirt in their faces. Huber had never endured such a wretched night. He thought of his nice soft bed at home and how he had taken it for granted all these years. The thought of soft warm sheets and fluffy pillows waiting for him brought Huber to the point of tears. He flipped over and saw Scott's mug scrunched up next to his. The night dragged on as he wandered in and out of consciousness but never really slept. Whenever he would doze, he would dream of either the creature chasing him in the dark tunnel or Salazar running after him with the knife. After the nightmares, it would take him five or ten minutes to calm down and convince himself that he was really alive and okay. The process repeated itself over and over throughout the night.

Sometime later, Huber was startled awake by a sound. His head instantly snapped up. The fog that had settled over the woods had become more dense, reducing visibility to a few feet. Then he heard it again. The crunching of leaves.

"Scott! Hannah! Wake up!" Huber whispered frantically. "There's something out there."

Instantly awake and on their feet, they scanned the perimeter. Quietly, they listened.

"What did you hear?" Hannah asked in alarm.

"Footsteps," Huber answered.

"Ya sure?" Scott asked.

"Positive."

In the shadowy fog of the trees, Huber caught a glimpse of movement.

"There!" he pointed.

Suddenly, Huber felt a hand rest on his shoulder from behind. A voice whispered in his ear, "Hello, Yoober."

"Run!" Scott yelled as Huber broke free from Salazar's grasp.

The three of them tore through the blanket of fog. The heavy breathing of Salazar echoed through the air as he ripped his way through the foliage after them.

"Split up!" Scott yelled. "He can't chase all of us!"

The three set out in three different directions. Salazar went after the closest target—Hannah.

"Yes, run, *jovencita*!" the Spaniard laughed from behind.

Terror gripped Hannah as she heard the man gain on her. She continued running as hard as she could, unable to see ahead more than a few feet. Stealing a glance behind, she made out Salazar's shadowy outline. Her legs threatening to give way beneath her as she relentlessly pounded the ground, she suddenly burst through the trees and skidded to a halt, nearly running straight into a deep chasm that prevented her from going anywhere but backward. The abyss below her feet appeared bottomless. She was trapped. Bending down, she gathered a handful of dirt.

Salazar emerged from the tree line and witnessed his trembling prey.

"No place to go, *jovencita*," he growled.

"Please! What do you want?"

"Fame. Fortune. But do you know what I really want?" he asked as he skulked closer.

Hannah said nothing. Her head shot back and forth between the gorge and Salazar.

"I want to imagine Yoober's face as he hears his sister's screams when she falls down that ravine." He chuckled and unsheathed his blade.

Backing up, Hannah's heels soon teetered over the precipice of the chasm.

"Please, don't—"

Before she could finish her sentence, Salazar lunged forward. Hannah flung the dirt in the man's face, temporarily blinding him. As he staggered forward, Hannah bolted back toward the trees without looking back. A bloodthirsty yell sounded from behind, and Hannah once again heard footsteps racing toward her. As she ran, a set of hands reached out from the trees and covered her mouth. Before she could scream, she heard Huber's voice. "Shhh, sis. Down here." He held a finger to his lips and pointed downward. A few feet away, a small recess was carved into the bedrock. Scott reached his arm out and helped them slide into the opening just as Salazar reached their location. Eyes level with his feet, they breathed a sigh of relief as he kept running past them.

CHAPTER 21

EVENTUALLY, THE SUN PEEKED over the opposite horizon of where it had disappeared, now burning away the fog. Huber had never been so grateful to see the light of day.

"Sun's up," Huber prodded the others lying on the ground.

Slowly, Scott rose to his feet and extended his hand to Hannah.

"Ya doin' all right?"

She nodded. "What do we do now?"

"Try to find our way back to the Waters of Life and back down the trail," Scott answered.

"Aren't you supposed to stay put when you're lost?"

"Yeah, when people know you're lost. Nobody even knows we're up here. I dunno 'bout y'all, but I don't like the idea of stayin' up here another night with that psychopath runnin' round. I'm gettin' outta here today."

"Sounds like a plan," Huber said. "Which way?"

"Dunno. Let's let the lady pick."

"That way." Hannah pointed randomly in front of her, not knowing why.

"Anything look familiar?" Hannah asked as the group trudged along the all too familiar scene of pine trees interspersed with quakies and knee-high grasses. Their stomachs growled with hunger.

"Yeah—everything," Scott replied. Hannah rolled her eyes.

"This reminds me of the corn maze we went through last year. Remember, sis? We got lost for hours."

"In a regular corn maze, you don't have wild animals and crazy Spaniards after ya," Scott said.

"Where do you think he is?" Hannah asked. Since the incident the night before, no one had really spoken about it.

"Now that he has the map, he's probably off treasure hunting," Huber muttered.

"What happens if we can't find our way out of here?"

"What do you think'll happen? We'll slowly starve to death," Scott said with a sly grin. "Ever hear of the Donner party? First one who dies, the other two getta eat." Scott moved his eyebrows up and down in his usual fashion after saying something smart.

"You're sick. Don't talk like that," Hannah responded tersely.

"Think of it as a final gift to those you love," Huber joined in, smiling. "If you died, sis, wouldn't you want your friends and family to survive? Your body would just rot and go to waste anyway."

"I call the ribs!" Scott laughed. "Just wish I had me some barbeque sauce."

"Knock it off."

"I call the calves. I bet they'd taste just like those big juicy turkey legs from Disneyland," Huber added.

"Shut up, you stupid jerks!" Hannah snapped. "Quit

treating this like a joke! A man is out there ready to kill us! We're lost, and nobody knows where we are! Don't you understand how much trouble we're in?"

"Just tryin' to lighten things up, buttercup," Scott answered.

"Don't call me that!"

"Hey, a buttercup is a delicate flower, just like you."

Huber stifled a laugh.

Hannah quickened her pace to get ahead of the two boys. As she distanced herself from them, she turned her ankle on a loose rock, falling sharply to the ground. Scott ran to help her.

"Leave me alone," she cried out.

"C'mon, let me help ya up, buttercup."

"Get away from me!"

It was amazing to her that the guy she had been in love with a few hours before was now the bane of her existence.

"Hey, I was just kiddin' back there. There's no way I could eat ya. Well, I wouldn't enjoy it, anyway," Scott said wryly.

"There you go again," she said, slapping his hand away from her.

"I had no idea you were so sensitive! Fine, just stay there! Don't forget we saved your life," Scott retorted as he threw his arms up in the air.

"I didn't need saving. I was doing just fine on my own."

Scott fell back in step with Huber as Hannah struggled to her feet and limped on in front of them.

"Man, she's just like a roller coaster—up and down," Scott complained loud enough so she would hear.

"Try living with her," Huber sniped.

"Dang, dude, I can't even imagine."

Hannah continued on as if she hadn't heard anything the boys were saying. One thing was for certain: Scott McCormick would never get another kiss out of her.

Despite their predicament, Huber smiled.

CHAPTER 22

"ANY SIGN OF THEM?" Robert yelled to Brad. When Robert saw Brad's ashen face, hope dissipated.

"Nope. Nothin'. Coulda gone anywhere," Brad responded, exasperated. The two fathers had split up in the morning and were now reuniting to update each other on their progress.

"Let's break for lunch, then we'll start up again," Robert suggested.

The men had been searching all morning. At the mouth of the canyon, they'd noticed footprints in the mud alongside the river and followed them until they disappeared at the bottom of the scree-laced escarpment on the opposite side. The two had ascended the slope and from there could only guess where the kids had gone.

"How was your wife doin' when we left?" Brad asked.

"Not good. Didn't sleep a wink. Tried to call her, but there's no reception up here. How about Scott's mother?"

"Haven't been able to reach her yet."

"Really? Is she out of town?"

Brad smirked and said, "Guess ya could say that. Been outta town for years now."

"Oh, I'm sorry to hear that," Robert said after an awkward moment of silence.

"Ahh, it's all right. We manage okay."

All of a sudden, they heard a sound behind them. Jumping from where they stood and turning around, the two fathers beheld a tall man in a white button-up shirt and blue jeans.

"Easy there . . . didn't mean to startle you," he said.

The smooth-faced man possessed an olive complexion, wore a cowboy hat, and looked to be in his mid- to late forties. His eyes hid behind thick sunglasses. A braided leather necktie decorated his shirt collar. Holstered to his right hip, a black .9 mm handgun caught Robert's gaze. A bushy salt and pepper mustache covered the man's upper lip. In his hand, he held a lead attached to a beautiful black and brown German shepherd, which sat obediently at his side.

"Who are you?" Robert asked.

"Gentlemen, my name is Anthony Rodriguez, federal marshal," the man stated as he flashed his credentials. "This is Jenkins," he said, pointing to the dog. "I think you may be able to help me out."

"What can we do for you?" Robert asked.

"I left town as soon as I got word you were up here. From what I gather, there was a man spotted around Carbondale over the last few months. Goes by the name of Juan Salazar. He came here from Spain and is a wanted fugitive. He fled his country before he could be detained. I've been tracking him ever since he entered the country," the marshal replied gravely.

"What does this man have to do with us?" Robert asked, perplexed.

The marshal took off his sunglasses and surveyed the men. The absence of the sunglasses revealed a face filled with anxiety and apprehension. His voice sounded heavy. "Well, we've researched this man and realized he has connections to your family. I learned he was seeking some kind of redress from your father-in-law, Nicholas Eldredge. I spoke with your wife before I came up here. Apparently, he came to your home not long ago, looking for some kind of letter."

"Yes, I remember her mentioning to me some strange man had dropped by."

"Your wife reported she didn't know what the man was talking about and that he left your home very agitated. She should not have let his man inside your home, Mr. Hill . . . you have no idea how dangerous he is."

"Look, all I know is what she told you. If you're looking for more information about him, I haven't the slightest clue. I wasn't even home when he came by. As you probably know, we're up here searching for our kids. I'm sure you've traveled a long way to talk to me, but now isn't the time. You're probably best off to talk to my wife again if you're looking for more details," Robert said, annoyed at the delay.

"Sir, I didn't come up here to question you about this man. I came here to find him," the marshal said, his brow furrowing and his features hardening again.

"Come again?"

"The owner of the Thomas Family Mercantile reported to Sheriff Brady that another man came into his store shortly after your kids. He also appeared to be going on some kind of excursion up in these parts. I found his rental car near the mouth of the canyon."

"This same man . . . this Salazar, who you said is a wanted fugitive?" Robert asked, now very concerned.

"Yes, sir," Marshal Rodriguez answered flatly. "Gentlemen,

this man is considered armed and dangerous, and by all accounts it looks like he's up here in the area. The fact that he visited your home and is now here at the same time your kids go missing seems highly suspect, wouldn't you say?"

"Are you sayin' this guy is after our kids?" Brad asked anxiously.

"Can't be certain, but could be."

"Why would he be after our kids?" Robert asked in a panic.

The marshal hesitated.

"Tell us!" Brad raised his voice.

The marshal looked at Robert with sympathetic eyes. A moment of silence passed before he nodded his head.

"All right, I'll tell you what I can."

"You said this guy's wanted. For what?" Brad asked.

"Back in Salamanca, Salazar tortured an old man . . ."

The fathers stood speechless.

"Worst part of it is, the old man was his uncle. Then Salazar used his uncle's passport to fly to New York, and from there to Denver. In Denver, he rented a car. That car is now sitting a couple of miles away from here. Like I said, I've been hunting him for weeks."

"Marshal, this letter he mentioned—does it have something to do with what's going on?"

The marshal once again hesitated.

"Tell us what's happening! We've a right to know!" Brad barked.

The dog began growling and baring his teeth.

"Jenkins, stop it," the marshal demanded, and the dog did so.

"The old man who was tortured . . ."

"Go on," Robert insisted.

"You see, this old man, Carlos Salazar, did travel here many years ago. While he was here, he made the acquaintance of one Nicholas Eldredge, your wife's father. Carlos wrote in his memoir that he gave a letter to your father-in-law."

"What's so important about the letter?" Robert inquired.

"According to the old man, it's not really a letter. It's a series of directions and diagrams."

"Directions?" Brad repeated.

"Directions and diagrams for what?" Robert prodded.

"The memoir said it leads to a place called *Tesoro de los Muertos*. A vast trove of Spanish artifacts and objects of monetary value."

"A treasure map?"

"Yes, sir, a treasure map."

"You're telling me that those stories about Spanish treasure up here in Mt. Sopris are actually true?"

"Well, whether they're true doesn't really matter, does it? This man, Salazar, seems to think so and has proved he will do anything to find the place."

"And he thinks our kids have this map? Why would he think that?" Brad asked.

"Because they do."

"What? How do you know this?" Robert stammered.

"Your father-in-law's caretaker, Maria. I questioned her thoroughly. She's a tough nut to crack, that one. She told me that Nicholas Eldredge left behind a box of items to your son and daughter. Inside the box were letters of correspondence, personal journals, and an old Spanish map, drawn on buck-skin."

"Even if that's true, how would this man know our kids had it?"

Rodriguez shrugged his shoulders. "Not out of the question to think he's been watching your family."

The thought sickened Robert.

The marshal continued. "It's imperative that I get going and find your kids before he does. I'm gonna have to ask you all to go home now. This is a criminal pursuit."

The two fathers' concerns about their children being lost in the woods now turned to sheer terror at the thought of them being stalked by a dangerous fugitive.

"If this is a criminal pursuit, where's the cavalry? We need as many people as we can, combing the mountains for this guy!" Robert said.

"Under normal circumstances, yes. However, this case is different."

"What do you mean, different?"

"The only thing I can assure you is that the fewer the people who get involved in this situation, the better. I was sent here for a reason. I am good at what I do. I'm a hunter. I will hunt this man down and bring him to justice. The more people we bring in, the bigger the chance we take of jeopardizing your kids' safety."

"Well, we ain't goin' nowhere," Brad remarked defiantly.

"Marshal, we're talking about our kids," Robert added. "You can't expect us to just pack up and go home. Do you have kids?"

"Two."

"Then you know that we can't just up and leave."

Marshal Rodriguez stared Robert and Brad down for a moment. "All right, fine. No time to argue. You can come with me. Just be ready for anything," the marshal admonished. He stroked the dog's head. "C'mon, boy, let's go get 'im."

CHAPTER
23

"THIS LOOKS VERY FAMILIAR. I think we're goin' in the right direction," Scott uttered as they passed a mound of boulders surrounded by brush and trees.

Hannah rolled her eyes. "How many times have you said that?"

"I'm serious this time."

"I think he's right. It does feel familiar," Huber said. Hannah shook her head in derision.

"Boys are so stupid," she murmured. However, as soon as she finished her sentence, she was stopped in her tracks by something she saw in the distance. She hobbled toward her left.

"Where ya goin', Speedy Gonzales?" Scott laughed.

"I think I see the meadow over there. I see our stuff!"

The hidden meadow suddenly materialized. They were back at Aguas de Vida.

"Nice eyes, sis!"

"Guess I'm glad we didn't eat cha now!"

Hannah simply smiled with a smug look of satisfaction, the angry feelings she harbored dissipating.

The three warily approached the carnage as the traumatic memories of the day before still haunted them.

"We'll be able to find our way back home from here. Just think, we won't be sleeping out with tree branches for blankets. We'll be sleeping in our soft warm beds," Hannah said.

The three of them absconded behind some trees and waited to make sure the coast was clear before venturing out into the open where their scattered gear lay. Once they were sure it was safe, they trotted the distance to the site and surveyed what was left of their supplies and gear.

As they shuffled among the ruins, Scott once again noticed the shattered pieces of his compass. His eyes burned with moisture.

"That son of a—" Scott began.

"Don't say it," Hannah stopped him. "He doesn't deserve us wasting our breath on him."

"My dad gave me that compass," he went on in a melancholy voice. "It was his when he was a kid."

Hannah's heart melted. The spiteful feelings she held an hour earlier were gone. She wanted to take his hand and hug him but couldn't do so in her brother's presence.

"Sorry, Scotty," was all she could say.

"It's okay," he said, trying to hold back, but unable. His tears flowed freely. Huber was surprised. Never in his wildest imaginations had Huber thought he'd witness Scott McCormick crying. There was something disconcerting about the notion. But in a strange way, it was also comforting. So Scott was human and he felt things like everyone else.

"If either of ya tell anybody 'bout this . . ." Scott tried to sound tough, but his statement came out as pitiful rather than threatening. Huber genuinely felt empathy for Scott. After all, Salazar had taken the map and he'd likely never get it back.

Hannah changed the topic. "Let's head down to the waterfall. We can wash off our food and stock up on some raspberries too. I think we can find our way back home from here. We just need to backtrack."

"I need a moment," Scott said and wandered off to compose himself.

Hannah and Huber walked to the waterfall. In the foreground, the sun climbed a cloudless, transparent sky and began to heat the cool air of the mountains. The forest was coming alive and seemed to add new energy to Hannah and Huber's exhausted bodies. They washed the nuts they had scavenged in the waterfall and ate about half of them. They put the remainder in their pockets as they gorged themselves on wild raspberries, struggling to restrain themselves from eating too many. Hannah listened as the waterfall sang from the rocky ledge above. It was hard to believe that it had been only a day since her romantic escapade with Scott.

"I still feel like Salazar is going to pop out any second," Hannah said, looking around them.

"He's gone now. We'll be fine," Huber tried to reassure her.

"Hey! Guys! Look at this!" Scott shouted, running up. He smiled as he pulled a small object from behind his back and held it up to see.

"My grandpa's guide! I figured Salazar must've taken it or ripped it to shreds. How did you . . . ?"

"Found it just now, lyin' on the ground. He must've missed it," Scott replied, handing Huber the guide.

Huber caressed the cover of the book.

"I was looking in it. Turn to the last entry," Scott suggested.

He flipped through the guide to the last page and began to read.

> *October 3, 1979*
>
> *All of these years I've been looking in the wrong place! The map, it seems, is inaccurate. The Spaniard, Carlos, was looking in the wrong spot too. The map indicates that the turtle's shell is about two miles northeast of the Waters of Life. I found today that it's actually around two miles straight north of the clearing. I discovered this purely by accident today hunting for deer. Had the animal in my sights, put my finger to the trigger, and then I noticed something strange in my scope. La Tortuga! It was unmistakable. The turtle's shell! There it was! Dead Man's Treasure must be near.*
>
> *Later same day:*
>
> *I scaled the turtle's shell. Now I need to find "Los Hermanos." I'm not sure what that means. The map has thirteen cross symbols—I assume this was the site of the Spanish massacre. I've been looking for gravestones or memorials, but so far, nothing. The final clue states that Tesoro de los Muertos is located west of where I will meet the brothers. The instructions then say, "Levanta el velo de la muerte donde, sin boca, la calavera te canta. Para entrar, recuerda por quién doblan las campanas." **Translation:** Lift death's veil, where without a mouth, the skull sings to you. To enter, remember for whom the bell tolls.*
>
> *I know I'm close.*

"That's the last entry?" Hannah asked.

"Last one. Looks like there was one more page, but it's

been ripped out. Grandpa must've given up after this."

"We can always come back someday, you know," Hannah suggested.

"But we've come all this way. We're so close."

"Hate to side with a gal over a bro, but she's right, Puber. We can come back and find it later. I just wanna go home."

"Just feels like a waste to go back empty-handed after everything. We probably won't even run into Salazar. He's looking in the wrong place." The rational side of Huber agreed with his sister, but as he rubbed the gold coin in his pocket, the emotional side of him took over. Hannah could see the determination in his eyes.

"We don't even have any supplies," Scott complained.

"We're close to the mine. I have the map memorized in my head. We know which way is north from here. We'll leave markers to find our way back. I bet we could get there and find our way back to the mouth of the canyon before it even gets dark." Huber sniffled as his allergies kicked up. He looked at his phone. One blinking bar left of the battery. "It's only nine."

"If you two go on, you're going by yourselves. Besides, have you forgotten? Our parents expect us back today," Hannah reminded him.

"C'mon, sis, if we don't find it within a few hours, we'll backtrack and go home," Huber said. "I promise."

"It's a stupid thing to do," she protested.

"It's the only thing to do," Huber said, meeting her gaze.

"Let's vote. Majority rules," Hannah suggested. "I say we go home."

"I say we find Dead Man's Treasure."

The twins both looked at Scott, pleading with their eyes. What to do? Side with his girlfriend or his best friend? Scott said nothing for a moment as he contemplated. The Boy Scout took over.

"We go home. It's too dangerous."

Huber grimaced as if he'd been stabbed in the back. Hannah's eyes shone brightly. If Huber wasn't here, she would've kissed Scott again.

Hannah and Scott started in the direction they'd originally come.

"How's your ankle?" he asked as they trudged along.

"So you care now?" Hannah quipped.

"Not really. Just thought I'd be a gentleman and ask."

Hannah couldn't help but laugh just a little. She tried to look angry but couldn't stop from smiling. "Thank you for making the right vote, Scotty."

As Scott and Hannah walked together, it took them a few moments to realize Huber wasn't with them. Looking back, they observed him still standing in the same spot.

"Huber, come on!" Hannah shouted.

"I'm not leaving! What if Salazar somehow finds it? I'm not taking the chance." Huber answered firmly. "My whole life, I've quit things when they got too hard. I'm not quitting this time. I'm going to find it . . . for Grandpa Nick . . . with or without you."

Scott and Hannah eyed one another.

"What do we do?"

"I can't leave him up here by himself," she said, sighing.

Reluctantly, they walked back to join Huber.

"Fine, Huber, we'll keep looking. It's a stupid thing to do.

If we get lost again or worse, it's on your conscience."

"We won't."

"You ain't gonna budge, are ya?" Scott asked.

"Not a chance," Huber answered unwaveringly.

"Well, let's get goin' then. We don't got all day to flap our gums."

The trio trekked off to the north and soon disappeared among the trees.

An hour and a half later, three men staggered through the foliage and stumbled upon the awful scene of destruction. It seemed that Robert Hill, Brad Nelson, and Marshal Rodriguez had arrived too late.

CHAPTER •24•

"WHAT HAPPENED UP HERE?" Robert asked as the group rummaged through the tattered materials strewn along the ground.

"Does all this gear belong to your kids?" Marshal Rodriguez asked the two fathers. They both answered in the affirmative by slowly nodding their heads, unable to process the scene before them.

"Was this done by some kind of animal?" Robert wondered, still dazed.

"No, sir. This was definitely done by human hands," the marshal replied. Grabbing one of the tent poles, he held it up for the men to see. "I don't know of any animals up in these parts that could do something like this." He then picked up the tent cover and stretched it out over his head, watching the sunlight filter through the tears and perforations. Squinting, he analyzed the rips in the fabric, "When an animal tears something, there's a series of short gashes that run parallel to each other—you know, from their claws. These tears are long, singular, and asymmetrical. There's no doubt a person did this. Most likely with a knife or sharp object."

"Salazar . . . ," Brad ventured aloud.

"I'd say that's a fair bet," the marshal responded anxiously.

"Huber! Hannah!" Robert began to yell in all directions, cupping his hands to his mouth, frantically calling out for his children. No reply. "Brad, we're too late, we're too late," he cried in hysteria. "My kids needed me and I wasn't here . . ."

Something on the ground glimmered in the sunlight and caught Brad's eye. He bent down and wistfully looked at the shattered compass. Unable to speak, he imagined the brutal scene that had unfolded earlier. "I'll kill 'im," Brad uttered in a barely audible voice. Staring into the thick forest, he belted out. "Ya hear me? I'll kill ya when I find ya!"

"Gentlemen, you both need to calm yourselves," the marshal demanded in a stern voice. "The good news is that your kids aren't here, which means they may still be out there somewhere."

"Or he's dumped them in some awful place," Robert remarked scathingly.

"There's no need to put yourself through that. We still don't know the whole situation. Jenkins'll sniff around. Maybe he'll be able to pick up their scent. There's no reason to lose hope. You both need to keep your heads. Your kids need you to keep your heads."

The two fathers' emotions subsided at the marshal's insistence. "You're right, you're right," Robert replied, wiping tears from his eye.

For over an hour, Marshal Rodriguez took pictures with a digital camera, trying to reconstruct what had happened. A small distance from the site, he noticed something. Walking over to it, he took out his camera and snapped a photo. Moments later, the two fathers approached.

"What is—" Robert began before seeing a bloody

handprint plastered over the trunk of a nearby aspen. He fell to his knees.

"I knew it," he whispered vacantly. "Huber . . . Hannah . . . I'm so sorry."

Brad, in shock, just stared in horror, the stare of a man who had lost everything.

"Now, just hold on. Something here isn't right."

"What do you mean? Our kids' bloody handprints are right there on that tree!" Robert cried out.

"Look closely."

The two fathers reluctantly approached the tree.

"Notice anything strange?"

Brad saw it first.

"It's too big! Like an—"

"Adult's," the marshal answered. "That handprint was definitely made by an adult-sized hand."

"So what in the world happened here?" Robert asked, dazed and confused.

"We'll find out," the marshal replied and then whistled for the dog. Jenkins bounded to his master obediently.

"I'm going to have the dog sniff around a bit."

Half an hour passed. Brad became agitated. "What is that dog doin'? We can't just sit here all day watchin' him sniff around for some spot to pee!" he bellowed. Robert sat on a log, chewing a piece of grass, watching the dog anxiously and waiting for something—anything—to happen.

The dog eyed Brad, growled for an instant, and then resumed sniffing. "He knows what he's doing. He's working, so just be patient," the marshal reiterated.

"You tell me to be patient while our kids are out there

somewhere?" Brad yelled at the marshal. The dog lowered its head and began snarling.

"Jenkins, knock it off!" Marshal Rodriguez shouted. "Get back to work!" The dog let out a slight whimper and resumed scouring the ground. "Sir, if you continue on like this, I will ask you to return home," the marshal said calmly.

Brad got up in the marshal's face, even though he was a good six inches shorter than Rodriguez. They both stared each other down.

"Will ya now? I'm not goin' nowhere!"

"You don't want to do this . . . ," the marshal warned, putting his hand on the .9mm pistol.

"Look!" Robert exclaimed during the confrontation.

The two men broke their stare and turned their heads. Jenkins was moving toward the woods. "Come on, let's go. He's caught the scent!" Robert yelled.

Marshal Rodriguez and Brad McCormick stared eye-to-eye for a few more seconds and then followed Robert in the direction the dog had gone.

CHAPTER
•25•

HUBER, SCOTT, AND HANNAH slogged along the forested area with necks craned upward, looking for anything that resembled a turtle shell. So far, they hadn't seen anything close.

"How do you know we're going in the right direction, Huber?" Hannah asked. "It's easy to veer off course without a compass."

"We've been going in a straight line north by the sun," Huber said, his voice carrying the irritation he felt. He sprayed a pink dot the size of a baseball on a quaking aspen. The group had been leaving markers every few hundred feet.

"I hope you're right."

As they traveled further west, the forest became denser, laden with an incalculable number of trees and shrubs. Huber led, with Hannah and Scott walking behind. A verdant sea of vegetation made the going very slow and very loud.

Whenever they could, Scott and Hannah held hands, if only for a second or two.

"How far do you think we've come so far?" Hannah asked.

"I'd say a mile and a half or so," Scott commented as he wriggled his way through a pair of shrubs. "We're making enough noise to wake the dead."

"Or living," Hannah added as twigs snapped underfoot.

"True. Hey, Puber, what are ya doin' up there, man?"

Huber had just pushed through some foliage in front of Scott and Hannah. Through the leaves, his outline was barely visible. He didn't answer.

"Huber?" Scott hollered.

"Huber?" Hannah yelled, and she tore through the bushes with Scott right behind.

Upon reaching the other side of the brush was a small twenty-foot clearing, and they quickly ascertained the reason for Huber's silence. Standing opposite their position purred a large, reddish-orange animal, its yellow eyes fixed on them. The cougar had found them!

The cat appeared as if it had recently been in some kind of skirmish with another animal. Dry blood mottled the fur around its neck. The tip of its right ear was curiously missing.

"You kiddin' me? Not him again," Scott whispered, terrified.

"It's been hunting us!" Huber said, breaking a branch off a nearby tree and wielding it like a sword. Yelling loudly, Huber waved his staff in the air, hoping it would scare off the beast. Undaunted and unnerved, it continued, now only ten feet away. Knowing they were too slow to outrun the animal, Hannah looked around at the ground and picked up a large rock. Hefting it like a shot-putter, she lugged it toward the cat. The cougar hissed and screamed out as the rock bounced off the ground and collided with its left leg. It eyed them momentarily before sprinting through the forest with a slight limp.

"Way too close," Huber groaned. "You saved my skin yet again."

"Yeah, thanks. Just so ya know, I woulda taken care of that thing if it'd got any closer," Scott said, puffing out his chest.

Hannah shot him a skeptical look. Despite the gravity of their situation, Hannah felt guilty for hurting the animal, but what choice did she have? Huber threw down the stick.

Hannah was about to reply when a rustling sounded from behind. Turning around in unison, they were greeted by the frame of a tall, slender man, his face hidden by a wide-brimmed hat.

"*Si, si, muchisimas gracias, jovencita,*" the man's voice boomed.

Sooner than they could respond, Salazar clutched Hannah by the arm and pulled her close, holding his shining blade at her side.

Scott picked up the tree branch they'd used to fend off the cougar.

"Ah, ah, ah. I wouldn't do that, *joven*," Salazar said, and he dug the knife ever so slightly into Hannah's side. She let out a gasp of pain that stopped Scott in his tracks.

"Scott, drop it!" Huber demanded.

Scott dropped the branch and stood helpless.

"Yoober, Yoober, Yoober . . . you thought you could break our deal and not suffer the consequences? Perhaps I should punish your sister instead."

"No! Please, let her go."

"Hurt 'er, and it'll be the last thing ya ever do," Scott threatened.

"Ohh, the boyfriend comes to the rescue."

"Scott, don't," Hannah implored.

"*Scott, don't,*" Salazar repeated mockingly. "Yoober, did you know these two share something more than just friendship?"

A look of confusion stole across Huber's face. "What are you talking about?"

"Is true. Before I came for the map, I saw these two walking in the meadow, how do I say . . . showing affection for one another."

"Shut up!" Scott bellowed.

Huber felt as though someone had socked him in the stomach. Hannah and Scott had been off on some romantic rendezvous while *he* had been kidnapped? What hurt the most is that they had kept it a secret from him. With pleading eyes, Huber looked at Scott and could see it in his eyes. It was true.

"You see, what I tell you is true, Yoober. You cannot trust anyone. Everyone betrays you in the end."

"How did you find us?"

"The pink markers were more than helpful. I must also thank you for ridding me of that constant nuisance."

"What are you talking about?"

"That animal has caused me nothing but trouble since I came into these mountains."

"The cougar?"

"*Si, ese puma maldito,*" Salazar spat.

Salazar held up his left arm. Sunlight shimmered off the scabby wound Huber had observed the night before.

"It did this to me the night I tried to enter your tent, but not before I took a piece of its ear, however. I thank you again, *jovencita.*" Salazar laughed raucously at Hannah.

The girl's heart plummeted to her stomach. The cougar wasn't hunting them; it was protecting them. How could she have known? The question didn't make her feel better as she derided herself. She couldn't stop the tears from flowing down her face.

"What do you want?" Huber demanded. "I already gave you the map."

Salazar seethed toward the boy. "Knowing it would lead me astray." With his free hand, Salazar dug into his shirt pocket and held the map in front of Hannah's face. Sunlight sifted through the paper-thin parchment.

"*Mire la concha.* Tell me what you see there, *mi amor.*"

"A . . . a . . . turtle," Hannah stuttered.

Salazar dug with the knife. "Look closer."

Hannah squirmed and squinted at the yellowed parchment. "It looks like something was written but erased."

"*Sí, sí,* closer. Tell me what it said."

Salazar brought the map within an inch of Hannah's nose. A leathery, musty odor filled her nostrils. Squinting harder, she tried to make out the erased inscription.

"P. Guide, pg. 87."

"P. Guide, pg. 87. What does this mean?"

"How should I know," Huber lied, thinking of the prospecting guide in his pocket. Upon all the times looking at the map, he had never noticed what Salazar was talking about.

The man wasn't convinced. "No?"

Although none of the three uttered a word, the expressions on their faces gave them away.

"I see. Secrets." Salazar refolded the parchment and tucked

it back in his shirt pocket. With great strength, he grabbed Hannah's left hand and pulled her pinky away from her other fingers. She screamed in terror as he brought the knife to the base of her finger.

"No, don't!" Huber and Scott both yelled in unison.

"Tell me your secrets," Salazar hissed.

"Okay, okay. My grandpa probably left that pencil mark. We've been using his prospecting guide. The guide said to come this way. I'll give it to you if you just let us go," Huber cried out.

"Hand it over!"

Seeing the sharp blade rest at the base of his sister's finger, Huber had no choice except to give in to the demands of Salazar yet again. He took the guide from his back pocket and handed it over to Salazar.

"Ya got what ya wanted. Now let go of her!" Scott insisted.

Salazar smiled wickedly.

Marshal Rodriguez and the two fathers agonized as Jenkins sniffed around. Picking up the scent, he'd bark and run wildly in one direction and then stop for ten minutes or so to sniff around again.

"Marshal, this is getting old. I—"

Before Robert could finish the sentence, his pocket vibrated. Retrieving his cellular, he saw the phone had one flickering bar, barely enough to get reception. A yellow envelope on the screen popped up, indicating he'd received a text message. The name of the sender read, HUBER.

"They're alive! Marshal! Brad, they're alive! I just got a text message from Huber!" Robert beamed with hope as the other two men gathered around. Just as quickly, the hopeful look turned to mortification. There were only four letters: HELP.

CHAPTER 26

IT FELT SACRILEGIOUS TO ALLOW Salazar anywhere near his grandpa's guide. Keeping Hannah at knifepoint, the Spaniard forced her to open it to page 87. As he busied himself reading the page, Huber snuck his phone out of his pocket. In the clearing, he had one bar of reception, and the battery bar was blinking. It was almost dead. He quickly thumbed a quick text message to his dad and pressed SEND. As he did, the phone beeped and died. Huber had no idea if the message actually made it out. Salazar heard the sound of the dying phone.

"What was that? Give it to me!"

Huber placed the cell phone in Salazar's free hand. With violent force, he flung it at the trunk of a nearby tree, and it shattered into pieces. He then turned his attention back to the guide.

"Hmm, interesting . . . so the map was mistaken," he mumbled before rolling up the guide and slipping it into his back pocket. Salazar retrieved his compass. He turned slightly to the right until the needle pointed due north. "*La Tortuga* won't be far from here." Salazar turned toward Huber and Scott. "Now turn around and stand in front of the girl. You will not escape this time."

"You have what you need! Just let us go!" Huber pleaded.

"Now, why would I do that? If I could get 500,000 dollars for you alone, think of what I can get for all three of you."

Hannah looked at Huber. "But our parents don't have that kind of—"

"Yes, they do! Remember, Grandpa's inheritance money?" Huber insisted.

"Oh yeah, I forgot about that," she muttered unconvincingly.

The awkward exchange was not lost on Salazar.

"Yoober, I hope you were not lying to me. For all your sakes, I hope your parents can come up with the money. Now, listen to my instructions. I will walk behind the girl. If you try anything, I will not hesitate," he warned, causing Hannah to let out a whimper as he dug the knife into one of her ribs. He motioned for Huber and Scott to line up single file in front of Hannah, Huber in front. Salazar slid the pack off his back, forcing Hannah to rummage through it until she found a small piece of rope. She handed the rope to Salazar, who lashed Hannah's right wrist to Scott's left, and Scott's right to Huber's left. Holding the end of the rope like a leash, he beckoned them forward.

Hannah grabbed Scott's hand and clung tightly.

"Keep walking until I say to stop. And you all will address me as 'sir,' understand? Even you, Yoober."

Silently, the four of them began to march through the thick shrubbery. When they veered off course, Salazar redirected them. They traveled a quarter of a mile when the ground sloped sharply upward. The peak of Mount Sopris loomed high above them. Humid air stifled their breathing.

"Hey, Salamander, when can we take a breather, sir?" Scott shouted.

"Do not be smart with me, *joven*."

"I'm just sayin' it's hot, sir. We need a rest."

Sweat was running down Salazar's face. Up ahead, a waist-high rock jutted out of the ground.

"Stop there," he ordered, pointing at the rock. "On the ground."

The three gratefully plopped down as Salazar slumped against the rock. He still held the knife to Hannah but seemed to be letting his guard down slightly.

Huber believed it a good opportunity to distract him. "What would your mother think of you now, sir?"

Salazar's face grimaced, full of rage. His hand shot forward and slapped Huber in the face. "Do not talk of my mother, ever! Understand, *joven*?"

Huber fell to the ground but felt powerful by eliciting such a response. He had to distract Salazar but not make him so angry as to snap completely.

"What about your uncle then? What would he think, sir?"

"My uncle?" Salazar snarled. "Why would I care what he thinks?"

"You said he raised you," Huber said.

Salazar stared wistfully at Huber for a moment before anger took over his expression.

"I despised my uncle. He only took me in because he had to. He would tell my cousins all about *Tesoro de los Muertos*. Showed them this map many nights around the fireplace. One summer he set off to find it, promising us that we'd all be rich and not have to worry anymore when he returned. He did return months later . . . with empty pockets. He told us that he could not find the treasure, that it did not exist, and that he gave the map to some stranger he found in the woods. He just gave up! Things became worse after that. The *tienda* went under, and we scraped by for years and years. I hated him for this! If he had just looked harder, he could've found *Tesoro de los Muertos*, I know it. With the map gone, it would be impossible to ever try again. Over time, the rest of my family forgot about the story. I never did. In the end, my uncle got what he deserved!"

"Wow, that's quite a sob story, Salamander, sir. Your uncle takes you in to care for you and you hate him for it. Makes sense," Scott said.

"You know nothing of it!" Salazar snarled. "You spoiled American children have it so easy. You know nothing of hunger, pain, or poverty."

"What do you mean, he got what he deserved?" Huber asked somberly.

Salazar turned his scarred eye toward Huber, sending chills down his spine. "As I grew up, I made my own way. I did not see him for many years. Times were not easy in *España*. I grew tired of just getting by. So I decided to pay my uncle a visit. He would tell me how to find the American man who had the map. I demanded that he tell me the name of the man. He refused, so I . . . *persuaded him*."

"What'd you do?"

A fearsome, pulsating grin broke across Salazar's face. "Nothing that I would not do to you." He waved the knife in Huber's direction.

Huber felt genuinely frightened now. If the man didn't

hesitate to harm his own family, would he really treat them any differently?

"What are you going to do, even if you find Dead Man's Treasure? Do you really think you can just waltz back into Spain like nothing happened, *sir*?" Hannah spat out.

"I do not plan to return to Spain. I will travel to Mexico and finally live like a king, like the *conquistadores* of old. And if I cannot find the treasure, then at least I'll have three children whose parents will pay anything to get them back. Now, I think we have rested long enough."

The group continued onward and departed the cover of the forest only to witness another massive escarpment impeding their way west. The slope grew rockier and steeper as it climbed upward. Trees and brush sparsely covered the hillside.

"*La Tortuga* should be near!" Salazar yelled angrily. "Where is it? *Miren!* Look for it!"

The three surveyed their surroundings, looking for a carving of a turtle on a rock or tree, but saw nothing out of the ordinary. Salazar flipped through the prospecting guide, looking for any kind of clue, but it failed to describe exactly what the turtle was. The Spaniard seethed with rage. He tossed Hannah aside, grabbed Huber by his shirt collar, and brought the blade to his neck.

"You know where it is! Tell me!"

Huber's eyes widened in fear. The sun crested over the eastern ridge, illuminating the hillside of moss-covered quartz opposite of them.

"There, it's right there! Look!" Scott exclaimed, pointing past Salazar.

Salazar turned around, still clutching Huber, and observed

the escarpment that lay before them. There it was, staring them in the face. The sun revealed dazzling patterns and hues along the greenish-white rock. A great, oblong, quartz boulder protruded sharply from the top of the slope—the turtle's head. They'd found *La Tortuga*.

"This is gonna be fun," Scott moaned.

Salazar laughed before replying, "Up we go! Over the turtle's shell, *jóvenes!*"

"Any answer, Bob?" Brad asked.

"No, nothing. Can't get through."

"Like ya said, the good news is we know they're out there, alive."

"But for how long?"

Jenkins had once again lost the scent and was trying to recover it.

"What kind of a search dog loses the scent so often?" Brad remarked.

"He'll pick it back up," the marshal replied confidently.

"Marshal, you saw that text. Our kids are in trouble, they need us now."

"I am aware of that, Mr. McCormick."

"Well, I ain't waitin' for that dog! I'm goin' on without 'im."

Brad started off into the wilderness.

"Brad, wait! You don't even know where you're going!" Robert yelled after him as Brad tromped through the forest, yelling his son's name.

"Let him go," the marshal responded. "He's been nothing but trouble anyway."

Robert and Marshal Rodriguez continued watching the dog.

"Tell me the truth, marshal. Do you think they'll be all right?"

"Wish I could tell you. I certainly hope so. Just hope for the best, but prepare for the worst."

"Marshal! Robert!" a voice echoed through the woods minutes later.

Jenkins barked and ran toward the voice with the other two men following. A few hundred yards later, they found Brad.

"What is it?" the marshal demanded.

Brad held out his hand, stained with a gooey, pink substance.

"Spray paint! It's fresh!" he exclaimed, pointing to a nearby tree.

A neon pink smiley face dotted the trunk.

"The dog couldn't find this!"

CHAPTER
•27•

HUBER, HANNAH, AND SCOTT journeyed arduously up the rocky slope, made all the more difficult by being lashed together. If one stumbled and slipped, they all did. Salazar continually barked at them to "go faster," "get up," and "shut up." They held their hands together to combine their strength.

Unbeknownst to the Spaniard, Hannah was tracing a phrase, letter by letter, onto Scott's palm as the three clambered up the mossy shell of the turtle. When she first began, Scott wasn't sure what she was doing. However, after the tenth or eleventh time, he understood and relayed the same message onto Huber's hand. The phrase she traced onto Scott's hand simply read "AMBUSH." At first Scott had no idea what the word meant. What was she talking about? He glanced behind to look at her. Limping along, she darted her eyes back and forth toward the ground. The second time Scott turned his head, he knew in an instant what she was looking at. Salazar was also limping.

As Huber received the message, he also felt confused until he glanced behind him and saw Salazar hobble.

An hour later, after nearing the turtle's head at the top of the hill, Huber wheezed. "I can't go any further . . . need to sit down . . . need water."

Salazar's chest heaved in and out as he appeared strained himself. "Fine, we will rest up at that flat spot," he said, pointing to a section of the hill where the incline decreased dramatically before resuming its ascent.

Upon reaching the even ground, they all collapsed, trying to catch their breath. The sun baked their skins as heat waves rippled off the rocks around them. Perspiration poured down their faces. Salazar took off his hat and flipped his ponytail back as he wiped the sweat from his forehead. When they looked down, they could see how high they had come. Even a small misstep could result in a nasty tumble all the way to the bottom from where they started. Still carrying his pack, Salazar replaced his hat and let go of the rope to fetch his canteen. As he did, he sheathed the knife along his waist. He found the canteen and drunk the cool water deeply. Huber's eyes stared longingly at the crystal clear liquid pouring into Salazar's mouth, desiring more than anything just one drop.

"*Les gustaría beber agua, jóvenes?*" he asked with a sinister grin. "Would you like some?"

Salazar held the canteen to Hannah's mouth and tipped it. He allowed a singular, tiny droplet of water to fall onto her cracked lips before laughing hysterically.

"Still thirsty? Not enough?" He picked up a handful of sand and tossed it in her face. "How's that?" He laughed and resumed gulping the water.

As he drank, his eyes closed in satisfaction.

"Hannah, now!" Huber yelled out.

Quick as a lightning strike, Hannah lifted her good leg as high as she could and brought down her heel square onto

Salazar's right ankle. Dropping the canteen, he wailed and bent over to clutch his foot. The three threw their collective weight into Salazar, causing him to lose his balance and fall backward. The trio watched as the man circled his arms wildly, trying to maintain his balance, but it was no use. He plummeted head over heels down the slope, screaming profanities all the way down. He disappeared in the brush at the bottom.

Scott found a sharp, thin rock and cut the rope binding them together. Huber picked up the canteen, and they all took turns bringing it to their parched mouths. Although they couldn't see him, Salazar moaned far below.

"Now's our chance. Let's go!" Huber directed the others. He dropped the canteen, and they began to ascend the slope. When they reached the turtle's head, resting precariously at the summit, the terrain turned flat again, and thick trees and brush covered the entire area. Peering over the ledge, a tiny speck, almost like an ant, crawled up the rocks. Salazar, angry as a hornet, had emerged from the bush, moving gingerly, fueled by high-octane anger.

"Ya gotta be kiddin me! Man, he is one tough—"

"Don't say it!" Hannah warned.

"He's tough, but he's hurt," Huber remarked. "Look how slow he's moving. It'll take him a while to get up here. When he does, we'll be ready. I think it's time we stopped being the hunted and become the hunters."

Scott nodded his head and grinned from ear to ear. "Now we're talkin', Puber."

Scott watched the sun gradually drift off to the west, above the trees and beyond the pond fifty or so feet away. He ran and gazed over the steep edge. Salazar was only about thirty feet from the turtle's head.

Grunting, spittle foaming from his mouth, Salazar caught a glimpse of him. "I see you, *joven*! When I get my hands on you, you will beg for mercy."

Scott sneered at the man, unafraid, and yelled at his companions behind him. "Almost here. Get ready!"

Picking up his wooden pole he'd broken off a healthy tree, Scott darted behind the turtle's head and placed one end at the base to use it as a lever. He watched behind him as Huber ducked and hid behind the bushes. Beyond Huber, Hannah crouched in the reeds next to a small pond. If Scott wasn't aware of their location, he would have had no idea they were even there. He felt in control, powerful. He looked over the ledge once again and could see Salazar approaching quickly. In a few moments, they would commence their assault. Scott waited until Salazar stood directly in line with the boulder. With sweaty hands, he struggled to grapple the pole. Ten feet away now, Salazar scratched his way upward. As their eyes met and locked, Scott smiled. The Spaniard's bloodied face screwed up into a ball of rage.

Salazar hissed, "You will not be smiling for long, *muerto*."

"Come on up then and get some!"

With all of his might, he pushed downward on the pole. The boulder budged just a smidgen. The pole splintered and cracked.

"C'mon, c'mon!"

With clenched teeth and a scarlet face, Scott pushed

harder. The vein on his forehead throbbed and threatened to explode. At last, the boulder moved toward the edge of the slope. One last gigantic effort toppled the gigantic rock over the precipice just as the pole shattered. He had decapitated the turtle.

Salazar's eyes brimmed with fear when he saw the colossal boulder hurtling toward him, end over end. At the last second, he dove out of its path, digging his fingers into the gravel to keep from sliding backward. Both he and Scott watched as the turtle's head continued to bounce down its shell, breaking up into pieces before crashing at the base below. Salazar's eyes filled with fury as he peered up at Scott.

"Nice try, *joven*! You'll have to do better!"

"C'mon up then! We've got s'more for ya!"

The comment enraged Salazar further as he struggled to his feet and resumed his climb. Scott picked up the bottom half of his splintered wooden pole, and he hid behind a nearby tree. Salazar soon reached the top of the summit where the turtle's head had once jutted from the ground. Hands on his knees, he let out a ghastly scream of frustration and anger. Surveying the area, he sensed that he was walking into a trap. He crept ahead, eyes darting in every direction.

"*Jovencitos, jovencitos* . . . where are you hiding? Come out, come out, wherever you are. I promise I won't hurt you. I just want to talk. Who am I kidding? I'm going to slowly cut you into little pieces and feed you to the birds," he growled, unsheathing his knife.

Scott hid five feet away from where the man hollered, leveling the broken lever like a baseball bat. Salazar inched forward. "Here, *niñitos* . . ." Salazar stood only two feet away from Scott when he jumped out in front of him. Startled, the man paused, and the boy swung the pole at his head. With lightning-quick reflexes, Salazar ducked the swing. Scott came back around with less force and belted him in the shoulder. Salazar bawled in pain and dropped his knife. Scott released the pole and ran toward the pond. Snatching up his blade with his tattooed arm, Salazar pursued him, trying to ignore the aches and pains.

Scott darted past the bush where Huber hid. As soon as Scott was clear, Huber pulled the fishing line he had tied between a tree trunk and a stick he used as a handle. He held it tight and braced himself. Seconds later, Salazar, moving swiftly, caught his bad ankle in the line. The force ripped the handle out of Huber's hands and catapulted Salazar face-first into the ground. The broken man moaned in agony.

"*Les mato!*" he screamed. "I will kill you all!"

Huber emerged from the bushes and ran toward Scott, who neared the pond. Salazar saw them both and struggled to his feet, dragging his bad leg behind him now. He steamed ahead like a locomotive. Scott ran parallel to the pond; Huber trailed fifteen feet behind. As he approached Hannah's position, Huber retracted the small pebble from his pocket and skipped it over the water. Seconds later, Hannah surfaced from the reeds and imagined herself pitching a championship softball game. Her appearance surprised Salazar, who stopped ten feet from the pond. A row of three smooth stones lay on the shore next to Hannah. She picked up the first one.

"Rise Ball," she cried out, flinging the stone with all her strength. The stone whizzed by and narrowly missed Salazar's face. He looked at her in fury and sputtered forward.

"Drop Ball," she yelled and tossed the second stone toward his lower body. The stone curved slightly, dropped, and knocked his left kneecap. Salazar fell to the ground in a wail of distress. Hannah grasped the last stone and leapt out of the reeds.

Salazar managed to hoist himself upon his good knee, nursing the rapidly swelling left one. The knife lay on the ground next to him. Picking it up, he pointed it toward his eye. "*Les corto los ojos, mi amor.*"

"Heat!" she roared and let fly the final stone. With great speed and accuracy, the stone cut through the air and slammed Salazar in the center of his chest. An audible *craaack* reverberated through the woods upon impact as it fractured his sternum. The breath went out of the Spaniard, and he collapsed backward.

Hannah ran to the boys, her feet muddy and soaked. "Had enough yet?" she yelled.

Salazar stammered and hissed on the ground like a wounded snake. He peered up, incensed. Slowly, he struggled to his feet once again.

Salazar dragged his injured body toward them. Stumbling through the leaf-riddled path toward the motionless trio, Salazar encircled the blade handle within his fingers and furnished a nefarious smile. Only feet away from them, the ground gave way beneath Salazar's feet. A look of surprise crossed his face as he crashed through dry sticks and a flurry of leaves.

Examining the hole they'd hastily dug and covered with forest debris, the trio observed Salazar slumped over, half his face covered in blood, his clothes in tatters. A swollen kneecap protruded grotesquely from his pant leg. He lay motionless.

"Is he . . . dead?" Hannah asked.

"Naw, he's breathin'. Just knocked his butt out!" Scott responded enthusiastically.

"What do we do now?" Huber asked.

"I say we leave him there to rot," Scott rejoined. "Deserves it, don't he?"

"Maybe. But then we're no better than him," Hannah countered. "I say we head back and tell the cops where he is."

Hannah and Scott continued to bicker when Huber saw something from the corner of his eye. He turned and walked toward the object, craning his head high in the air toward a tree. Could it really be? His memories flashed back to the prospecting guide. He mentally flipped through the pages until he reached the correct entry. Closing his eyes, he concentrated and visualized the page. When he opened them, he knew what he was looking at. Etched twenty-five feet in the air, upon the trunk of a massive pine tree, a cross symbol stared him in the face.

"Guys! C'mere! Look at this!" Huber cried out, pointing to the Spanish insignia inscribed high upon the tree trunk. Below the scarred cross, the letters G. H. were etched into the tree along with the date, 1711. Based on the height of the initials, the inscription had been placed there many years ago.

Scott and Hannah, still arguing over what to do with Salazar, sauntered over to Huber and immediately ceased their contentious conversation.

"Oh my gosh!" Hannah exclaimed and covered her mouth. "Look! There's another one over there," she yelled, pointing to another tree twenty feet away to the north. There was another cross with the letters P. D. S.

"What are they?" Scott asked.

Huber's voice became excited. "I think they're the initials of the Spaniards who were ambushed by the Ute and killed here."

"What was that last clue in Grandpa's journal?" Hannah asked.

" 'Dead Man's Treasure is located west of where you meet my brothers.' These men were Pedro Salazar's friends and companions . . . his brothers. We just need to keep following the symbols and head west!" Huber ran to the next tree. A short distance away to the west, they spotted another one and ran toward it.

"Huber, Scott, wait!" Hannah shouted.

"What?" Huber asked impatiently.

"What about Salazar?"

The two boys looked at each other momentarily and sprinted back to the hole. They peered into it, and Huber's stomach dropped to his feet. Scott's face turned ghastly white. An empty hole filled their view. Their eyes darted back and forth. Instinctively, they stood back to back, searching for any sign of the Spaniard.

"Where'd he go?" Hannah murmured.

"Maybe he got wise . . . decided to book it back home," Scott whispered.

"Not likely . . . He's close," Huber whispered back. "Be ready."

Their senses keen, the sounds of the forest turned deafening. Sounds of crickets and birds became jackhammers. Minutes passed. No sign of the man.

"C'mon, where is he?" Scott groaned.

"Over there." Hannah pointed to a spot near where they found the first symbol. Something was rustling around behind the tree, disturbing the leaves and twigs.

"It's him . . . ," Huber said.

"Be quiet!" Scott shushed.

Their eyes locked in on the movement as they braced themselves for another confrontation. The rustling grew louder as the foliage shook profusely and then stopped.

"What the—"

Scott's statement was interrupted by Hannah's ear-piercing scream as something emerged from the shrubs. The sound caused them all to jump in the air like rabbits. A sigh of relief ensued, then a chuckle. A small raccoon moseyed out of the shrubs and looked at them inquisitively, standing on its hind legs and putting its hands together as if asking for their pardon.

"Sorry," Hannah said.

"You almost gave me a heart attack, sis."

"Your sister's got some pipes, dude. She can really scream."

"You should hear her when she sees a spider."

While they watched the raccoon scurry away, they didn't notice Salazar creep up from a tree and stand behind them. But as he inched closer, they all sensed his presence. Collectively, they turned and saw Salazar within striking distance, clutching the knife. He grabbed Scott by the neck.

"Now, *joven*, you will die." Salazar seethed through clenched teeth and brought the blade to Scott's throat. Before he could do anything, the group heard a low rumbling behind them. Salazar glanced toward the sound, and his eyes conveyed sheer terror, his mouth agape. The growling sound turned to a loud scream. Salazar's muscles went slack, and he dropped

Scott to the ground. The three turned their heads to behold a one-eared cougar baring its razor sharp teeth at Salazar. In an instant, a blur of fur flashed over their heads and pounced on top of the Spaniard.

The three watched in awe as Salazar wrestled the cougar in a flurry of man and beast. A swipe at Salazar's face connected. Three more scar lines would be added to his already disfigured face. The Spaniard threw the cat from his body and wielded the knife. The man and beast circled one another in slow motion.

"Here, kitty, kitty," he growled as blood oozed down his face.

The massive cat continued to snarl, and its lips quivered. Glued to his spot, Huber couldn't take his eyes off the spectacle. The cougar hunched its head between its shoulder blades and let out an ear-shattering scream. Salazar's face turned pallid. Turning his back to the animal, he trampled the ground as fast as he could, his bad leg acting like a dead weight. Still perched in the same position, the cougar held its head forward, eyes locked on the man, readying itself to pounce.

"Huber, Hannah, now! This is our chance!" Scott bellowed.

Hannah bolted with Scott into a thicket of trees. Mesmerized, Huber couldn't take his eyes off the cougar. Hannah finally grabbed her brother by the arm and pulled him from the scene. As they ran in the opposite direction, Huber turned to look at their savior one last time. As he did, the cat turned its head and made eye contact with him for a split second. Then it leaped after Salazar.

Terrified, Salazar turned and prepared himself to make his final stand, still clutching the knife. The cat slammed into him like a bullet, knocking him flat. Salazar pushed the creature off him and rose to his feet. He swung his knife at the beast, missing its throat by inches. With the swing, Salazar overextended himself, leaving his backside vulnerable. The cougar pounced again and dug its claws into the backside of his ribs. Both man and animal toppled over the edge of the precipitous bluff where the turtle's head had once stood.

CHAPTER 28

"SHOULD WE GO BACK and look?" Hannah asked.

"Why in the world would we wanna do that?" Scott asked.

"He saved us. What if he's hurt and needs our help?"

"I think you're forgetting the fact that that thing is a *wild* animal."

"Why did it go after Salazar and not us?"

"I dunno. Maybe it didn't like the way he smelled or something. Not hard to believe."

"You have to admit it's not normal behavior for a wild animal to do something like that. Cougars hardly ever attack people," Huber remarked.

"That's why they're called *wild* animals . . . cuz they're unpredictable. Even if the thing is hurt, what are we gonna do? Are you a vet? What if the thing decides to turn on us now that it has taken care of Salamander? What if Salamander came out on top? Ya really wanna come face-to-face with him again?"

Deep down, Huber knew Scott was right. Even if the cougar were hurt, there wasn't anything he or anyone else could do for the animal. After ten minutes of walking, they were unable to spot any more tree crosses. They looked around for another hour in vain. It had to be close to 5:00 now. In a few hours, it would be getting dark again.

"Huber, we have to find this thing before it gets dark," Hannah commented.

"Why? So you and Scott have time to go off and make out again?"

Scott and Hannah went red-faced.

"Hey, dude, like I said, we were gonna tell ya. It just kinda happened. We didn't make out, by the way. It was more like a peck . . . a long peck."

"Right, it just happened. You know what, I don't even care at this point. I just wanna find Dead Man's Treasure, then you guys can do whatever the heck you want."

"C'mon, Puber . . ."

"Just drop it. I don't wanna talk about it. And don't call me that. You know I hate it," Huber said with fiery eyes.

"C'mon, you guys, let's focus," Hannah said. "The guide said it should be right around here, 'where without a mouth, the skull sings to you.'"

After trekking along for twenty minutes, the group broke through the tree line to behold a stunning vista. The summit of Mount Sopris towered only a hundred feet above them along a rocky ridge. Off in the distance, the town of Carbondale sat in repose.

"Hey look!" Huber ran toward the summit's wall. The others followed his lead. "I can see our town from here. We're near the top of the mountain. It has to be close. See any skulls?"

"Over here! Look!" Scott yelled.

Huber ran to where Scott and Hannah stood. Along the rocky bluff, someone had carved the words, *Tesoro de los Muertos—Anno Domini 1711*. Scott and Hannah marveled as they traced the Spanish etching. Scanning the baseline, they saw nothing that resembled a skull.

"It's here somewhere," Huber whispered reverently. "Lift the veil of death where the skull sings to you . . . to enter, remember for whom the bell tolls."

"So where is it?" Scott complained. "Where's the mine?"

"It's here. It's close. Gotta be. Help me look around."

The group pushed and prodded their way along the base of the cliff. Forty-five minutes later, they were worn out and frustrated.

Hannah blew out a sigh and sat down on a boulder covered in orange fungus. "Huber, I'm not spending another night out here. You said we'd find it and be back home before it got dark."

"I'm not leaving till we find it!" Huber shouted. "We've come too far!"

"Well, I am!" she yelled back. "The thing's probably collapsed, anyway."

A cold wind blew in their faces and scattered some nearby leaves.

"Shhh, listen!" Scott commanded.

The twins ceased their arguing and listened as the wind whipped the air.

"Do ya hear it?"

"Hear what?" Hannah asked.

As the wind continued, they heard it—a low-pitched whistling sound that was barely audible.

"Where's it coming from?" he wondered aloud.

"It's comin' from over there," Scott pointed toward a section of the cliff covered in thick, perennial vines twenty feet to

Hannah's left. Running to the spot, he inspected them more closely.

"Trumpet creepers!" he said, fondling the vines.

"Huh?" Hannah scrunched up her face.

"The vines . . . they're trumpet creepers. They'll climb and cover anything. Rocks, telephone poles, small children."

"Listen!" Huber demanded.

The wind picked up again. As it did, a whistling sound filled their ears. Hannah marveled. "It's almost like . . ."

"Singing!" Huber exclaimed. "It's here! This is it!"

"But where's the skull?"

They began clearing away the vines, pulling them off of the rocky wall. As they did, the whistling grew louder. With a hard tug, Scott fell backwards, taking down a clump of vines with him, unveiling what lay beneath. Two large, hollow eyes looked down upon him from ten feet above the ground. A triangular indentation was carved out below the eyes. A gust arose and broke against the rock wall. As it did, air whooshed through the hollowed depressions, creating a whistling sound.

"Lift the veil of death, where without a mouth, the skull sings to you," Huber remarked solemnly.

"So, where's the mouth? Where's the entrance?" Scott said.

"Look! You can see the outline of an opening," Hannah pointed and traced the outline of an archway, recessed a quarter inch from the rest of the wall's face. "It's sealed shut."

"Stand aside," Scott said. "Lemme put some muscle into it." He flung himself against the wall. A second later, he was sprawled out on the ground, nursing a sore shoulder. "Thing's solid. Anyone got some dynamite?"

"Hold on! Over there!" he pointed to a rectangular slot

carved at chest level, five feet from the skull. There appeared to be letters etched into the stone below the slot. Huber used his fingers to dig out the dirt and soon a sentence materialized. *Recuerde por quién doblan las campanas.* Below the inscription was an etching of a severed arm. "Remember for whom the bell tolls."

"Maybe it's got somethin' to do with that Metallica song," Scott joked.

"It's from John Donne," Hannah replied flatly.

The boys looked at each other and shook their heads.

"Never paid attention in Mr. Morris's English class, did you? John Donne was an English poet in the 1600s. Parts of this passage stuck with me. It's so beautiful: *Tribulation is treasure in the nature of it . . . A man may be . . . sick to death, and this affliction may lie in his bowels, as gold in a mine, and be of no use to him; but this bell, that tells me of his affliction, digs out and applies that gold to me. No man is an island . . . and therefore never send to know for whom the bell tolls; it tolls for thee.*"

"Was that English?" Scott asked, bewildered.

"You seriously have that memorized? You stole all the good genes," Huber remarked.

"No, I just study."

"What's it supposed to mean, anyway?"

"No one knows exactly, but I think it means that real treasure is gained through tribulation . . . through hardship."

"What's all that about the bells?"

"When people died, churches would ring bells. I think he's saying that when we hear a bell toll for someone who has died, we don't need to worry about who it's ringing for . . . because in a way, it's really ringing for all of us."

A shudder rippled through Huber's body at his sister's comment.

"I still think he's talking about Metallica. Da-da-da-da, da-da-da-da, da-da-da-da-da-da-da-da. Time marches on! Awesome song."

"I think I know what we need to do." Huber walked to the slot in the wall. He closed his eyes, took a breath, and slid his arm inside, up to his shoulder. "It's here! I feel it!"

"Feel what, Puber?"

"It's metal . . . there's a bell inside here. Trying . . . to find . . . Got it. There's a rope hanging down in the middle." As he grabbed hold of the rope, a grinding sound belched from deep inside the wall. Huber felt his arm become sandwiched between two slabs of stone. "My arm! It's stuck!"

"Why'd you put your arm in there, dude!" Scott yelled, tugging on Huber's torso. Huber didn't budge. His arm was wedged tight.

"It's okay! Hannah, do you remember how many Spaniards died in the ambush?"

"I . . . I . . ."

"How many? Tell me quickly!"

"I think Grandpa said there were thirteen."

"I hope you're right."

"Why?"

"If I'm right, we have to ring the bell thirteen times to get in. If I'm wrong, you're going to have a one-armed brother."

Hannah brought her hands to her mouth. "You're such a moron, Huber. If your arm gets chopped off, I'll never forgive you."

"Well, here goes." Huber closed his eyes and pulled down

on the rope. A muffled chime sounded from beyond the stone wall. "One, two, three, four, five, six, seven, eight, nine, ten, eleven, twelve . . . thirteen." The reverberation slowed until it was silent. The two slabs pressing in on Huber's arms didn't move. "What the heck, nothing happ—"

A deafening, grinding sound interrupted Huber. The rock beneath the nose of the skull began to recede into the ground, leaving behind an arched entrance. As it did, the slabs of stone encasing Huber's arm also retracted, allowing him to slide it back out.

Above the din, Hannah squealed. "Huber, you did it!"

A full, open mouth now appeared below the two hollowed eyes and nose. *A skull.* At last, they'd found the entrance to Dead Man's Treasure!

"Huber, do you still have your flashlight?"

Huber pulled out the small flashlight from his front pocket and stooped inside the opening, feeling a bit unnerved about stepping inside the mouth of a skull. Once inside, he could see that the ground curved downward and led to a larger opening, about six feet high and four feet wide. Within the opening, he viewed broken timbers, rusted iron nails, and an elaborate pulley system that must've controlled the door to the mine.

Huber crawled back out, smiling from ear to ear.

"What's inside?" Scott asked jubilantly.

"I think we've found ourselves a gold mine!" he said before stepping back in.

"Ladies first," Scott said to Hannah as if he were ushering her into a formal theater.

As Huber waited for the others, a chill tickled his spine. He thought about the massacre that occurred nearby long ago. In his mind, the murderous scene that had unfolded years earlier reenacted itself. The legend suggested that the bodies of the Spanish miners had been dumped inside this place. The cave had been awakened from some ancient slumber, and it seemed hungry. A cold, claustrophobic sensation racked Huber's body as the face of the old Indian man momentarily flashed within his mind.

"Stay outta that mine," his voice repeated. Huber quickly pushed the thought aside and focused on the treasure that surely lay deeper within.

Hannah harbored similar sentiments. "Now that I'm here, I'm not so sure I want to go in." She hesitated before stepping inside. "Remember what that old man said?"

"Seriously? I can't believe you're gonna let some ghost story from an old kook scare ya off," Scott huffed.

Hannah's pride took over. "I'm not scared," she said bluntly.

"Let's go then."

"We don't have a ton of time before it gets dark. We'd better hurry," Huber insisted.

Hannah steeled herself and stepped inside the darkness.

"Bob, what's that up ahead?"

The three men ran to the littered spot that rested in an open clearing beneath a steep slope.

"Huber's cell phone." Robert's words landed like death-blows.

"This doesn't look good," the marshal said gravely.

"Thanks for that insight, marshal," Brad replied.

"Hannah, Huber, where are you?" Robert yelled at the top of his lungs.

A series of barks interrupted the fathers' grief.

"What is it, boy?"

Without waiting, the dog bounded up the slope toward something. Jenkins stopped about halfway up the slope and waited as the men struggled upward. Minutes later, the men, catching their breath, came upon the scene.

"What in the world happened here?" the marshal asked himself curiously and slipped the dog's lead around a heavy boulder. Jenkins whined and barked in protest.

"Sorry, boy. Can't have you barking up a storm. Stay here and be a good boy. I think we can take it from here."

The dog pulled his ears back and slid to the ground, letting out one last whimper.

"I think I'm gonna be sick," Brad uttered when he passed a bloody mass of yellowish-orange fur.

CHAPTER 29

THE LONG, DARK TUNNEL filled its visitors with a cold foreboding. Blackness seemed to have actual substance here and dampened the group's earlier jubilance.

"Are we sure about this?" Hannah asked again. "There haven't been people in here for a long time. If this thing collapses on top of us, it'll be our grave, and no one will be the wiser."

"At least we'll all be together," Scott said in a wavering voice. "And it'd be quick."

"Actually, it probably wouldn't. We could be buried alive in here for days, as long as there were some oxygen pockets," Huber added dismally.

"Just a big ray of sunshine, aren't ya, Puber?"

Huber's flashlight illuminated the path ahead, revealing that the tunnel was much larger than Huber initially thought. He could easily stand, and there was probably a foot or two above his head. The tunnel was narrow though, only about four and a half feet wide. The flashlight highlighted particles of falling dust, reminding Huber of a gentle falling snow during a winter day. Breathing became laborious. His eyes burned, and the urge to cough became almost impossible to suppress. He knew that unless he gained control of himself now, he would begin to panic. Trying to calm himself, Huber took longer, more controlled breaths. The others experienced similar sensations. Huber's anxiousness subsided somewhat as he tore a piece of his shirtsleeve off and held it to his mouth to filter the dust.

"Careful when you're walking to not kick up too much dust," Huber yelled at Scott and Hannah, who were behind him. Shining the light on the wall next to him, Huber noticed a vestige of the Spaniards' ill-fated journey—the same large cross they'd observed on the trees.

The group walked for a distance of fifty feet or so before peering back at the entrance. A comforting light led to a world of safety, a world of comfort; a world of freedom. The group then turned their backs to it and looked ahead of them in the blackness, a world of unknowns, a world of fear, a world of captivity. The tunnel seemed to keep going and going into an infinite expanse. The darkness was so thick that the light only penetrated ten or so feet ahead of them. Spaced five feet apart, splintered beams struggled to support the many tons of earth above their heads. Spiderwebs waved everywhere and clung to their hair and clothing. Shells and skeletons of insects and mice dangled within them.

"Oh, I hate spiders," Hannah whimpered.

The three continued on. Huber shone the light in all directions as they walked. He didn't want to miss anything. While he shone the light toward the ceiling, his foot caught hold of something, causing him to trip. As he went sprawling, the flashlight spun around on the ground until it came to a stop, illuminating the obstruction.

"Is that a . . . ?" Scott trailed off.

They all let out a collective scream. Huber scurried away from the object frantically, trying to stand up. Lying on the mine floor and looking straight up at them was the corpse of a man, his face illuminated by the flashlight. Shards of skin and hair still clung to the dusty bones in many parts. The man wore some kind of leather armor, which had mostly deteriorated. Tufts of black hair projected out of his cracked skull. A semblance of a beard still remained on the papery tissue covering his face. Two arrows protruded from his ribs.

"It's one of them Spaniards!" Scott exclaimed, bending down to get a closer look. "What's lefta 'im, anyway."

"It's like a mummy," Hannah said, suddenly more fascinated than afraid.

"Must be because it's so dry in here," Huber derived.

"Incredible!" Hannah gently touched the cold, hard face of the man, near his temple. As she felt the corpse's face, a large hairy spider, almost as big as her fist, crawled out from the right eye socket and onto her hand. At first, she made no sound. Then her body began to shake like a leaf. Two seconds later, the mine was once again filled with a bloodcurdling sound.

"Get it off, get it off!"

Huber tried to shine the light on her hand, but she twisted and turned frantically.

"Shhh, hold still," Scott commanded. Huber looked on, amazed at the spider's size.

Almost beside herself, she instantly froze and started taking deep breaths.

The large hairy arachnid crept up Hannah's arm and

onto her shoulder. It scaled up her neck and climbed over her mouth until it reached her forehead.

"Mmmm, mmmm," she uttered, trying to hold in her screams.

"Don't move a muscle," Scott whispered slowly.

"Mmmm, mmmm," she cried with pursed lips.

Scott cautiously picked up a piece of a broken beam and gently placed it against her forehead. The gigantic spider slowly clambered off her head and onto the wood, leg by hairy leg. As soon as it left her body, Hannah crumpled to the ground. The spider clung to the timber in Scott's hand. Slowly moving the end of the stick to a nearby web, it disembarked.

After calming down, Hannah stood up and slugged Huber in the shoulder as hard as she could.

"Ouch! Why'd you do that?" he asked.

"You didn't even try to help me! You just sat there, gawking at the thing!"

Scott interjected. "If it had bitten ya, it woulda hurt, but ya probably wouldn'ta died . . . probably."

"Oh, that's comforting!" Hannah shot back. "That was the most terrifying thing that's ever happened to me in my life. I am leaving! Now! You can keep my share of the treasure."

She pushed her brother out of the way when he tried to stop her, causing him to stumble over the dead miner once again and fall against the wall. A massive amount of dust fell from the ceiling, and they all heard the old timbers groan in contempt at being disturbed. The group held perfectly still, hoping their lives were not about to be snuffed out by an avalanche of debris and rock. Slowly the timbers returned to their silent state, and the dust quit falling quite so fast.

"You two be careful! Ya almost got us all killed," Scott complained. "No fightin' allowed in here."

Relieved that they were still breathing, Hannah helped Huber up, gave him the flashlight, and shot him an apologetic look. Huber simply nodded and took the light.

"I'll be outside. I'm not going any further. Besides, if this thing collapses, someone needs to go get help," Hannah reasoned.

"You're wimpin' out, eh? That's not the girl I know," Scott said.

Huber tried not to get angry at the comment—talking to his sister like he knew her so well.

"I'm done."

"Don't cry when we get your share," Scott retorted, disappointed at her departure.

"At least I'll be alive. C'mon, you two, this is insane. No amount of treasure is worth our lives."

"We'll be careful. See you when we come out, sis."

"Please, don't," she implored. The boys gave no response.

"Fine, get yourselves killed then," she said in exasperation and turned to head back to the mouth of the mine. "See if I care."

The two boys could vaguely see her silhouette against the bright light of the entrance. Eventually she reached the end of the tunnel and walked out into an open world filled with blue sky and oxygen. They heard her desperate yell echo toward them, "Please be careful!" She sat on a boulder outside the entrance and whispered, "Please come back."

The boys propped the Spanish skeleton up against the wall so it would be out of the way when they came back. Huber felt a deep sense of foreboding and fear as he looked upon the face of the corpse, fearing for a moment that his sister was right.

As the two crept ahead into the darkness, the light toward the entrance shrunk until it was only a tiny dot and then disappeared. The dust kept falling and the tunnel careened sideways, climbed up, dropped down, and became wider or narrower in places.

"Ya get the feeling we're just diggin' ourselves into a deeper grave?" Scott mumbled.

"Then go back and make out with my sister. Quit being a wimp," Huber whispered angrily.

The same thoughts as Scott were running through Huber's mind, but he had resolved to find the treasure and wasn't turning back. They had come too far and fought too hard to just give up. He walked on in silence, afraid if he spoke too loud, the walls would collapse.

"We just have to keep following these," Huber said after holding up the light to one of the cross symbols.

They kept walking further and further into the tunnel. After twenty minutes or so, Scott began to worry.

"How far do ya think this thing goes?"

Breathing became harder and harder.

"Doesn't matter how far it goes. We'll keep going till we find it," Huber replied defensively. "My grandpa spent his whole life trying to find this place."

Scott feared that Huber was becoming consumed with the

desire to reach the treasure, at any cost. He noticed the air becoming thicker, almost acrid as he struggled to breath.

"Ya ever been to Carlsbad Caverns?" Scott asked.

"No, what's that?"

"They're these huge caves in New Mexico. M'dad took me there once a couple of years ago. The ranger told us the number one danger of goin' into caves is bad air."

"Bad air?"

"It's when there's hardly any oxygen to breathe. He talked about these cavers who went in a section no one had been to before. They started breathin' bad air, so their brains didn't get 'nough oxygen, and they started actin' all weird and makin' stupid decisions. Ended up gettin' lost, and by the time someone found 'em, it was too late."

"What's your point?"

"What if that's happenin' to us? What if we're breathin' bad air right now?"

"If that were happening to us, you wouldn't have been able to tell me that story. We're still thinking straight, so we're fine."

"Are ya sure? If we were thinkin' straight, we probably woulda turned around when your sister did."

"The only crazy thing is to come this far and turn back," Huber snapped.

"We should turn back," Scott said. "Ain't worth it."

"We'll flip this coin," Huber said and pulled out his grandpa's golden piece. He shined the light on it. "This side with the cross is heads. The one with the shield is tails. Heads, we keep going. Tails, we go back."

"I dunno," Scott whispered.

"The coin won't lie to us. It'll tell us what to do," Huber reassured him.

"It's happenin' to ya, dude. You're acting all crazy-like. It's getting too hard to breathe. I ain't goin' no further, no matter what some stupid coin says. I ain't lettin' you go either," Scott said determinedly.

Huber shone the light straight on his own face. Beyond the light, Scott could see there was a faraway look in Huber's eyes, half glazed over, like he was walking in his sleep.

"I'm not going anywhere. Now call it! Heads or tails?" Huber demanded in a deranged fashion.

"You're losin' it, dude. C'mon, your sister was right. Let's get outta here!" Scott grabbed Huber's arm.

Huber knocked Scott's arm off and shoved him backward. "And who made you king of the universe? You won't call it? I will. Heads, we go forward. Tails, we go back."

He flipped the gold coin with his free hand. It landed in the dirt.

"See! The coin says to keep going. You were wrong!" Huber said with a twisted look of satisfaction as he picked up the coin.

"You've lost it, Puber! We're goin' home," Scott said sternly.

"You'll lose your share too then. More for me, I guess. Go back to my sister. You guys can kiss each other till I get back. You never really liked me anyway. Just used me to get to her," Huber uttered angrily.

"What are ya talkin' about?"

"It's true. I saw it all along. The way you looked at her, talked to her. You used me the whole time, from day one," Huber replied, becoming more and more upset.

"Puber, you're goin' nuts. I like the both of ya. If I have to not like your sister for us to be friends, then it's done. I won't like her no more. C'mon, let's get outta this death trap 'fore we suffocate," Scott implored.

"You're a liar and a backstabber!" Huber yelled. "I'm not leaving here without the treasure. I've changed my mind, anyway. I don't want you to come with me anymore. Go back to my sister, *lover boy*."

"That's enough!" Scott said as he grabbed Huber's arm again and tugged toward the direction they had come.

As soon as Scott touched Huber's arm, Huber snapped, swinging the flashlight hard against the side of Scott's head. Scott tried to wrestle the flashlight from Huber's hands. As they struggled, it flew from both of them and crashed into the wall. The bulb shattered. Darkness, black as pitch, enveloped them instantly. Scott's ear stung, and he could feel the warmth of the blood trickling down his neck. Scott rubbed his ear and brought his hand in front of his face. He couldn't see it.

"Huber!" Scott yelled in the darkness. "Where'd ya go?"

"I'm not going back, Scotty!" Scott heard Huber laughing from somewhere in the blackness, his voice trailing off.

"I'm going on like it told me to. The coin doesn't lie—it has no reason to lie!" he heard Huber yell. "It wouldn't betray me. It wouldn't stab me in the back."

"Huber! Please come back! Please!" Scott yelled into the nothingness. No response. No sound. Many minutes passed. The concept of time didn't exist in this place. Each second seemed an hour.

Panic infused Scott's insides as he realized that he was totally alone in the dark and didn't know which way to go in order to get out. He dropped to his knees and began to hyperventilate. Curling up into a ball, he wondered if he was already dead. The madness that had taken Huber now began to take hold of him. He rocked back and forth, laughing hysterically. Pink spiders danced before his eyes and then disappeared. A myriad of different colored shapes flew above his head in strange patterns. The shapes disappeared, and the darkness resumed.

Then came a sound—a screeching, terrifying sound. Footsteps. Then the screeching sound again, like metal being drug against metal. Out of the blackness, a figure materialized just a few feet in front of him. The shape came into focus, and Scott let out a gasp. The dead Spanish miner they'd passed earlier in the mine limped lifelessly toward him. The head tilted grotesquely from one side to the other as it came face-to-face with him. The corpse dragged a long, rusty sword at his side. A bony hand reached toward Scott's face and caressed his cheek. Scott screamed in terror and closed his eyes. "It's not real! It's not real!" he sputtered over and over. When he opened his eyes again, the corpse remained, staring through him with eyeless sockets. The screeching sound came from its mouth as an inky tongue slithered out like a snake, wrapping itself around his neck.

Just my imagination. Just my mind playin' tricks on me, Scott thought. "You're not real!" he shouted before the snake-like tongue covered his mouth.

The corpse vaporized. The loneliness and fear were overwhelming. He could still feel the craziness welling up inside of him. Even with all of the madness pervading his senses, a small, rational voice was trying to break through. It told him to find the broken flashlight. Still reeling, he dropped down on his hands and knees searching for the shattered remnants. After feeling around for a few minutes, his hand touched a piece of the broken plastic that led him to the rest of the object. He felt both sides of the wall, which were about five feet apart from each other. "I was standin' with my back to the entrance when he hit me on the left side of my head with his right hand. So if I'm facin' the direction I was hit, the broken flashlight should be closer to the wall on my left."

He felt the distance between the pieces and both sides of the wall. He determined which way he was facing when he was hit with the blow of the blunt object and placed himself in the same position.

"Okay, now all I have to do is turn around and go in that direction, and I'll find my way out." The sane part of his brain slowly began to overtake the insane. "Yeah, makes sense. Should work."

Scott began to feel his way in the direction he had chosen, hoping and praying he had done the right thing. As he traveled along, the air became less dense, and he was able to breathe more freely. "I'm goin' in the right direction. There's more oxygen this way," he said aloud, becoming more excited. "I'm gonna live, I'm gonna live," he told himself over and over while edging along.

After for what felt like hours of inching his way out, he saw a tiny white light ahead of him. "Either I've died and am goin' to heaven, or that's the way out," he laughed. He moved more quickly, taking in deep breaths now. The light up ahead grew bigger. Finally, he reached the end of the tunnel and stepped outside. Light blinded his eyes. Falling to the ground, he gulped the fresh mountain air, filled with the scent of pine. His lungs filled with oxygen, and he was overcome with happiness.

After a moment, his pupils constricted, and he could see more clearly. Rolling on his back, he looked up at the bright blue sky with its puffy white clouds. He had never seen anything so beautiful in all of his life. He sat up and rubbed his eyes, his vision still a little blurry. Was he still hallucinating? Hannah, tied to a tree with a bandana in her mouth, was trying to yell something. Still dazed and confused, Scott wondered what was happening. With all of her effort, she was able to spit the gag out of her mouth.

"Run, Scott, run!"

Before he could respond, a powerful force tackled him from behind, taking him to the ground. With his face in the dirt, Scott felt someone grab his arms and bind them. He rolled over. Juan Hernán Salazar loomed above, smiling. He clasped Scott's throat within the fangs of the tattooed serpent.

"Miss me, *joven*? Good to see you again. Shouldn't there be two of you, however? Where is the other boy? Where is Yoober?" He eased his grasp.

Scott wheezed, then spat in his face. "Go in and get 'im yourself."

Salazar grinned wider and replied, "I will, boy. You and the girl will accompany me. Only this time, you will not be coming out."

"No! Don't touch me!" Scott yelled out in frustration as Salazar dragged him through the dirt toward Hannah. Salazar, badly wounded, could barely walk. In addition to the damage they'd inflicted, the cougar had left deep gashes on his face, chest, and arms. There didn't seem to be a square inch of his body that was not bruised or cut up.

"Sit here and shut up. I will do what I wish. Who will stop me, now?" Salazar barked.

"You . . . killed him?" Scott muttered in disbelief.

"Not a him. A her. And yes, she is dead, I am afraid. We took quite a tumble over the ledge, as you no doubt saw. Lucky me, she landed on my blade." Salazar held up his knife. Clumps of blood and fur clung to its surface. Scott felt a sense of deep grief for their protector. His face turned pale as he eyed the knife. Hannah's eyes grew large, spilling over with tears.

"A slow and painful death." His lips curled into a full smile as he sheathed the knife.

"Shut your mouth!" Scott screamed in anger.

Salazar caressed Hannah's cheek. "Thanks are in order again, *mi amor*. Without you all, I do not know if I could've found *Tesoro de los Muertos*. Let's go for a trip, shall we?"

"If you take us in that cave, we'll all die! There's no oxygen. You'll suffocate right along with us," Scott yelled at Salazar in contempt.

"You think I did not know this?" Salazar responded and threw his trail pack off his shoulders. He retrieved the small, green oxygen tank. Attached to the nozzle dangled a clear, plastic breathing mask. "Do not fret, I will not allow you to suffocate, *jóvenes*. I will share my oxygen with you on our way. I want to see the look on your faces when I find the treasure and leave you in its place." Salazar retrieved a couple of empty rucksacks from his trail pack along with a battery-powered lantern.

Scott attempted to cry out for help, but before he could do so, Salazar shoved a cloth rag into his mouth, muffling any sounds. He untied Hannah from the tree and bound her wrists together with the rope. He pushed the two in front of him until they reached the skull's entrance.

"Go on, *jóvenes*. We have no more time to lose." Salazar grinned as he turned the valve on the oxygen tank and holstered it to his side. It made a hissing sound as he fastened the mask around his face.

Obediently, Scott and Hannah marched back into the blackness with Salazar close behind, holding the lantern and the knife.

CHAPTER •30•

HUBER'S HEAD SWAM WILDLY. He walked blindly through the gloomy darkness. As he twirled around and around, he realized that he had no idea which way he was going. Ten feet ahead of him, he saw his mother and father standing with their arms folded, scolding him. His mom, wearing her pink Sunday dress with a flower on the shoulder, glared in his direction. His dad was wearing his white shirt, black slacks, and favorite blue tie.

"Don't you know we've been worried sick about you?" Huber's mother chided him.

"We know you lied about where you were going," Huber's father added. "It's time to come home now. You need to feed Hobo."

"Mom, Dad, I'm sorry. I knew you wouldn't let me go if I told you where I was going. I have to find the treasure Grandpa Nick told me about. I know it's around here. I came all of this way. Can't I just stay a little longer?" Huber pleaded. "I'll feed him later."

The hallucination lasted a bit longer, with his parents glaring at him, saying nothing. Then slowly, their eyes began to bulge and pulsate until they exploded, leaving empty sockets in their place. Their skin fell off as they morphed into the aliens Huber read about in his comic books. The two ghastly apparitions ran toward him, chanting in a low, distorted voice, "Come home with us, come home with us."

Huber let out a scream, closed his eyes, covered his ears, and, curling into a ball on the dirt floor, yelled for the figures to go away. He counted to ten. When he opened his eyes, his parents were gone, but in their place was the all too familiar blackness. He didn't know which was more terrifying.

"Hannah . . . Scott!" he yelled into the nothingness. "Please help!" he cried out. "I'm sorry for not listening to you. Please come back! Help me! I'm sorry!" he sobbed.

"You should've listened to me Huber," Hannah's voice whispered.

Huber looked up and saw his sister where moments earlier his parents had stood.

"Hannah! Are you real?"

"What do you think?"

"No. You're not holding a light. I shouldn't be able to see you," Huber replied logically, his hopes dashed.

She held up her hands and smiled. "Got me there, brother. I'm really outside, making out with Scotty." She then laughed wildly. Scott walked up next to her. He raised his eyebrows up and down at him.

"Stop it!"

"Calm down," a low, raspy voice sounded next to his ear. He turned to see Mr. Mendoza's face beside his. "No reason to get upset, buddy. Just calm down. You realize that none of this would have happened if you had listened to your sister, don't you? She's the smart one in your family. Then you push away your friend who tried to help you? Bad form."

Principal Harris now appeared. "You're the one responsible for your current predicament, young man. What kind of example are you setting for all the other students? You disappoint me greatly."

Hannah and Scott held hands and kissed in the background.

The louder he yelled for the hallucinations to depart, the more severe they became.

All of a sudden, other people from school began to appear out of thin air, joining in the laughter. Alison Harmon, his longtime crush, appeared. She shook her head sadly and said, "You poor thing." They all laughed harder and began to shoot spit wads at him. In unison, they all chanted, *"Puber is a goner! Puber is a goner!"*

The chorus continued as the old Indian man from the store appeared in their midst. His eyes were downcast. Pointing to all of the people, he said, "I told you kids to stay away from this place. It's filled with . . . evil spirits."

"L-l-leave me alone. Go away! Just let me die," he cried as he shut his eyes. Then his voice became quiet. "Help me . . . someone, please help!"

"Huber!" he heard a voice louder than the others. It sounded vaguely familiar, comforting somehow. "Huber! Listen to me!" he heard the voice say. It couldn't be.

As he opened his eyes, all of the people around him disappeared and a tall solitary figure materialized in front of him. There stood a man, clean-shaven, wearing a cowboy hat, and smiling. On his back was a prospecting pack with a fly-fishing pole at his side. In his right hand, the man carried a gas lantern. Orange flames flickered within the glass compartment, highlighting his blue eyes, which shone like sparkling jewels. His voice carried a deep, rich, and soothing tone.

"Come now, my boy. Don't give up on yourself. You're closer than you think. Get up! Follow me."

"Grandpa Nick?"

"Come along now. Gotta get moving."

"I don't want to get up," he answered lethargically.

"You have to listen to me, Huber. You need to follow me or you *will* die here," Grandpa Nick said. His voice no longer was mechanical sounding. It was the smoothest, most comforting voice he'd ever heard. And he appeared much younger. "There is a time to talk, a time to walk, and a time for action. This is a time to walk. Now stand up and dust yourself off."

"Okay," Huber said. "Okay, Grandpa. I'll try."

"That's the spirit," Grandpa Nick said, slapping his grandson on the shoulder and helping him up. "Come along now. I know the way."

Grandpa Nick walked ahead of him briskly.

"Grandpa, slow down . . . I can't keep up with you."

"You have to keep up, my boy. Got to hurry."

"Why?"

"Because you're running out of oxygen and where I'm taking you, you'll be able to breathe."

"Oh," Huber gasped, trying to catch up with his grandpa.

He kept following him through the darkness, for what seemed like miles without end. Sometimes Grandpa Nick would get too far up ahead, and Huber would yell for him to stop. Grandpa Nick would always turn around and hold up his lantern for Huber to find his way. Grandpa Nick's warm, leathery face flickered in the orange afterglow and brought hope to Huber's heart.

"Just a bit further now," he called.

Grandpa Nick stopped shortly thereafter and waited until Huber stood at his side. "Almost there now, my boy. I can't go with you any further, but you can make it, I have no doubt."

"Why can't you come with me?"

"I wish I could, but I've got to get going. Got things to do. Keep heading that way about fifty feet," he advised, pointing down the dark path with his fishing pole. "After that, you'll be all right. *Adios, muchacho.*"

He turned and started walking back the way they had come.

"Wait!" Huber yelled. Grandpa Nick kept walking. "Please, wait!" Grandpa Nick stopped and turned.

Huber ran and embraced him. Nothing had ever felt so real. "I miss you every day, all the time," Huber said, unleashing a torrent of pent-up emotion.

"I know, I know, my boy. I miss you too," Grandpa Nick said lovingly and stroked Huber's head, bringing him close. "That's what memories are for, you know? They bring us hope and sustain us in our darkest hour. June roses during the December of our lives."

"So you're just a memory, then?"

"I bet you'll be trying to figure that one out the rest of your life." Grandpa Nick smiled compassionately at Huber before becoming more serious. "Now, get going."

After another brief hug, Grandpa Nick squeezed Huber's shoulder, turned around, and kept walking in the darkness until he faded away into nothingness. Choking back more tears, Huber followed his advice. He turned and walked quickly in the direction his grandpa had pointed with the fishing pole. As he walked, he noticed that he was becoming weaker and weaker. His lungs constricted as he gasped for breath. He coughed wildly and wheezed. Panic filled his senses as suffocation gripped his body. Dropping on his hands and knees, he crawled. The thought of his Grandpa Nick, his parents, Scott, and Hannah gave him strength to inch forward. Each effort was agony.

I am not going to die in here. I'm not done living yet. I want to go to school. I want to see my family. I want to get married. I want to be a dad. I want to be a grandfather.

Lungs burning and mind racing, he kept crawling forward. It felt as if he were dragging fifty heavy chains behind him attached to hundred-pound dumbbells. Finally he collapsed in the dust, unable to go any further. The dust circled around his mouth as his lungs ached for air.

Just as he resigned himself, he looked ahead in the darkness and felt it: a small breeze of cool air. Mustering all of his strength, he lunged forward a bit further and then a bit further. The breeze grew stronger. It was becoming easier to breathe.

With added strength, he felt around and found the cave wall. The draft was coming down from somewhere up above. He stood up and found that the air flowed from a tiny opening in the wall, a fissure that had become exposed through a fault line. The opening, about the size of a football, let in cool, oxygen-laced, fresh air. Placing his mouth to the opening, he sucked in the air from the outside world. As he did, sanity came back to his mind and calmness to his body. He put his back against the wall of the mine and slid down until he was sitting comfortably, relieved to be alive, trying to forget the horrible visions he'd experienced. His grandpa seemed so real, however. As he pondered on the reality of his experiences, he remembered something. The lighter! It'd been in his pocket the whole time! In the madness that took him after the flashlight broke, he'd forgotten about it.

He fished it out of his pocket and sparked it until a small orange flame with blue hues ignited. The light revealed he was in some kind of cavern. Brushing his hand through the dirt beside him, Huber heard a metallic clank as his hand touched something cold and hard. It was the kind of sound made when two pots bang together. He looked down where his hand was and picked up the metal object. Startled by what he saw, he yelled out and dropped the object.

The light revealed an eighteenth century Spanish helmet, dented badly above the forehead. Inside the helmet remained the skull of the person who donned it hundreds of years earlier. Strands of gray hair undulated from the base of the skull. Large, eyeless sockets stared him in the face. A surprising number of teeth were left intact. As he mustered the courage to pick up the helmet again, he rotated it in his hand. As he examined it closer, the skull fell from the helmet and crashed on the floor, breaking the lower mandible and scattering teeth all over the rocky floor.

"Oops, sorry 'bout that."

Huber rotated his lighter to see underneath him and realized he had been sitting on the torso of the skull's owner, obviously another Spanish miner. This body was not as well preserved as the one they'd found earlier. Next to the skeleton rested a long sword still partially sheathed. With spots of rust, the sword was, amazingly, still sharp as he unsheathed it. As he looked around the cavern, Huber realized that the room was full of similar corpses lining the walls. He began to count and identified the remains of twelve different skeletons, all of them wearing Spanish-style attire. With the addition of the miner he'd met on the way in, that made a total of thirteen. For a moment, Huber wondered if the Spaniard he'd crossed paths with earlier had tried to crawl his way out before dying.

"So the legends really were true. This is where they dumped all of the bodies after the massacre. Grandpa, I wish you could see this," Huber said out loud. His excitement was short-lived as it dawned on him that the dead surrounded him. They all seemed to be watching him. Old horror movies and comics came to his mind, and he prepared himself for one of them to jump at him. He took a few deep breaths, trying to rid himself of the nauseous feeling that riddled his body.

"The dead can't hurt me. The dead can't hurt me," he repeated. "They've been here for hundreds of years now and haven't moved. I'm sure they're not about to change their minds."

In the center of the room, he noticed a shiny gleam. He nervously turned his back to the skeletons and approached the source. The gleam was coming from a latch attached to some kind of chest, which was camouflaged in the darkness. A surge of adrenaline raced through Huber's body, and he ran to it, still holding the Spaniard's sword in one hand and the lighter in the other. Any fear of the Spanish corpses vanished instantly.

Dropping the sword beside him, he used the lighter to reveal that it was only one of three chests sitting adjacent to each other. They were about three feet wide, two feet in depth, and about two and a half feet high. Hands trembling, he caressed and unlatched the chest in the middle. He opened the lid slowly. The glow of the lighter revealed a veritable sea of gold inside. Bars—all stamped with the same Spanish insignia that was on his grandpa's coin—filled the chest. Beneath the bars, he observed gold doubloons, bearing the same symbols. Quaking with excitement, Huber opened the other chests, which revealed more treasure the Spanish had produced from the mine.

"We did it, Grandpa! We found it!" Huber yelled excitedly. All of the Spanish skeletons looked on, almost like they were smiling that someone finally found the fortune they could not use.

"For which I cannot thank you enough, *joven*," Salazar's voice boomed from behind.

CHAPTER 31

HUBER DROPPED THE GOLD and turned around. This was no hallucination. Salazar had entered the cavern, with Scott and Hannah in front of him. Salazar held a bright lantern that temporarily blinded Huber and illuminated the entire room. It was as if someone had flipped on a light switch in the middle of the night. The skeletons and gold now stood in full view. Huber dropped his lighter in the dirt.

Salazar, Scott, and Hannah stood awestruck at the scene before them. As his vision adjusted, Huber saw that Scott and Hannah's hands were tied and holding empty bags, like trick-or-treaters on Halloween. They appeared exhausted. Salazar's right hand held his long, sharp knife to Scott's neck.

"Ay caray! Qué magnífico!" Salazar looked upon the skeletons reverently. "These men are my ancestors," he said, pointing with his quivering knife toward the corpses now. "They mined this gold with their bare hands, and you dare try to take it for yourselves?" His voice turned violent. "Insolent, greedy *Americanos.*" Salazar declared with a hateful stare.

Panic returned to Huber's chest. He had just come through an impossible battle within his own mind. Now he faced another precarious situation with a real, dangerous human being, intent on stealing the treasure and leaving no witnesses behind. He tried to think quickly.

"Please, you can have the gold. Take it all. Just let us go, and we'll never tell anyone about you and what happened here. We swear!" Huber pleaded. He saw the look of panic in the eyes of his friend and sister. Their hands shook as they held the empty burlap sacks.

Salazar looked at Huber with a smile absent of any mercy. "Take heart, Yoober. I am a compassionate man. I will not kill you with my own hands. I will bind and leave you here to remain with my brothers forever. They will keep you good company . . . and no one will *ever* find you. You will die slowly," he said wryly. "Now back up and stand against that wall, next to my ancestors."

Huber complied with the request, and in moments, he was bound and gagged, hand to foot, lying next to the skeletons, looking squarely into one of the Spanish miner's faces. Salazar sheathed his blood-stained knife, snatched the burlap sacks from Scott and Hannah, and bound them similarly. Approaching the treasure in the middle of the room, Salazar's hands shook wildly as he pilfered through the gold.

"*Tesoro! Tesoro! Tesoro!*" he cried out.

Huber, unable to move, watched helplessly as Salazar rifled through the chest, laughing hysterically and dancing around. He futilely tried to move his wrists back and forth to loosen the cloth bands.

After examining the contents of the first two chests, Salazar noticed something out of place in the third chest as he opened it. "*Qué es esto, mi amor?*" he asked curiously. On top of the gold coins rested a sealed envelope, yellowed with age but obviously from a more modern time than the eighteenth century. "Someone has been here already," Salazar uttered with suspicion, looking around. Huber, Scott, and Hannah watched, unable to speak. Salazar tore open the envelope and pulled out a piece of white lined paper, looking suspiciously similar to the lined pages in Grandpa Nick's prospecting guide. Salazar began to read the letter out loud.

> *July 18, 1980*
> *Dear Friend,*
>
> *Congratulations on finding Dead Man's Treasure. As you no doubt have figured out, it was no easy feat finding this location. I have searched these mountains for many years. Today, I finally had some luck. I have sat in this room for several hours now, ideas wildly running through my mind about how I will spend the treasure. Visions of a large house, fine automobiles, and clothing . . . no more scraping by month to month on a meager income . . . however, a recurring thought continues to surface in my mind: "This treasure belongs to the mountains." You may find this thought strange, but let me explain.*
>
> *This gold was ill gotten by greedy men who shed the blood of Ute to obtain it. The blood of the Spanish was shed by the Ute to hide it. So much pain and suffering over what? Pieces of metal? I'm not so sure the value of this gold is worth the weight upon my conscience.*
>
> *I have also come to the realization that if I remove this treasure, I will essentially be stealing away a precious gift from many others. Fathers and sons, grandfathers and grandkids, mothers and daughters will no doubt spend many precious hours scouring these mountains for what I*

have found here today. Do I have the right to deprive them of such memories?

So what you do with this treasure now is up to you. I hope you will reach the same conclusion as I have. A verse from the good book comes to mind: "Lay up for yourselves treasures . . . where neither moth nor rust doth corrupt, and where thieves do not break through nor steal." We can't take it with us, friend, as these poor gentlemen in this cave have found out. However, there are lasting treasures that no one can take away from you. So I exit this place minus any treasure, but a much richer man.

Yours truly,

N. E.

Many thoughts raced through Huber's mind as Salazar read the letter written by his grandfather. At the end of the letter, Huber felt a sense of confusion mingled with respect at Grandpa Nick's foresight and self-control. Huber still could not believe that he had found the treasure thirty years earlier and just left it here. Why didn't Grandpa Nick ever tell him he had found it? It was a question he'd never be able to ask.

"N. E.? It must stand for Nicholas Eldredge. Blah, blah, blah . . . your grandfather was a strange man," Salazar said smugly. "Please do not take the treasure," he mocked while waving his hands back and forth, laughing. "He could have had it all. *Idiota!*" He eyed Huber viciously. "When you see him in the afterlife, tell him *gracias* from me, okay?" Salazar crumpled the letter into a ball and threw it at Huber's feet.

Upon hearing such blasphemous words pouring from Salazar's mouth and witnessing such blatant disrespect, rage replaced the fear that Huber felt. He looked over at his two captive companions and could tell they felt similarly. Salazar could not get away with this. A voice of reason advised Huber to not abandon himself to anger, but to think logically. Trying to calm himself, he looked around to find resources within his vicinity, and there it was, shining clearly in the light of Salazar's lantern. The sword!

Salazar stuffed two of the burlap sacks with treasure and cinched them up at the top.

"Don't worry, *jóvenes*, I'll be back. I'm afraid this may require many trips. Now, do not go anywhere!" Salazar laughed uproariously. He flung one of the sacks over his shoulder, inhaled a few breaths of oxygen from his canister, and carried the lantern away as he exited the room. The room immediately returned to darkness.

When Huber could no longer hear Salazar's footsteps, he began to squirm toward the sword, remembering how a boy at school did "the worm" to impress a group of girls. With all of his might and concentration, Huber picked himself up off the ground by sending a ripple of energy from his knees to his head. As he did so, he flopped forward until he smacked his head into one of the wooden chests. The impact smarted, but he was too focused on the task at hand to dwell on the pain.

After feeling around a few minutes, he finally felt the hardness of the blade. Carefully, he lipped his fingers around the edge of the sword and forced it up on its side. He cautiously worked the blade downward until he was holding the end of the sword with his fingertips. Huber grabbed the blade handle with his heels. He rubbed the cloth around his wrists against the sharp edge of the blade, vigorously moving his arms up and down as fast as he could to cause friction. Huber felt the cloth starting to give. Half way through the cloth, Huber heard footsteps and saw shadows dancing off the cave wall in the distance. There would be only seconds before Salazar returned with the lantern. Doubling his efforts, Huber worked the blade through the remainder of the knot. Finally, the knot snapped, and Huber quickly dropped the sword back in place and crawled back to his spot, hiding his hands behind his back and out of sight.

Seconds later, the light of the lantern quickly brightened the cavern as Salazar reentered the room. Placing the lantern on one of the chests, he eyed his captives and wiped the sweat from his forehead. "Whew! Gold is very heavy, my friends. I should have bought myself a horse. I suppose I do not have to collect it all right now. Maybe I'll come back in a few days, just to check up and see how you're all doing, eh? What do you think?" Salazar laughed and filled another sack, slinging it over his shoulder before exiting again.

When Salazar was out of earshot, Huber yanked the gag out of his mouth and cut the bonds around his ankles. He then felt around the dirt until he found his lighter. He ignited it and then made his way over to release Scott and Hannah.

"Nice work, dude," Scott said gratefully to Huber.

"Hey, sorry for not listening to you and kinda going nuts back there."

"Always knew ya were nuts, so don't worry about it," Scott replied. "I was startin' to lose it too. It wasn't your fault. What are we gonna do now?"

"We better think of something fast. He'll be back soon," Hannah reminded them. "I say we hide and sack him."

"Hold on now. Let's think about this. He's gonna see us if we try to pull anything. What if we just lay here, pretend we're still tied up, and wait for 'im to leave? Then we can book it to town and report 'im to the cops," Scott reasoned.

"What if he changes his mind and decides to do away with us now?" Hannah worried.

"He's too evil for that. He wants us to suffer," Scott said.

"I don't want to take the chance," Hannah squabbled.

"So you want us to get ourselves killed then?"

"It beats putting ourselves at his mercy!"

"Quiet! Hannah, quit arguing with him!" Huber hissed.

"Talk some sense into her, Puber," Scott said.

"I agree with my sister." While he couldn't see Hannah's face in blackness, Huber was sure his sister was gloating. "We can't take the chance that he'll just leave us here. Even if he does, we could easily run out of oxygen trying to get out when he's gone. Plus, you heard my grandpa's letter. We can't let the treasure leave this room."

"Fine. I guess I'm outnumbered. For the record, I think you two are morons. What are we gonna do?" he asked in a defeated tone.

Huber smiled to himself. "I know exactly what we're going to do."

CHAPTER
•32•

AFTER TOSSING THE SECOND bag of gold behind some vines outside the mine's entrance, Salazar stopped to catch his breath. In his wildest imaginations, he never dreamed there'd be so much gold. He'd pack all he could down the mountain and come back over the next few days for the rest. As he formulated his plan, the chirp of a robin, perched on a nearby limb, interrupted his thoughts.

"*¿Que piensas tú, pajarito?* Let them suffer or end their misery now? Perhaps it is better to end it. To be merciful." The bird tilted its head as if trying to understand his words. Salazar unsheathed his long knife as the bird flapped away. "Don't worry, *pajarito*, I will make it quick for them." Salazar reentered the cave, his final objective now firm in his mind.

Salazar marched past the dead Spaniard, took a few hits of oxygen when the air turned sour, and relished the idea of his revenge. The sound of his footfalls echoed through the mine shaft. At last he reached the cavern, readying himself for the malicious deed at hand.

Salazar's face contorted in confusion and shock.

Empty. His captives were nowhere to be seen. Their bonds lay in the dirt. Confusion turned into comprehension as Salazar swung the lantern around the room. The lantern light revealed only the ghostly grins of the skeletons looking on. A gloomy chill crept up the man's spine.

"¿Dónde están, jóvenes? I know you are here! There is no way out!" he cried out nervously.

Scanning the room to detect any movement, Salazar noticed footprints that wound around the room. Following one of the sets, they led him to the center chest. The same chest he'd looted. Scattered coins littered the surrounding ground. A small person could easily hide.

Salazar tiptoed toward the chest. Raising his knife in the air, he flipped open the lid. Hannah quivered inside.

"Please! No! Stop!" she cried out.

"It ends now," Salazar growled.

A rustling sound startled him from behind. Before Salazar could register what was happening, Scott emerged from the shadows of a small niche and swung a rusty, iron helmet toward the Spaniard. There was a loud *smack*. Salazar groaned and crumpled to the dirt floor as the heavy helmet collided with his lower back. The lantern slipped from his grasp and rolled on the ground, casting eerie shadows along the cavern walls. Echoes of pain-filled moans reverberated around the room.

"How's that feel, sir?" Scott yelled.

Salazar let out an angry bawl and raised himself up to charge toward Scott. As he did, Huber emerged from a pile of armor and skeletons lying on the ground, holding a large femur bone in his hands. Huber swung like he was trying to hit a home run. Landing with a flat thud, the femur shattered Salazar's nose. A bloody mist sprayed through the air. Salazar lay motionless on the ground, only semiconscious, loosely clutching the knife. Hannah emerged from the chest and picked up the lantern. Salazar stirred like a piece of half-cooked bacon sizzling on a hot pan.

"Tie him up. Let's see how he likes it," Scott suggested, and the three moved toward Salazar. Huber kicked the knife out of the man's hand and in moments had tied his wrists and ankles together. Propped up against the wall, Salazar's head wobbled from side to side. Huber retrieved the map and his grandpa's prospecting guide from Salazar's pockets, placing them within his own, finally safe and sound. A few moments passed before Salazar regained full consciousness. Hannah shone the light on his face, pupils constricting in the bright light. The Spaniard's face grimaced painfully, eyes reflecting defeat.

"*Buen hecho, jóvenes.* Well done," he said softly. "*Jóvenes* . . . it's not too late. Release me. We'll split the treasure evenly and all be on our way. If you do this, I will never return."

Scott stared at him momentarily. "Hmmm, let's think 'bout that. Kiss my—"

"Don't!" Hannah interrupted and turned toward Salazar. "What he's saying is that we don't trust you as far as we can throw you. There's no promise you can make that we'd believe. Besides, like my brother said, it belongs here."

"If that's how you prefer it," Salazar replied flatly, blood still dripping from his nostrils. "So you are going to leave me here to die. I do not blame you."

"I'm sure you'll wish that when you're rotting in prison. You're coming with us," Huber scorned.

"C'mon, dude, let's just leave 'im here. He was gonna do the same to us," Scott protested.

"Yes, you should leave me . . . I will not forget should I survive," Salazar remarked coldly. "I will come back one day, and when I do, I'll make a special trip to see you. I will find you. I will have my vengeance and take the treasure. I will fill my cup,"

"It doesn't belong to you. It doesn't belong to anyone. It's blood money," Hannah shot out.

"Money is money, little girl . . . you'll find that out soon enough."

Huber thought about all the fights his parents had over money. Would this treasure solve all of his problems? Or would it create more?

"Where's that gag? I've heard enough from this puke-bag," Scott picked up one of the loose gags off the floor and tied it roughly around his mouth. Salazar screamed in pain as he did so.

"Scott, take it easy. We're not like him," Hannah chastised.

"Right, be nice to the guy who just tried to kill us!"

"I'm just saying . . ."

"She's right, Scott. We're not like him," Huber said.

"Whatever ya say, Puber. Ya know, Salamander does make a good point. It's a lot of money," Scott ventured to Huber. "Nobody's usin' it."

Huber thought for a moment. "It stays here. Period."

"Sure ya don't wanna take just a lil bit . . . ya know, one or two souvenirs?"

Hannah and Huber both shot him a glance that conveyed their answer.

"Actually, there is one thing," Huber said. He snatched the

lantern from Hannah and walked over to the crumpled mass of paper on the ground. Picking up the letter, he smoothed it out carefully. Taking out his grandpa's guide, he flipped to the end of the book. Lining up the crumpled paper with the spine, Huber recognized that the tear marks matched precisely. The missing page.

"What about the gold that Salamander already took?" Scott asked. "We can take that home, can't we?"

"I'm sure he didn't hide it far. We'll bring it back inside."

Scott's shoulders fell. "We should at least take somethin' for a museum?" Scott whined. "They'd pay us for it, I bet."

"No," Huber and Hannah answered in unison.

"So we went through all of this, for what? Nothin', basically, is what you're sayin'," Scott muttered.

Hannah looked with playful eyes and brushed his hand lightly with her fingertips. "Nothing?"

Scott's knees became weak and the darkness prevented anyone from seeing how red his face had become.

"Well . . . maybe some good came of it."

Huber rolled his eyes. "All right, let's get going," he said and unloosed Salazar's ankles, motioning for him to get up. Scott stepped behind him and pressed the blade tip gently to his back.

"Not so fun bein' on the other end of the stick, is it, Salamander, sir?"

Salazar turned his head around and glared in contempt, but the gag prevented him from speaking. When he turned his head back around, Scott smiled and whistled the tune of "Zip-a-Dee-Doo-Dah." The trio paced behind Salazar, passing around the oxygen mask when someone needed it. No more evil spirits came. Huber stood to the right of Scott, who held the lantern high. As they proceeded through the shaft, Scott relentlessly harassed Salazar.

"Beautiful plan, dude. Did ya see Salamander's face when he came back and we were gone? Priceless! Bet you messed your britches, huh, Salamander?" He laughed. "How's your back? Probably wanna put some ice on it and take it easy for a few days once you're in prison. I'll bet it'll be tough to relax when Bubba's your cell mate though."

Huber and Hannah couldn't help but snicker. Salazar's eyes burned with anger as he blew air from his nostrils. Ten minutes passed. They must've been two thirds of the way through the shaft. A tiny dot of light glimmered in the distance. Hannah passed the oxygen tank around and everyone took a few more breaths as the air became stale.

"Hey, Salamander, thanks for bringing this thing along. Couldn'ta made it back without ya," Scott said, breathing in the oxygen deeply. "Ahhh, good stuff," he exaggerated. Scott handed the tank to Huber, who took a few breaths. Salazar dropped to his knees, desperately trying to breathe through his broken nose.

"Huber, we need to give him some. He can't breathe," Hannah cried out.

Scott harbored no such sentiment. "Guy deserves it. Let 'im crawl the rest of the way out."

"He'll suffocate, Huber! He's a terrible man, but I don't want murder on my conscience," Hannah pleaded.

"He woulda killed you in a second. Ya forgot that?" Scott quipped.

"No, I haven't forgotten. Like I said, *we're not like him.*

Huber, give him some, now!" she yelled as Salazar's eyes began to roll behind his head.

"Take the gag off," Huber motioned to Scott.

Scott hesitated, glaring at Salazar for a moment, then begrudgingly removed the gag. Huber placed the lantern on the ground and the oxygen mask next to Salazar's open mouth. The Spaniard inhaled deeply and slowly, eyes returning to their proper place. For a moment, Huber felt a sense of compassion toward the man.

"*Gracias, gracias*, my friend! Yoober, you are a man of honor, and for this, I respect you," he said.

Salazar looked at Scott and spat at his feet. Scott simply shook his head back and forth at the sorry sight. "Please, just a little more?" Salazar asked politely.

"Fine," Huber replied.

As he brought the mask to his face, Salazar's right leg booted the lantern against the wall. Chaos ensued. Huber felt himself being pushed over. The lantern spun wildly on the ground. There were yells and struggles. Mere seconds passed before Huber snatched up the light and illuminated the area. Scott lay on the ground, the heel of Salazar's steel-toed boot pressing down on his throat. Scott gasped desperately for air. The knife lay on the ground four feet from Scott's position, just out of reach. Hannah had been knocked out of the way during the commotion and watched the scene, too dumbstruck to believe what was happening.

"Loose my hands, *por favor*," Salazar demanded coolly.

"Huber?" Hannah pleaded to know what to do.

"Just a little more pressure and this smart one will never utter a word from his filthy mouth again." Salazar pressed a little harder with his foot. Scott began to flail his arms about and grab at Salazar's foot, but the more he struggled, the more pressure Salazar applied.

"Stop!" Huber yelled out. "Hannah, untie his hands."

"Are you sure?"

"Do it!" Huber barked.

Hannah loosed the man's bonds. Salazar rubbed his raw wrists for a moment. "That's better. Now, please be so kind as to hand me my knife, *angelita*."

"No!" Hannah refused.

"No?" Salazar asked incredulously. "Do you not care for your friend here? More than a friend, I think. Give me the knife now or he loses what little breath he has left."

Scott, unable to utter a word, tried to shake his head to deter her.

"What are you going to do to us?"

"The knife, or he dies," Salazar reiterated.

Hannah picked up the knife from the ground and walked toward Salazar. Huber had to do something now. But what? What could he possibly do? Hannah gently placed the blade within the fangs of the tattooed serpent. Grandpa Nick's words came to his mind: *Time for action.* In an instant, he knew what to do. With Salazar distracted by Hannah, Huber extinguished the light of the lantern and threw it as hard as he could in Salazar's direction. A loud crash echoed through the tunnel, immediately followed by a yelp from Salazar. The lantern had made contact. As if in a dream, Huber charged toward Salazar, colliding with a wiry mass of flesh and bone.

"Hannah, Scott, run now! Run!"

Huber heard their footsteps pound the dirt floor as he

grappled with Salazar. The man's powerful arms held Huber in a headlock. Huber bit down, hard. Salazar screamed but maintained his hold. *This is it.* At least his last act would be a noble one. Stars appeared before his eyes. Maybe people would talk of his bravery years from now. Survival instincts kicked in and gave him the will for one last-ditch effort.

Mustering his remaining strength, Huber snapped his head backward. The back of his skull connected with Salazar's already broken nose. A deafening scream entered Huber's ears as Salazar released his death grip. *Run! Run!* he commanded his sluggish legs. His feet slapped the ground and propelled him forward. It all happened in slow motion, just like his dream.

Salazar gained on him from behind, breathing heavily, adrenaline masking the effects of his injuries. The light at the end of the tunnel grew larger and brighter. Huber glanced back for an instant. Salazar's bloodthirsty eyes seemed to glow in the semidarkness like some wild animal. As he looked ahead toward the light, Huber willed himself forward. Even if he made it out of the tunnel, what then? At least dying outside would be better than dying in a dank, dark tunnel. Huber could feel the man's foul breath on his neck. The entrance to the tunnel loomed just ahead, but his legs started to give out. *How sad*, he thought. *I almost made it out.* Huber collapsed.

CHAPTER
33

SALAZAR WAS INSTANTLY ON TOP of him. The light of freedom shone brightly through the tunnel just a few yards away. Pleasant aromas filled Huber's nostrils. Birds sang their cheerful song. Maybe he was dreaming. Maybe he was already dead. Huber looked toward the light, when sure enough, a silhouette of a man appeared. *Grandpa Nick*. Huber felt comforted. He'd come to take him to the beyond.

To his surprise, a loud angry voice boomed from the silhouette, "Get your hands off of my son!" Huber's eyes adjusted to the light, and the shape came into focus.

"Dad!"

Robert kicked the knife from Salazar's hand and grabbed the man by his shirt collar, pulling him off Huber. Salazar, caught off guard, fell hard as Robert slugged him in the stomach. As the Spaniard gasped to catch his wind, Robert threw him onto the ground outside. As Salazar's eyes adjusted to the brightness, he realized a group of people surrounded him. A man in a white button-up shirt and cowboy hat pounced on top of him. In a split second, Salazar's hands were handcuffed behind his back. When the Spaniard rolled over on his stomach, he spotted Scott and Hannah in the background, watching smugly as the scene unfolded.

Huber ran toward his father and clung to his side, tears rolling down his dirt-stained cheeks.

"Are you hurt?"

"No, not bad. I'll be okay. How did you . . . ?"

"Jenkins."

"Who is Jenkins?"

"A dog," he pointed off in the distance. "He's tied up back there a little ways. He picked up your scent when we found your gear. Are you sure this man didn't hurt any of you?"

"We're okay. How did you know we were even up here?"

Brad answered, "Your dad and I ran into each other at the grocery store. Toilet paper aisle."

"Oh . . . ," Huber said slowly.

Robert continued, "How could you all be so thickheaded to wander up here all alone?"

"It was my fault," Huber said. "I convinced them to come with me. I had to get away."

"Why?" his father asked and then answered his own question. "Your grandpa."

Huber said nothing.

After hugging his son, Brad looked at Scott and said two words, "Military school."

Scott shot Hannah a wry smile, and she almost laughed out loud.

"What were you kids doin' in that hole, anyway?"

"Dad, we found it!" Hannah burst out. "We actually found Dead Man's Treasure! Grandpa Nick's stories were true!"

"Where'd you hide it?" Huber demanded, pointing at Salazar.

"Hide what?" he snarled in response. However, his eyes inadvertently darted toward some vines a few feet from the mine entrance. Hannah noticed the glance and dashed to the spot.

"Found it," she called out.

Salazar sighed heavily.

"I'll be, is there really gold inside there?" Brad asked, amazed.

Hannah lugged the heavy sack toward the group.

"Little miss, can I see that?" Marshal Rodriguez asked her.

She hefted the bag of gold over to the marshal and plopped it down near his feet. As she did, the bag opened at the top, spilling several gold doubloons which gleamed in the fading sunlight. Several gold doubloons spilled out and gleamed in the sunlight. Spellbound, the men only stared, unable to believe their eyes.

"You actually found it," Robert replied, still unbelieving.

In astonishment, Brad looked back and forth at his son and the gold, speechless.

Marshal Rodriguez, seemed unimpressed. "How much more is in there?"

"A ton! There's—" Hannah exclaimed.

Before she could finish her sentence, the man leveled his pistol at Huber.

"Rodrigo! What are ya doin', man?" Brad yelled.

Marshal Rodriguez turned toward Scott's father and tossed him a small key. "Uncuff him." He pointed at Salazar.

"What's going on here? Get that gun away from my son!" Robert demanded, pale-faced and helpless.

Huber quaked beneath the barrel of the marshal's gun.

"Do it!" he barked.

Salazar smirked as Brad loosed him from his bonds. "*Gracias, mi amigo*," he said. He arose and socked Scott's dad in the stomach. Doubling over, Brad fell to his knees.

"Dad!" Scott screamed and rushed to his side.

"All of you on your knees!" Rodriguez demanded.

They all knelt down in a semicircle.

Salazar turned to Rodriguez. "*Hermano*, good to see you."

"Good to see you as well, brother. Looks like they did quite a number on you."

"Nothing that won't heal. Don't worry, I will soon return the favor."

"Brothers?" Hannah mouthed quietly.

"You're no marshal," Robert seethed under his breath.

"Got me," Rodriguez replied and threw off his hat and sunglasses, revealing an uncanny resemblance to Salazar.

"You're late," Salazar laughed. "I was afraid you would not find me."

"Brothers . . . ," Brad mumbled.

The imposter sneered. "Yes, brothers! Unjustly torn apart when we were children. Now reunited! Allow me to introduce myself. Antonio Rodriguez-Salazar." Then turning to his brother he stated, "We can finally do it, Juan. Live like kings!"

"Please, take it all! Just don't hurt our kids!" Robert begged.

"We'll do whatever you want!" Brad pleaded.

Salazar retrieved his knife and approached Robert with a sadistic grin.

"Whatever we want? I have something in mind."

"I can't do it." Robert trembled, holding the knife to Huber's face.

Salazar's brother held the gun to the back of Huber's head.

"It's okay, Dad," Huber whispered as tears stained his cheeks.

"I . . . I . . . won't!"

"Antonio, pull the trigger," breathed Salazar.

"NO!" Robert and the others gasped in unison. Hannah, Scott, and Brad watched the scene unfold, powerless to intervene.

"Then do it! You refuse again, your son dies."

"Why are you doing this?"

Salazar remained silent.

"It's okay, Dad," Huber repeated. *Water off a duck's back.*

"Give your son a scar to match mine. Cut your son as my father cut me."

Robert gripped the blade in his palm and steeled himself with a breath. Shakily, he pressed the blade to his son's cheek.

"I'm sorry, Huber. Please forgive me," his father whispered.

"It's okay."

"I love you, son."

"I know . . . I love you too."

Blood trickled down Huber's cheek as the tip of the knife pierced his skin. Huber winced as his weeping father inched the blade upward a few centimeters.

Unable to watch, Hannah squirmed and turned her head. Brad grimaced and closed his eyes.

Salazar's lips quivered in sadistic pleasure. Bending down

low, Salazar whispered into Huber's left ear.

"While we are revealing secrets . . . here is one more," he said so only Huber could hear. "To his dying breath, your grandfather refused to reveal the map's location. Little good it did him. He didn't even put up a fight. Do you know what he said to me right before I disconnected the tubes from his machine? 'You'll never find Dead Man's Treasure.' He was wrong. They both were wrong."

Huber felt ill. He seemed to float away from his body. An anger and sadness beyond words raged within him, yet he could do nothing.

"Stop it! Get away from him!" Scott suddenly screamed and charged toward Huber.

"Scott! No! Stop!" Brad yelled.

Taking the gun from Huber's head, Rodriguez aimed at the boy and pulled the trigger. A puff of white smoke accompanied by an acrid odor filled the air.

Searing, excruciating pain overtook Scott's senses. His T-shirt turned crimson red around the shoulder.

Distracted by the commotion, Rodriguez swung his pistol toward Brad and Hannah. Robert, still clasping the blade, pushed Huber aside and plunged the knife into Rodriguez's thigh. Pain-riddled screams floated through the forest as the impostor collapsed, clutching his leg with both hands. The pistol fell to the ground next to Huber.

"The gun! Get the gun!" Hannah screamed.

Salazar and Huber dove for it simultaneously. Salazar held the advantage. His long, lanky arms, combined with unnatural swiftness, helped him sweep the gun up just at the moment Huber reached it.

"Enough!" Salazar yelled and leveled the pistol at Huber.

As the last word fell from his lips, a "click" sounded near Salazar's ear.

"Get away from them kids," a deep voice demanded.

Unable to believe his eyes, Huber peered up to see the old Indian man from the Mercantile. In his hand was an old six-shot revolver.

"*¿Que maldad es esto?* Who are you?" Salazar growled.

"Hawk. Guardian of this place."

"Guardian?" Salazar snorted.

"Knew you Spaniards would come back sooner or later. We've been waiting for a couple hundred years."

Rodriguez stirred on the ground and let out a scream as he drew the knife from his thigh.

As Hawk averted his eyes, Salazar swung around, and in one swift motion brought his own pistol to face the old man.

"You won't stop us, *viejo*."

"Maybe they will," Hawk replied.

As the old man uttered his words, a slew of fifteen Ute men stepped from their hiding places and surrounded the group. They all held rifles and pistols, their sights trained on the two Spaniards.

"*Tesoro de los Muertos nos pertenece a nosotros!* The treasure belongs to us!"

"Belongs to the mount'in . . . along with your ancestors. Whether you join them's up to you. Put down your weapons, and we'll let you live."

Salazar and Rodriguez looked at each other momentarily. Rodriguez clutched the knife in his hand. Salazar lowered the pistol to his side.

"Drop it," Hawk commanded.

Salazar studied the faces surrounding him. Their eyes did not blink. Their hands did not waver. Gazing into Huber's eyes, Salazar whispered, "When you look upon that scar in the mirror each morning, Yoober . . . remember me, *joven.*"

The Spaniard flung his firearm upward at the old man. A single shot fired. A quiet thud hit Salazar in the chest. A young man, maybe in his twenties, lowered his pistol. Salazar collapsed to the ground, motionless. Rodriguez looked upon his brother and then attempted to charge toward the young man. A chorus of fifteen rifles discharged simultaneously, disrupting the still mountain air. Rodriguez fell.

CHAPTER 34

THE TWO FATHERS GATHERED their children close as a small group of Ute men drug the Spaniards' lifeless bodies into the mine along with the gold Salazar had brought out. No words were spoken. None were needed.

Still bleeding somewhat, Scott held a rag to the wound. The bullet had just grazed his shoulder.

"What did he whisper to you, Huber?" Hannah finally broke the silence.

"Nothing that needs to be repeated."

Hawk approached.

"How did you kids find this place, anyway?"

The three took turns telling the story. It was all so incredible; they wouldn't believe it themselves if they hadn't experienced it. They spoke about the many narrow escapes with Salazar and how they had sabotaged him in the forest and in the mine. Hannah began to sob as she told Hawk about the cougar that protected them.

"He killed her!" she cried.

"Did you find her on your way up here?" Huber asked somberly.

The two fathers looked at one another. Brad answered the question. "We found a mess of blood and fur and saw some bloody tracks trail off into the brush."

"I'm sorry, kids . . . looks like she didn't make it," Robert added sorrowfully.

Tears streamed down Hannah's face. Huber and Scott simply stared at the ground.

"Now, don't be sad for her," Hawk said softly. "She was a mother protecting her young. She died a happy death. You know, the Ute believe that animals commune with the spirit world. Maybe someone sent her to watch over you."

The statement sent chills through Huber's body.

"You kids take anything outta there?" Hawk asked, pointing toward the mine.

Huber pulled out the crumpled letter and handed it to the old man.

"This it? No gold?" Hawk probed further. They all shook their heads. The old man read aloud Grandpa Nick's letter. When he finished, he folded the letter reverently.

"You all agree with the letter then?" he asked them.

Huber, Hannah, and finally Scott all nodded their heads in the affirmative.

"When I was younger, 'bout your age," Hawk pointed to Robert and Brad, "the elders trusted me with a great secret. They brought me to this place. Told me if I made it past them evil spirits, and got to the end, I'd become a sentinel, a protector of Dead Man's Treasure. I made it through and found my way out. From that day, I promised to protect this place from outsiders. A few months later, I came back here with my uncle. We'd been tracking this guy who was getting close to the mine. He got to it and went inside 'fore we could catch him. Waited outside for 'im to come out. When he did, he wasn't carrying any gold. He put his hands up, and we asked 'im how he found this place. Showed us that same old map there." He pointed at the parchment sticking out of Huber's pocket. "We asked 'im why he didn't take any of that treasure. Gave us these same reasons I just read. We decided to let 'im go if he made an oath that he'd never tell anybody about it."

Hawk now smiled. "His name was Nicholas Eldredge."

Huber turned to his sister. "That's why he never told us he found it. He wouldn't break his oath."

Hannah's eyes were swimming.

"I think he took one of the coins," Huber murmured and brought out the gold doubloon from his pocket. He handed it to Hawk.

Hawk grinned. "Guess he snuck one past us."

"A souvenir," Scott shrugged and then winced, having momentarily forgotten his injury.

"Now I must ask all you to take the same oath as your grandfather."

"Oath?" Brad raised his voice in alarm. "What do ya mean? Some kinda blood oath? Cuz I'm not down with that."

"No blood required," Hawk said, smirking. "Just promise that you'll never tell anyone where Dead Man's Treasure is."

One by one, they all promised, including Robert and Brad. "Long as you keep that promise, you can come back here anytime. Just let me know, first. Otherwise, you might find a couple o' guns pointed your way when you come out. Well, better get goin' 'fore it gets dark."

As they readied to depart, Hawk lightly touched Huber on the shoulder. Turning around, Huber looked up into the kind coal-colored eyes of the man. "Better take this with you," he whispered and slipped the gold doubloon back into Huber's palm. Huber nodded, affirming his thanks. As he did so, a bell began to chime. After thirteen, the sound of grinding stone filled their ears as the mine sealed itself shut. The Salazars had joined their ancestors.

Continuing down the mountain, Robert kept his hand on his son's shoulder but said nothing. The waning sun splashed an array of spectacular color across the sky, reflecting upward in the slow, meandering stream swimming beside them. Suddenly, a movement caught the corner of Huber's eye. Craning his head upward, Huber stared in disbelief.

"Hey, look up there!" Huber yelled, pointing to a rocky ridge that towered ahead of them.

Hobbling alongside the purple horizon, a beat-up, one-eared cougar looked down upon them.

CHAPTER
•35•

"SO, WHAT'LL IT BE tonight, *Blood Wars 2* or *Kings of Chaos?*" Huber asked. It was a stormy Friday night, and the two friends were celebrating the weekend with one last all night video game session on Robert's massive TV. It was hard to believe that almost three month had passed since finding Dead Man's Treasure.

For the few weeks following the ordeal in the mountains, stories graced the front pages of local newspapers about the efforts and determination of two loving fathers who found their missing children lost in the wilderness. There was no mention of Salazar or Rodriguez. Huber's mom sobbed and scolded her children as they came through the front door. Where had they been? How had Huber got that cut on his cheek? They'd all rehearsed perfectly plausible answers to her questions. The siblings had just wanted to get away. Huber had fallen into the river and sliced his face on a rock. They had wandered off and gotten lost until Robert, Brad, and his dog, Jenkins, had found them.

Huber regularly experienced vivid nightmares of Salazar. Sometimes he'd wake to find the Spaniard standing over him, half-skeletonized, gripping his blade. As Huber would scream, he'd awake a second time in reality and find himself alone in his room. He'd then amble into the bathroom and gaze into the mirror at the quarter-inch scar decorating his right cheek. It would always be a reminder.

"So, how about it?" Huber asked Scott again.

"Huh?" Scott asked, lost in thought. "Oh, I dunno. Don't really feel like doin' much of anything."

"Why not? 'Cause my sister isn't interested in you anymore? I tried to warn you she wouldn't be your girlfriend forever."

"No, it's not that. I'm way over her."

"Sure you are. So you didn't mind when you saw her sitting with Beau Atkinson at lunch last week?"

Scott's jaw clenched. "Nope, she can do whatever she wants. I just feel bad for that fella, Beau what's-his-name."

"Atkinson."

"Poor dope. Doesn't even realize his heart's about to be thrown in a blender, does he? He's just a moth attracted to the flame."

"That's what I've been trying to tell you. Girls are nothing but heartache. That's why I only have two loves in my life."

"Yeah? What's that?"

"Taco Bell and *Blood Wars*."

"Yeah, I guess that's smart."

"Taco Bell and video games will always be there for you. See my point?"

"Yeah, I guess so. Where's your sister tonight anyway? Not that I care."

"I think she's sleeping over at a friend's house."

"*Kings of Chaos* sounds good, I guess."

Huber popped out the disc and was about to insert it into the console when the doorbell chimed.

"Weird. Wonder who that is?"

"Maybe it's Alison Harmon!"

"Funny. Come with me just in case it's a serial killer or something."

The two hoisted themselves from the sofa and sauntered to the door.

"I'm telling you, it's her, Puber."

Huber laughed and flung the door open. As he did, lightning flashed in the sky and briefly illuminated the figure standing on his front porch.

Huber fell backward and couldn't breathe. The grotesque and emaciated corpse of Juan Hernán Salazar limped forward. His bony fingers clasped his rusty blade. Scott disappeared into thin air as Salazar lunged through the door and loomed over Huber. Everything went dark. Huber was suddenly in the mine again. The Spaniard's dry bones splintered and cracked as he collapsed toward Huber, who was cowering in fear. Skeleton fingers clasped Huber's collarbone. His entire body seized up. He was paralyzed like a scared rabbit. Huber's tongue froze in his mouth. Salazar's jaw twisted in bizarre shapes. A deep, guttural sound gurgled up as his mouth opened. He gasped, "I . . . will . . . fill . . . my . . . cup . . ." Salazar raised his blade high and brought it down. Huber's tongue loosened as he let out a scream and shut his eyes. He awoke, thrashing in his bed, yelling for help.

Scott, asleep on the floor next to him, bolted upright and shook Huber by the shoulders. "Dude, snap out of it! You're having a nightmare."

Huber's surroundings came into focus. His room. Scott sleeping over. Yes, this was real. After several deep breaths,

Huber composed himself. "Sorry . . . I was dreaming . . . about him."

"You too, huh?" Scott nodded. "Happens to me every once in a while."

"It's never felt so real before."

"What do you mean?"

"I don't know. I just feel like something bad has happened."

At that moment, the boys heard the front door downstairs open and slam shut. Footsteps hastened up the stairs. Huber glanced at his clock radio. It was just after midnight. A rapping came at his door. Huber and Scott looked at one another worriedly. "Who is it?" Scott called out.

Without warning, the door flew open. Hannah stood there, trembling.

"Hey, sis. What's wrong?"

"I was at Jana Brady's house. I ran over as fast as I could," she panted.

"What's the matter?"

Hannah tried to catch her breath. "Jana's dad . . . Sheriff Brady. Something's happened."

Huber felt his stomach knot up. "What?"

Hannah's eyes brimmed over with tears. "It's Hawk . . . he's . . . dead."

The air went out of both boys. Huber blinked quickly and glanced up. "What? How?"

"I don't know . . . he was attacked up in the mountains along with two others. I heard Jana's dad talking about it on the phone with someone."

The room was spinning. Huber had to force himself not to throw up.

"He said he died on the way to the hospital and that he kept repeating something."

"What did he say?" Scott whispered.

Hannah gazed into Scott's and then her brother's eyes before dropping to her knees. "*They took the treasure.*"

LA AVENTURA CONTINUARÁ EN ESPAÑA—
HUBER HILL AND THE BROTHERHOOD OF CORONADO
—COMING FALL 2012!

DISCUSSION QUESTIONS

1. At the beginning of the novel, Huber was harassed by Scott. How do you think he and the adults around him should have handled the situation? Have you ever experienced anything similar? What can people do to stop harassment and bullying?

2. When Huber and Hannah's grandpa dies, they profoundly feel his loss. Have you or someone you know ever lost a family member, friend, or even a pet? What emotions does a person feel when they lose someone they love? How would you help a friend who is in the grieving process?

3. Although Huber and Scott were enemies in the beginning, they became friends. Have you ever made friends with someone who was previously an enemy? How did it happen?

4. Scott McCormick is labeled early on as a bully. What are the dangers of labeling people? Have you ever been labeled as something you didn't like? How did it affect you?

5. Toward the conclusion of the story, Salazar tries to make Huber experience the same pain he endured when younger. Why do some people want to hurt others when they've been hurt? What are some healthy ways to get through an emotionally painful experience?

6. At the end of the novel, Huber, Scott, and Hannah choose to not take the treasure. Why do they do this? What things in life do you think are more valuable than money? Why?

ABOUT THE
AUTHOR

B.K. BOSTICK RESIDES AMONG the magnificent Rocky Mountains. In addition to writing, he has spent his career in education. He earned his bachelor's degree in psychology from the University of Utah and his masters in psychology from Utah State University. He has worked as a teacher, after school program coordinator, junior high school counselor, and most recently as a teacher mentor for a university. He loves spending time with his lovely wife and two dogs. In his spare time, he enjoys eating Cheetos and watching old episodes of the *Twilight Zone*.

CMA DEL
MONTE

MIS
HERMAN

TESORO DE
LOS MUERTOS

AGUAS
DE
VIDA

ESCALE
DE

EL OJO DE
DIOS TE GUÍA